The Stargazer's Journey

Mark Reed

authorHOUSE®

AuthorHouse™
1663 Liberty Drive
Bloomington, IN 47403
www.authorhouse.com
Phone: 1 (800) 839-8640

Published by AuthorHouse 04/27/2017

ISBN: 978-1-5246-8980-3 (sc)
ISBN: 978-1-5246-8978-0 (hc)
ISBN: 978-1-5246-8979-7 (e)

Library of Congress Control Number: 2017906400

Print information available on the last page.

This book is printed on acid-free paper.

1

They say opposites attract, and boy did we prove that adage true.

My name is Adam. My partner, Wayne, and I have been together for eight years. I couldn't ask for a more loving, caring, and wonderful man to share my life with. Not to mention, he's sexy as hell in many ways. He speaks his mind also, where I tend to be quiet or more reserved about expressing my ideas or opinions. He's always telling me to be more forthright and aggressive. Maybe someday I'll be more like him.

We met through social media and live in St. Louis, Missouri. After several phone conversations, we finally decided to go out to dinner one evening. That night changed my life forever.

Both of us are extremely hairy, a bit burly, and bearish type of guys. We're each around six feet tall, give or take half an inch. I have a bit of a tummy, whereas Wayne is much more defined than me. He's a muscular man and strong. We both spent time in gyms throughout the years, but Wayne worked much harder on developing his body into a work of art.

He's got shoulders to die for, with sculpted biceps, toned thighs, a shapely ass, and a powerful chest above an awesome tummy that bulges out just a smidge. He's got hairy, yummy feet, too. I can't tell you how many times we've lain in bed opposite each other, sucking each other's toes with lots of added kisses and tons of lickings. It feels so good when he rubs my feet. He does it tenderly and slowly with a lot of care.

Every Sunday he brings me flowers. There's a florist right down the street from our house. He grabs me roses or lilies, or sometimes a hanging basket with a variety of flowers, green leaves, and stems. It always puts a smile on my face even though I know my weekly gift is coming. Sometimes he adds some chocolate, which he eats most of. Later in the evening, he makes love to me. He tends to get a bit aggressive and rough in the bed, but I enjoy his love for me. Wayne makes me feel special and cared for. We occasionally argue, but it always comes out clean. We've had a few loud arguments. But I usually feel bad about things like that, so I apologize before it gets worse.

My handsome man is thirty-one years old; I'm thirty. I have close-shaved, dark hair on my head, but he is bald. His face is very manly. He has dark eyebrows and a thick, full beard he enjoys brushing over my naked body, especially my back. My facial hair is nowhere near as impressive as Wayne's, but he prefers me to keep it trimmed shorter since he says I have a cute and adorable face. He's always kissing my cheeks or playfully tweaking the tip of my nose with a silly smile aimed right at me.

I have tattooed sleeves along my arms, extending from my shoulders to my wrists. They're composed of colorful flowers (a blend of purples, pinks, and greens) mixed with swirling yellow vines and a few dark leaves. Wayne has never gotten a tattoo. I keep suggesting he should, but so far, he hasn't. I think they're sexy on a man. He always tells me how attracted he is to mine, which might be why he always buys me flowers.

I work as an accountant in a casual office environment; khaki pants and a tucked-in shirt are the norm. It's not a bad job, but it gets boring sometimes. I keep my cell phone and earplugs close, so I can listen to music when I want to. Wayne does lawn and garden maintenance for a large company that keeps him on the move Monday through Friday, except on those days when it rains. Then he gets to stay home, where he relaxes or makes a great dinner for me before I get home.

I enjoy the fact that we have weekends together. It makes me smile knowing we can spend an afternoon cuddling on the sofa or in bed. Wayne loves to wrap his arms around me and hold me close, either standing or lying down. I always get lots of kisses, too. For being tough and forward, he's also very affectionate.

He loves to softly brush his lips over my neck and then kiss the side of my head, nibble on my ears, or lightly run his beard against my skin. Nothing feels better. He whispers beside my ear how much he loves me and how thankful he is for having me in his life. It melts my heart when he says those things, and I almost always collapse against him, cradled in his arms and love.

Now when I define us as "opposites," I'm referring to our likes and interests. Although we aren't entirely different, Wayne is a huge science fiction and horror movie fan. He's also an avid stargazer. I can't begin to tell you how many late nights we've spent out in our backyard, gazing through his telescope at the constellations above. My fun-loving man has shown me many beautiful things hidden in the night sky, most of which I had never heard of before, such as the seven sisters or the Galilean moons of Jupiter. I've seen the rings of Saturn, too.

Nothing is more beautiful than his eyes in the moonlight. Even the tiniest glimmer warms my heart. We'll take turns staring up at the stars before he wraps me in a warm hug, and we spend a few minutes kissing followed by some minor groping of my butt or crotch. Wayne loves taking hold of my ass with a firm grip.

During the summer months, we're usually up late and in barely any clothing when peeking through his telescope. A few times after I bent over to glance in the eyepiece, Wayne knelt behind me, pulled my shorts down, and dove in with his tongue between my cheeks. I'm the bottom. He's the top. But my sexy muscleman enjoys sweetly licking my tender spot, especially outdoors beneath his beloved stars. He can seriously get aroused while treating me so well. I've savored feeling his meaty mammoth inside me many times under the night sky. I've stared at the moon many times while lying on my back as he makes love to me.

* * *

"So what's on tap for tonight," I asked.

It was six thirty in the evening. We had showered and eaten dinner after coming home from work. Wayne is such a great cook, and he can whip together a meal fairly fast. Today was Friday, and we just started a seven-day vacation. We timed it just right.

Wayne decided to plop down on the center of our couch with the TV on, so I took the opportunity to sit opposite of him along the left side of the sofa. I slipped off my sneakers and stretched my legs across his toned thighs with the intention of getting my feet rubbed. I wore a tank top with cargo shorts, but Wayne preferred to wear silky athletic shorts with matching shoes and socks. He seldom wore a shirt inside our house, especially during the hot and humid days of summer.

The site of his mouthwatering hairy chest made me smile. In fact, I reached over and slowly moved my hand through his sea of fur before playing with his nipple. My teasing attention put a smile on his face. And when I refer to him as "hairy," I mean he is covered in thick, delicious fur on his front and back, plus his shoulders, arms, thighs, and butt. I can never get enough of him. I love rubbing my hands over his body. It feels amazing, and he always delightfully sighs while I touch him.

A pro at giving foot rubs, Wayne started by squeezing his hands against the top and bottom of a single foot. Then he moved his thumb along the bottom, pressing it hard, twisting right and left at times, and then slowly working all the sensitive spots that needed some love.

For a second, he leaned over a bit and raised my leg so he could sniff my black and blue socks. "Nice," he said in his deep voice before adding a couple of kisses. "Like fresh out of the dryer."

I wiggled my toes against his lips, and he chuckled before answering my question. "I figured we could relax tonight," Wayne told me. "We can watch a movie, have some wine, and then maybe take the telescope outside for some late-night viewing."

I stared straight into his eyes with a questioning, yet pleased grin. "Are you going to fondle me in all the right places while I'm gazing at the stars?" I thought that was a fair question.

Wayne let out a minor laugh while he rubbed my feet. "I like fondling you, sweetie, especially your tasty butt." He poked his tongue out several times. "And since we're both off tomorrow, maybe when we come back inside tonight, I could fill you up with some hot and juicy love. Would you like that?"

Was he kidding? Of course I'd like that! "Hell yeah! Feeling your thick, meaty boy inside me is the best thing ever. You really know how to work that sucker in and out of me. And then there's all the cuddling afterward. That's the best part."

He casually took hold of my ankles and maneuvered himself out from underneath my legs and crawled on top of me. Wayne and I both enjoyed sharing sloppy kisses, so we stuck our tongues in each other's mouths over and over again, savoring the feel of our tongues against each other.

He spread his legs over mine, cradling both of my thighs between his. While I sat on his knees, he gently rested his gorgeous hairy body against my chest. Along my leg, I could feel his erection growing from within his silky sport shorts. Wayne's manhood was considerably larger than mine in length and thickness.

My handsome man raised his arms then braced himself against the edge of the couch. I cradled his head with my hands as we kissed, and then slowly lowered my arms, moving my hands over his hairy shoulders then down his back. I absolutely loved running my fingers through all the dense hair that covered him. His back was almost as furry as his chest.

"So would you like to grab a bottle of wine while I put the movie in?" He licked my lips after asking me. His sweet affections always put a smile on my face.

I teased my sexy man, reaching around him where I firmly squeezed his butt. "Sounds like a date, hot stuff!"

He sat up, then smiled at me before drumming his hands lightly over my chest. I couldn't resist reaching up and stroking his hard wiener beneath his silky blue shorts. A long white stripe ran down the sides of his shorts. From the thrilled look on his face, he suddenly slowed down and didn't seem in such a hurry to leave the couch.

"Oh, that feels good," Wayne uttered. He closed his eyes, tilted his head to the side, and lost himself in this pleasurable moment. Since he wasn't a fan of wearing underwear, I could feel every detail along his erection; the prominent rim around its head, the filled veins along its shaft, its firmness and girth.

"What kind of movie did you rent?" I wasn't eager to spoil our moment, just curious.

"That horror film I told you about," he said. "I figured I'd hold you close in my arms while you freak out from all the blood and violence."

I stopped stroking him, then tapped my hand against Wayne's tummy. "I don't freak out that much. Do I?"

He raised his brows signaling that I did. He leaned down to give me another kiss before jumping up from the couch. He was always full of energy. I did the same before heading into the kitchen, where I grabbed two glasses and a bottle of red wine from the refrigerator.

We had a nice home in Spanish Lake. It was a two-story with three bedrooms, two full bathrooms, and a finished basement, which had a sectional sofa and a big flat screen TV mounted to the wall downstairs.

In our spacious and modern style-living room, stood patio doors which opened to a roomy deck, with a few steps leading down to our backyard. Living at the end of a dead-end street proved nice over the years. There was no traffic or noise at all. Plus, we were just a stones throw away from the lake and park. A lot of worn trails and tall trees were nearby. Many times we took a hike on a Saturday or Sunday morning, and got lost in the woods. We enjoyed the scenery, the lake, and lots of private moments together. We've had sex many times out in the woods beside the lake, either in the early morning or beneath the starry night sky.

While holding the remote control, Wayne made himself comfy on our soft brown couch, leaning against the side with one leg stretched out along its cushions. He enjoyed leaving room for me to sit back against him, so he could hold me in his arms and kiss my neck. Horror films tended to make me jump at times. I knew he liked to keep me close while wrapped in his warm embrace. He was my protector, my strong man, my hero. I'd always let him take charge.

Two mahogany end tables sat on either side of our sofa. Wayne sat his drink on the top of one. His drink was easily within arms reach. I placed my glass on the coffee table in front of us. We had a large, flat-screen television mounted on the wall, with surround sound speakers positioned throughout the living room. Wayne always enjoyed turning up the volume, which shook the floors, the wine in our glasses, and me, too.

He turned off the lights which made it mostly dark. He also lit a few scented candles next to one of his gifted floral centerpieces on the table. They had a lilac scent to them, and they each shimmered and glowed inside small glass containers.

Sure enough, I jumped a few times during the movie. It was a bloody zombie riot, filled with people getting their guts ripped out or limbs torn off, and their bodies chewed on while they screamed in agony. My hairy muscle-man held me close and secure, adding some occasional kisses along my neck.

Those types of movies entertained Wayne. He would laugh at times or blurt out "Holy shit!" or "Did you see that?"

While the credits rolled, I turned around a bit so I could lay the side of my face against his chest. He kissed the top of my head while rubbing my back and side. He had such strong hands. It felt incredibly relaxing when he would touch me. My heart melted every time while lying against him.

Through the patio door I could see stars in the distance above the trees, and I knew Wayne would want to go out for some views. He was originally a science major in school, but he couldn't get through advanced chemistry, so he decided to pursue a physically demanding job and just enjoy his own interests at freewill. At times, I could tell he would have loved a different kind of life and job, but overall he was happy. I always made sure he kept a smile on his face, in one way or another. I would never deprive him of pleasure.

"Ready for some stargazing?" I ran my hand over his hairy chest while staring in his eyes. Every strand was so thick that each one bunched up between my fingers.

"Yep," he answered with enthusiasm. "Jupiter should be right above us. We'll get a great view of its moons."

I slid off the couch, grabbed my sneakers, put them on, and then tied the laces. Wayne turned on one of the lamps sitting on the side tables, then put on his tank top which was lying over the edge of the couch. I got a nice view of his hairy armpits as he worked it over his chest. Right after that, he went to the closet and grabbed his telescope, while I opened the patio door.

Wayne's telescope was lengthy and oversized. Even with his formidable muscles, he needed two hands to carry it.

"Be careful," I told him. It had gotten seriously dark outside. The moon was nowhere to be seen, and our deck wasn't exactly level. Over the years it had shifted some as it settled in the backyard. We had always meant to fix it, to level it again, but we never got around to it. There was always much more entertaining things for the two of us to do around the house.

"I'm okay. I got it," he told me.

After I closed the doors, we made our way down the steps and out to the yard. We owned a large piece of land, with plenty of space for an in-ground pool and surrounding patio. Unfortunately, again, we never got around to installing such luxuries.

Maybe someday we'll get there, I hoped.

Wayne opened the telescopes tripod legs, then sat it down in the grass, making sure it was stable. It had thick legs and wide feet, so it stood with little effort on his part. He positioned the lens toward the sky he knew so well, aiming it directly at Jupiter.

"There we go," he uttered, while gazing through the eyepiece. "Take a look at this, honey. Two moons are on each side of the planet."

He stepped back, and let me take a glance at Jupiter, although as soon as I bent over for a view of the planet, Wayne stepped behind me and continuously rubbed my butt with a single hand. Even though I had on cargo shorts, I imagined he got a good feel of my behind. I actually had on underwear, whereas he just hated wearing stuff like that. He said it kept his privates too confined and bunched up, being so huge and all. Not a problem with me. I enjoyed his lack of undergarments.

"The moons look really nice." I was enjoying the view of Jupiter, and his fondling of my rear. "And your hand feels great, too."

I stood up, turned around, gave him kiss, and then let him go back to his viewing. He turned the telescope around to get nice shots of the constellations.

My phone chimed with a text message. I pulled it out of my pocket and responded. It was from my mother. She usually checked in on me to see how things were going. She divorced my father when I was seven years old, and she had never remarried. She lived in a retirement community about twenty miles from our house.

"What the hell was that?" Wayne blurted out. He was still gazing through the eyepiece.

Quickly, I slipped my phone back into my pocket, and placed my hand on his back. "What happened?" I had no idea what he was talking about.

Wayne stood up and stared at the sky. He appeared lost in his own moment, with a curious yet confused look on his face.

"Something big and dark just moved through the sky, and it didn't make any noise," he explained.

Before I could even reply to his outburst, a clap of thunder sounded along with a quick flash of light that appeared in the distance, right where Spanish Lake sat. But it wasn't merely a white light. It had a hue of blue and yellow to it, and as quickly as it appeared, it vanished.

Both of us stared at each other. Wayne's narrowed brows and expression showed an intense curiosity.

"What the heck was that?" I asked. "I've never seen any kind of flash like that before, or heard a loud noise coming from the park at his hour."

Wayne gazed up at the night sky. He also glanced over at the woods. "I think we should go and see if everything is okay," he suggested. "Maybe a plane crashed our something. Are you okay with going over there?"

Even though the park and lake were closed, we had access along the trails behind our house, all of which led into the area. Following the paths through the woods would dump us off right near the waters edge.

I nodded. "Yeah, but let's be careful. I don't want to get shot by some police force that might think we're the bad guys, or something else."

Wayne chuckled at me while shaking his head. "We'll hide in the woods, and stay back out of sight. Nobody will see us. I promise."

I followed his lead. We held hands while making our way through the backyard to the wooden fence, where Wayne unlocked the latch then opened the wooden gate. Both of us had come this way many times before (in daylight and the pitch black of night), so we were able to carefully and quietly follow the trails leading to Spanish Lake.

Often he or I would step on a dried twig or branch, which produced a loud cracking sound. I imagined him rolling his eyes with each noisy crunch I made.

"Be careful," Wayne told me. "We're trying to be quiet."

"Duh," I replied in a mild laugh. "You're stepping on them, too."

He squeezed my hand before reaching up with his other, where he tickled the side of my minimal beard.

"I know," he said. "I'm just kind of freaked out."

"Well that makes two of us."

We took our time moving along the dirt and grass trails, passing by stumps and bushes, small trees and tall ones with dense canopies. A bug or two sometimes flew around our faces. We swatted them away. The evening songs of insects filled the background in the distance, along with the occasional frog or two.

To our left, I could see the lake glimmering between the trees. Even without a full moon shining from above, the stars glistened along its still surface. But Wayne came up with a clever idea.

"Let's go quietly through the trees," he told me. "That way we can reach the edge of the water, and see if any police or lights are flashing along the shore."

"Okay." I wasn't about to argue with him. He always came up with good ideas. I knew he wouldn't let anything happen to me, and I would do my best to protect him.

I followed him through the woods, and we slowly made our way to the edge of the lake. The trees were so large, and the branches so thick, that we each needed two hands to push them away to make our way to the waters edge. Soon, we came to a stop, and knelt behind a dense row of bushes.

"Let's see what we can see." He raised his hands, sliding them into the bushes, and then parted the branches so we could gaze through the opening toward the lake.

We both gasped.

"What the *fuck* is that?" I mumbled.

After a short pause, Wayne whispered with ample amounts of wonder, "It looks like a ship... a spaceship."

Hovering motionless, directly above the surface of the water, was an enormous metal craft, a spaceship like Wayne had said. It had the rounded and broad shape of a crab's shell, but appeared extremely thick. It also had two long extensions poking out from its forward section that resembled pinchers or claws.

Starlight shimmered off of its shiny metallic hull, as well as the water below it, and the ship stood out against the distant, starry night sky.

My breathing became heavy and labored as I stared. I felt awestruck, yet afraid of this craft above our beloved lake.

"Can that be real?" I rested my hand along Wayne's shoulder. He laughed at my comment.

"Sweetie," he said in a delighted tone. "Either it's real, or our government has been keeping a shit ton of secrets from us."

The craft began to slowly move over the surface of the lake. It floated no more than a few feet above the calm surface, making no sound at all.

"The government," I replied with uncertainty in my voice. "I seriously doubt a ship like that is from any country on Earth. It's fucking alien, and you know it. You're the science-fiction geek."

He chuckled at my response.

But then, from behind us, I heard footsteps approaching through the dried leaves on the grassy ground. Immediately I squeezed Wayne's shoulder to grab his attention. But, the instant both of us stood and spun around to see who it was, we found a handgun pointed right at us.

I raised my hands in fear like any normal person would have done, but Wayne stepped to the side and stood in front of me, shielding me with his body since he was my tough guy.

"Who... and *what* are you?" Wayne asked.

Before us stood a human male (the one holding the gun), who was about five and half feet tall. He had dark short hair and a bit of scruff for a beard. He wore black pants with a single red line running down each outer thigh, and both legs were tucked into knee-high, black leather boots. I could see the collar of what looked like a tank top beneath his textured, long-sleeved jacket.

A good looking man, his face appeared rugged yet inviting. But the real surprise, the one Wayne had exclaimed about, was this man's companion who stood towering beside him.

At least eight feet tall and wearing no shirt, a massive muscular creature stared at us. He had a hairy chest and face like a human, but starting at his arms (right around his biceps), he was covered in thick dark fur which literally ran all the way down to his fingertips. He had a dark though short beard, and the hair on his head was full with a small amount of length to it.

This towering furry guy wore dark cargo shorts, but I couldn't really tell if he had shoes on or not in the dark. His legs blended in with the darkness all around him.

"I'm James, captain of that ship," the shorter male said. He sounded direct and intolerant of disobedience. He slowly slipped his gun back into the holster strapped around his thigh. "And this is Willie, my partner. We only stopped here to take a break." He paused for a moment before asking us, "So who the hell are you two?"

"I'm Wayne, and this is my boyfriend, Adam." My man sounded just as defensive as James did. "We live right down the street. I'm guessing both of you aren't from around here. And how do you know English?"

The huge bear looking guy laughed, and then spoke in a gruff voice. "We know many languages, and *many* different races." He rested his oversized furry hand on the smaller guy's shoulder, which was easily the size of his chest. "I'm part human and part growda ha'tar, which is a race of humanoid bears. James and I come from a universe known as the Expanse, and we are here hunting rogue agents."

"Rogue agents?" I'm sure I sounded as curious as the expression that covered Wayne's face.

"The universe we come from," James explained, "has gone through a change in the governing leadership. The Masters of Science and Technology, or MST for short, are no longer watching over its citizens, which is a good thing because they're all assholes. But, unfortunately, a ton of their soldiers fled into other universes, including yours. They are power hungry and can't be trusted. So, Willie and I, along with the help of my crew, are going to eliminate them before they cause a bunch of problems for you."

Wayne looked somewhat perplexed, yet intrigued to learn more. "How do you move from one universe to another? Do you use some kind of wormhole?"

In my mind, I smiled at my sweet man. His love of science fiction started to show, and the abundant amount of love I felt for him calmed my heart.

"We use what are known as shifting engines," Willie, the half-bear explained. "Our ships are designed to instantaneously move from one location to another, which includes parallel dimensions."

"Can you show us these engines?" Wayne asked bluntly.

I forcefully nudged the side of his arm. "I don't think we need to bother them while they're searching for these agents."

Willie laughed. "You're more than welcome to visit the ship. My tough little man here has a diverse crew, to say the least." He raised both of his furry arms, then slid his hands over James's shoulders before moving them partially down his chest.

I assumed when James explained their relationship as "partners", he actually meant boyfriends. An obvious amount of love showed between the two of them, especially from all the touching by Willie. But, I wondered how two different individuals could satisfy their sexual urges. Of course, this wasn't really the first thing to be concerned about. But, what I thought about was how does someone so small accommodate someone so huge? I imagined this Willie guy had an absolutely monstrous sized wiener. That is, if James was the bottom and not the top.

Come on, Adam... focus. Aliens are standing in front of you. Now is not the time to think about how they have sex.

"Like Willie said, the two of you are welcome to come aboard my ship," James told us. "But we'll have to be leaving soon, so you can't stay long."

"How would we get over there?" Wayne asked. After all, the ship sat hovering out above the middle of the lake.

"We have motorcycles that can fly," James informed us. "They're noisy enough to rattle your balls loose, or we can put them in stealth mode so no one can hear their engines."

"That's awesome!" Wayne sounded like he was in heaven. I could only imagine all the geeky thoughts that were tumbling around inside his bald head right now.

Our house was already locked up, so there was no need to run back home for anything, and we kept keys hidden outside under a rock in the backyard.

"Where are your bikes parked?" A necessary question Wayne asked.

Willie pointed toward the woods. "Right over there." He had a deep and gruff voice. "And yes, they're in stealth mode. No one will hear us flying over to the ship, unless one of you screams and waves your hands in the air like a little girl from the thrill of it all."

Wayne and I both laughed. So did Willie. However, James kept a serious look on his face the entire time. He was obviously devoted to his duties before anything else.

"Let's go." James led the way, and Willie followed close behind him.

Wayne eagerly took hold of my hand, jerking me forward step by step, moving over the trail while cutting through several bunches of tall grass, until we appeared in a small clearing with James and Willie standing beside one regular bike and one extremely oversized bike.

Willie plopped himself down on the long leather seat, then tapped his hand on the rear, inviting me to join him.

"You go ahead with Willie," I told Wayne. "You deserve the more stunning and unusual experience."

Wayne leaned in and gave me a quick kiss on my cheek. I could feel the love he had for me pouring out of the tender look in his eyes, along with the thrill of a science-fiction moment that had come to life.

"Thank you, sweetie," he whispered. "You're awesome. I couldn't ask for a better man in my life than you."

I reached up and gently massaged his beard, in a sweet and caring manner.

"This is all for you," I told him. "I want you to get the best experiences with these guys."

He smiled at me, massaged my shoulder, and then headed over to jump on the bike behind Willie.

I watched as Wayne sat down on the huge seat and spread his legs wide apart. There was no way in hell he would ever get his arms around Willie's waist, so he raised his arms and reached up high so he could hold on to Willie's massive shoulders.

I hopped on the back of James's bike, and was able to lock my hands around his waist for the ride.

A minor vibration coursed through the frame and seat after James started the engine. But like he said, it was quiet. Not a sound came from the bike. There were only some minor jiggling sensations.

Slowly, each motorcycle rose into the air, passing by tree branches, making our way along the canopies, rising higher and higher until we were some sixty or seventy feet above the ground.

What I could see of the park looked so different from our birds eye view. I felt nervous being up so high, but also overjoyed for Wayne. Even the stars appeared brighter. Willie kept his bike close beside us, and I could see the look of wonder mixed with excitement plastered all over Wayne's face. I was certain he was in heaven right now. What science-fiction fan wouldn't have been captivated by this experience?

Side by side, James and Willie slowly moved us through the sky. There were no wheels on the motorcycles. In place of them were components which powered the bike, I assumed, however, they were made to resemble wheels. Both were capable of sitting on the ground like any ordinary motorcycle, but they couldn't roll over the land. However, flying proved to be more fascinating than driving. I could have sat on it all day long and enjoyed cruising through the sky.

"This is amazing!" Wayne shouted out.

James immediately turned around to see what the hell was going on. Willie and Wayne were both laughing together. And, I had to admit, I did find his outburst kind of funny.

We sped up, then took a step dive toward the lake. Just a few feet above the waters surface, we leveled out and breezed along, swaying a bit to the right, then the left, making our way toward the ship, which only got larger and larger the closer we got to it.

A growing light appeared along its hull. Some kind of cargo door had opened, and James steered us directly into its bay, where a row of several similar bikes sat lined up next to each other.

A roomy place with full overhead lighting, desks or workstations lined one side of the bay. I could see several green and blue holographic displays floating above their consoles. I turned my head to make eye contact with Wayne, expecting him to be overwhelmed, and sure enough, he was totally captivated. He stared in awe at everything.

Our drivers landed both bikes, and allowed Wayne and I to hop off first before lowering their kickstands, and hiking a leg over the seat where they both stood before us.

The ceiling in here was a smooth metal with lower beams attached along it every few feet. The floor was polished steel, and a wide double-sided door split open from the far side of the bay, after which two guys and one alien entered. All three were dressed like hardcore, biker dudes. Each of the guys stopped beside James and Willie. They stared at both of us.

"This is Kurt, Reese, and Amp." James introduced them to us, and each one offered a handshake.

All of them were dressed in blue jeans, black leather boots, and gray or white tank tops. Kurt was a tall and burly sort of man. A bit older than the others, he had a dark beard and short hair with some gray in it. Reese appeared young, maybe in his mid twenties, and he had short blond hair with a thin build.

But the best part was seeing Amp. He was from a reptilian race, and had all the features of such a creature. Close to seven feet tall, scales covered his entire body, and he was a pleasing shade of dark browns and sandy beige. He had a short tail which stuck out through his pants, just above his butt, and it wiggled happily as he shook our hands. His mouth was kind of lengthy, and a few times he licked his lips, which gave me a good view of his long, reptilian tongue.

"Welcome aboard." Amp smiled at me, but Wayne was so captivated by his alien presence, that he had become utterly speechless.

"Thank you," I replied. "You have an impressive ship, James."

"These three are my maintenance team," James explained. "They know their shit, and they keep everything working topnotch."

"What race are you from?" Wayne was overwhelmed. I could see bewilderment written all over his face.

"Well, my full name is Ampsamparin, but everybody calls me Amp," he explained. "I am from the iddian race."

"And you have a tail," Wayne pointed out.

Amp turned around and jutted out his rear. He shoved his hips to the side, then reached behind himself and quickly stroked his tail several times. "I sure do. Feel free to touch it if you'd like to."

Before I could say anything, Wayne rushed over and wrapped his hand around Amp's tail. My captivated man spent a long moment examining it, feeling it, and stroking it no less than he would me when I had an erection.

"Amazing," Wayne uttered. "I've never imagined seeing anything like this in real life."

Kurt and Reese both chuckled, and then Kurt added, "Just wait until you see the Devil Bunnies up on the bridge. If they don't get you hard, I don't know what will!"

James gave Kurt a disapproving glare, but overall, I could tell they both had enjoyed his off-color remark. I felt certain James and his crew shared in a lot of good times with each other. I could see that much already in their interaction.

"Speaking of the bridge," Willie announced. "Maybe we should head up there."

"Good idea." James smiled as he gave his tall boyfriend a playful nudge against his extra-large arm. To me, that was definite proof the captain wasn't entirely grim and serious. He certainly loved his tall, furry boyfriend.

However, I still wondered how both of them had sex. It wasn't the most pertinent of answers I needed, but it definitely left me curious.

All of his crew (the ones we had met so far), seemed to be such remarkable individuals. I never thought in a million years that I'd actually get to stand on a spaceship, and surround myself with friendly aliens. I could only imagine what sort of remarkable adventure Wayne and I were about to have.

2

James and Willie paused for a moment in front of the bay doors, which slowly parted down the middle before sliding into the walls. I could see a pristine white corridor behind them. His ship seemed warm and inviting. So far, everyone we had met also lived up to those standards.

Willie raised his arm, then flipped his furry index finger several times, signaling for me and Wayne to follow them. "Come on, you two."

As soon as we stepped out in the corridor, both doors closed behind us, and we then followed James and Willie down the hallway.

The polished steel floors shimmered from the overhead lights, and our reflections showed upon their surfaces with every step we took. I could see a vague image of us along the subtly curved white walls, too. I assumed most of the doors we passed were rooms for crewmen, or they served some other purpose. Maybe they were offices, or maintenance rooms of some kind?

We reached an elevator, and it turned out to be spacious after its doors opened. As soon as we stepped inside, Wayne and I got a much better view of Willie's anatomy, and fur covered arms from being so close to him. He was incredibly tall and burly, a tower of strength and muscle. I felt like a munchkin standing next to him. He stood at least two and half feet taller than I did. I got a view of his furry legs, too. He was wearing short brown boots without any socks. I guess with all that fur on your legs you really didn't need to wear socks. I wondered if he sweated like the rest of us did. I wasn't sure if bears did or didn't.

"So are you the only half-human and half-bear of your kind?" Wayne sounded so intrigued.

"I am," Willie replied, with an amiable nod. "My father was growda ha'tar and my mother was human. If you ever meet my race, you'll be astounded by their height. I'm actually short in comparison to any full-blooded bears."

Wayne smiled happily. I could tell he was absolutely thrilled to be here, to experience such a fantasy come true. And that's exactly what this was for him. My handsome man had stepped inside one of his television shows, or Hollywood movies, and bathed in all the wonders and thrills.

The elevator came to a stop, and its door opened to yet another long white corridor. However, this hallway appeared much wider, and it rose slightly the further we walked up it.

Ahead of us stood two oversized, dark steel doors, which parted and then slowly opened, revealing a variety of people within the impressive and spacious bridge.

The four of us entered before the doors closed with a mild hissing sound. Designed as a split room, at the center I could see a gapping hole that led to a second floor on the bridge, just below the level we stood upon. However, a massive green and orange holographic display of Earth floated directly above the rounded stairways leading down to the lower section. Workstations and desk-type tables lined the circular room, with several of them positioned around the main holographic image. Each workstation had black and smooth glossy tops, resembling polished glass, and I imagined fingers tapping all sorts of futuristic controls or switches.

But the most captivating sight, the one that left Wayne's mouth hanging wide open with shock and awe, was the sight of James's diverse crew.

A male and female approached us and offered a handshake to me and Wayne. They were definitely non-human. "I'm Bray," the female said. "It's nice to meet you." A very beautiful, fit, curvaceous, and classy looking lady, she had reddish colored skin with long flowing auburn hair, and stood a couple of inches taller than us. Dressed in a sleeveless jacket, her pants were tucked into knee-high boots, all of which were a dark, red color.

"And I'm Woofa... her boyfriend."

This guy was definitely the more interesting of the two. Shorter than Bray, Woofa wore a black sleeveless jacket which allowed us to see his fur covered chest. And, I mean furry as in like a dog or cat. Rich and silky black hairs covered him. However, his arms appeared human just like mine, even though his eyes did not. He had vertical pupils like a cat, mixed with lengthy black hair on his head, and a rough face to match. He had a ready-to-fight stance about him. Even his voice sounded a bit abrasive. He was definitely a badass, if I had to pick a word to accurately describe him, because he certainly looked the part.

"Holy crap," Wayne blurted out. He pointed at the far side of the bridge where four crewmembers were working at one of the stations. "Look at them!"

I had to admit, I did slightly gasp with surprise when I saw who my captivated man was pointing at.

Beyond the huge holographic image of Earth, three female demons stood with a blue alien male right beside them. One of the females was taller than the other two, but all three were busty and shapely, wearing tight-fitting, black sleeveless bodysuits which showed off their shapely bodies. They each had light purple skin, long and black stylish hair, with two devilish looking, dark pointy horns growing above their temples.

The male was actually dressed in a nice pair of blue jeans, with a gray T-shirt that had some sort of huge tattoo-inspired, dragon design printed on it. I somewhat laughed when I saw this guy walking around and noticed he had on colorful bright blue sneakers.

Of all things for us to see on an alien spaceship.

"I think you two could use a tour of the bridge," Willie said.

"Woofa and I will be happy to take them around," Bray offered. She sounded and acted so sweet and kind.

We followed Bray and her smaller boyfriend around the bridge, while James and Willie pressed some glowing buttons hovering in the air above a nearby workstation. The console was several feet long and a few feet wide with an angled top, so whoever stood before it could see what the screens were showing.

"Are you enjoying yourself," I whispered beside Wayne's ear as soon as I had the opportunity.

He glanced in my eyes for a brief moment with a broad smile. "Oh, you know I am, sweetie." He grabbed my hand and gave it a tender squeeze. Nothing felt better than his love for me, and I expressed the same right back at him.

Bray and Woofa stopped near the alien crewmembers to introduce us.

"These are the Devil Bunnies," Bray announced, "Mortenna, Skiss, and Neese. They recently joined our team, and have proven to be outstanding in many ways."

All three of them stood beside each other. I couldn't stop staring at the small dark horns above their temples. It was so unusual to see such unique individuals. I glanced at Wayne and he seemed ten times more captivated than I did.

"I'm Adam, and this is my boyfriend Wayne," I told them.

The smaller blue alien male walked over to us with a smile on his face. He shook both of our hands. "I'm Dean," he said. "I'm sort of the computer expert on the ship. Welcome aboard."

The Devil Bunnies were all taller than Dean, and one in particular, Mortenna, was the tallest of her kind. But, they all looked like scantly clad models from some glamorous magazine. All of them were very fit with the neckline of their bodysuits unzipped fairly far down, which showed off their bountiful cleavage.

"Why are you called Devil Bunnies?" Wayne asked.

All three of them smiled flirtatiously before flicking a finger against their horns. Then each of them did a quick little dance, shaking their hips, and showing off their well-formed bodies.

"I think you get the point," Mortenna said happily. She had her hands locked around her shapely waist. "There are many of us but we agreed to join James's crew and help out with the rogue agents."

Each of them acted sweet and fun, but in the back of my mind I could tell if the shit hit the fan, each of the Devil Bunnies would come out fighting. They looked hardcore and more than capable of kicking some ass. I imagined them using their horns to stab people.

All four of them went back to their workstations, where they pushed glowing buttons or tapped holographic displays that floated in midair. Streams of data ran along some of the smaller digital displays that floated above each console.

We followed Bray and Woofa back over to James and Willie. Both the captain and his boyfriend had serious looks plastered on their faces.

"Is something wrong?" Woofa asked in his mildly gruff voice. As soon as he raised his questioning hands, I noticed he had padded palms like a feline. How incredible was that? He must have been part cat, or tiger, or something else from some alien world.

"Well," James said, "You know Dean was able to connect us to distant transmissions throughout this galaxy, and a few of them we've been monitoring seem kind of odd." He continued touching controls or running his finger over displays.

"What do you mean by odd?" Bray sounded concerned.

"Several unrelated planets are reporting minor attacks from unknown assailants," Willie explained in his deep voice. "We're thinking it might be rogue agents trying to infiltrate their societies."

"I don't understand," Wayne asked. "Why are they attacking people? What's the purpose in that? Why don't they just go their own way and leave people alone."

James and Willie both shook their heads with long sighs.

"Like I told you both," James explained. "There was a change of leadership in our universe so the rogue agents fled, and I'm sure their intentions are to take control of lesser developed cultures, and try to repopulate their military. They're hungry for power, nothing more."

"Plus they're all assholes," Willie added with a smirk.

Bray and Woofa laughed at his outburst.

"Well, if there's anything Adam and I can do," Wayne offered, "Just let us know."

James stared straight into Wayne's eyes with his head tilted and a single brow raised. "Actually, I think it'd be best if we took you back down to the woods and said our goodbyes."

Wayne's expression changed from joy to dismay in a heartbeat. I felt bad for him. He looked devastated.

Willie had noticed Wayne's sudden disappointment. I could see it on his face. "No offense toward you or Adam," he explained, with his huge furry hand raised respectfully. "But we've all dealt with rouge agents many times before. We know how to handle them."

An alert of some kind suddenly sounded. It displayed a flashing button that appeared in midair beside a holographic screen. The huge representation of Earth that floated between the decks of the bridge had changed too. It now showed an image of our galaxy, and then zoomed in toward a distant planet where I assumed trouble had started.

I grabbed hold of Wayne's hand. He gave mine a tender squeeze. It was always a pleasure for me to feel how much he cared about me. Bray and Woofa immediately headed over to a workstation located near the gigantic holographic image, while James and Willie kept analyzing the readouts streaming across the screens hovering in front of them.

"Looks like they've attacked a planet in the Torbin system," Dean announced out loud. His voice was calm and mild, which matched his appearance. "It's a slightly less advanced world. And, from these readings, it looks like they've only developed space exploration about one hundred years ago, or so."

"Well, let's get the hell over there and stop them!" Wayne actually shook his fist in the air. He sounded as determined as James's crew did.

"Wayne." I squeezed his hand, and gave him a mildly disapproving glance. "We don't belong here. Let them handle it, okay?"

He sighed, then shook his head. He let go of my hand too. From his stance and restlessness, I could see a great deal of frustration building inside of him. We had been together long enough that I could read his emotional state. Exploring space had been something he had always dreamed about being a part of. I felt bad for crushing his joy, so I brushed my hand along his arm in an attempt to comfort him.

Wayne moved closer to James and Willie. "Please let me and Adam come along," Wayne begged. "We promise to stay out of the way. I can't tell you how exciting all of this is for me... your ship, the alien crew, and *you*." He raised his hand and patted Willie's furry forearm, which made our half-bear friend smile.

James took a deep breath, then slowly let it out while he considered Wayne's pleading. He tilted his head, then gazed up into Willie's dark eyes. They both quietly contemplated his request, grinning happily at each other after a short moment.

"Okay," James finally said, "You both can come along. But it's going to be a short trip. Don't expect a lot of sightseeing."

Wayne almost jumped into the air he was so delighted. In a subtle display, he happily tapped his sneakers a few times over the floor. I patted him on his shoulder while feeling just as pleased as he did. To see him so excited warmed my heart. I wanted only the best for him in life.

"Have any people in the Torbin system had contact with outsiders before?" Willie had turned around and asked Dean.

Their computer expert hit several buttons, and took a moment to gather his data. "I'm showing records of brief encounters with other races," Dean explained. "But overall, they haven't had a lot of interaction with aliens." His blue skin really stood out against the rest of the bridge. I couldn't stop glancing at him.

Willie turned around, locked his furry hands around his hips, and then stared at James. "Our showing up shouldn't be too much of a surprise for them. Wouldn't you agree?"

James nodded. "Dean, do you have the coordinates entered into our navigation system?"

"I just input them," Dean informed our captain. He raised his blue hand, and scratched the side of his face. "We can shift to their world whenever you want to. Let me pull up a bio scan of their race." He pushed more buttons on his workstation, and swiped a few holographic ones glowing above in the air. "I'll put the data on the main projection. Their race is called elshon."

The gigantic hologram between the two decks changed. A representation of the race in question instantly appeared which showed a very detailed display of them. They stood upright with humanoid shaped bodies, but they were covered in fur from head to toe, just like Willie's arms and legs. Their faces resembled a gopher, to some degree. They had pitch-black eyes, small pink ears, and long whiskers on both sides of their stubby noses.

"We're ready to shift to their world," Bray announced.

James gave her a few confirming nods. "Let's do it."

Bray pushed several buttons, and the midair screens above her workstation showed columns of rapidly scrolling data. In less than a minute, the main image changed to a holographic representation of the elshons home world. In the back of my mind, I wondered if another light show had appeared above their world, similar to the one Wayne and I had witnessed from our backyard. I remembered hearing a clap of thunder, too. Were those common characteristics when their ship shifted to a new location? I assumed they were.

A ringed planet appeared between the decks of the bridge, and even though it was a holographic display, I could see continents, oceans, and a variety of sweeping clouds, which included some flashes of lighting. The details were impressive.

"Amazing." Wayne sounded utterly captivated. "We just crossed thousands of light years. Didn't we?"

"Ten thousand, six-hundred, and twenty-seven, to be precise," Woofa informed us. He added a crooked smile with his announcement.

Wayne shook his head. His expression showed complete and utter fascination as he stared at the images on the main display.

I stood beside him, feeling thankful for our adventure and experience. Wayne always dreamed of seeing the stars someday, and now it had finally come true. I was delighted to be experiencing all of this with him beside me.

"Are there any rogue ships in the area?" James sounded concerned. He and Willie scrutinized all the displays and screens in front of them.

"I'm not detecting any," Mortenna said, one of the Devil Bunnies. She and her two companions kept busy analyzing readouts as they appeared above their workstations. "However, there *have* been several small attacks. Dean, can you translate the global news reports that are coming in?"

"Sure, give me a few seconds," Dean answered.

Their computer expert quickly translated the news reports, channeling them to run along the main display. They had the same type of news media coverage as Earth did. News casts and visuals of isolated destruction, mixed with dead bodies lying here and there scrolled down the data stream. Streets had been demolished. Homes had been destroyed, with scenes of crying individuals huddled together showed up in every report. All their furry faces were soaked from tears.

"Why would these rogue agents do all of this?" Wayne was shocked and disgusted. I noticed his overjoyed feelings had noticeably diminished.

"Because they're power-hungry assholes who won't stop until everyone is bowing before them." Willie sounded incredibly pissed. In fact, everyone on the bridge looked disgusted from the reports, visuals, and streaming data. The Devil Bunnies had angry looks on their faces. I could tell they were ready to beat the shit out of someone.

"So, how are we going to stop them?" Wayne sounded resolute. Both of his fists were closed, and ready for some serious punching.

James tilted his head, raised a brow, and glanced at Wayne as if he were crazy.

"I think our fist priority should be trying to help these people," Bray pointed out. "I'm sure they had no idea an attack was coming." I think she tried to pacify the situation, before James said something harsh to Wayne.

Woofa nodded in agreement while standing beside his tall girlfriend. She seemed pleased with his reaction. "We should take a shuttle down to their planet, and assist them with whatever they need," Woofa added.

"They'll probably shoot at us," James said. "They might think we're more rouge trash. Dean, see if you can tap into their communications network somehow, and give them a heads up about why we're here."

"Okay." Immediately, Dean got to work on sending out a message. He must have had topnotch skills at translating alien languages. His dark blue fingers moved fast over the control panels. He quickly tapped and pushed all kinds of buttons, with a determined look on his face.

"But despite stopping here, we're still going to kick the shit out of these rogues, right?" Wayne asked. He sounded eager to fight.

"*We* are going to take care of them." James bobbed his pointed finger against his chest, and then stared at Wayne as if my boyfriend had a screw loose in his head. "I don't want you *or* Adam involved in any of this. It's too dangerous."

"I've sent a message to their primary military command center," Dean explained. "We should get a response in a few minutes."

"Adam and I both promise not to get in the way," Wayne told James in a pleading tone. "I would be thrilled to see a planet like this, and help its people. Seriously, we'll behave."

I saw James roll his eyes after hearing Wayne's suggestion. It seemed he wasn't about to budge. But, his towering boyfriend who stood to the side rested his huge furry hand on James's shoulder, and sort of eased his lover into submission from the amiable looks they exchanged.

James raised his head and faced us before letting out a long sigh. He raised his arm, and tenderly brushed his hand along Willie's arm, thanking his lover for his tender and caring support.

"Alright," James said, "You two can come along. But, *please* don't act all freaked out or dance around like kids in a candy shop. Stay calm, and just take in everything from a distance. Okay?"

Wayne nodded happily. "We will. I promise."

"Thanks, James." I gave our captain a satisfied smile before slipping my arm around Wayne's waist, and giving him a kiss on his cheek. His confidence and determination was so incredibly adorable to me. Wayne was more straightforward than I could be.

"We're receiving a transmission," Dean announced in an excited tone. He took a moment and pushed more buttons in order to decipher the message. "They're saying we can come down to the city of Porpanel to provide assistance. It's the capital of their planet. They've sent the coordinates where we should land."

"Dean and the three of us can stay on the bridge. We'll keep an eye out for any rogue ships," Mortenna suggested. Her two companions both nodded in agreement. I wasn't sure which one was Skiss or Neese, but I gave them all a satisfied smile, and they returned my compliment.

"Good idea," Willie added. "Any problems show up, contact us immediately."

Mortenna gave an approving nod, and then went back to tapping her purple fingers over the workstation she and the other two Devil Bunnies occupied. Dean did the same at his desk.

Bray followed Woofa over to me and Wayne. She gave both of us a tender pat on our shoulders. "I guess you guys are about to see your first alien world. Are you excited?"

Wayne's eyes opened wide with desire. "I'll admit, I'm kind of nervous."

"Don't be," Woofa said, with a shake of his head. He also patted Wayne's shoulder. "Trust me. It'll be more fascinating than frustrating. Although, I'm not exactly sure what damage we'll see. Hopefully, it's nothing too extreme. Just be prepared."

James and Willie had finished at their workstation. They stepped away about ten feet from it, then stood beside each other.

"Lets all get down to the shuttle bay," James announced. He waved his hand through the air, inviting all of us over to him.

Wayne and I made our way over to the doors. We stood beside James and Willie. Safe to say, I could see an ample amount of excitement written all over my sweet mans face. And, while holding hands, Bray and Woofa soon joined the four of us. He was so much shorter than she was, but they went together perfectly. I could clearly see the love they shared for each other.

"What are you guys going to do if we see a lot of dead bodies or injured people?" Wayne asked. He sounded worried. I could hear it in his voice.

Bray raised her hand, then rested it on Woofa's shoulder. "Well, my furry man isn't a healer," she informed us, "But he can cast a few rejuvenating spells which will help minor injuries."

I looked as shocked as Wayne had. His mouth had fallen wide open. "You can cast spells?" Wayne asked Woofa. He sounded completely in awe.

Bray's boyfriend nodded several times.

"So, you're like some kind of wizard?" Wayne added. "What other kinds of spells can you cast?"

Woofa laughed. "Well, my specialty is destruction spells, or impenetrable barriers. Those are my area of expertise."

I stared at Wayne. He had become so captivated he stood speechless.

"Plus, Bray can summon spirits from her past lives." Woofa patted her arm while smiling at her the entire time. "Just wait until you see them. She's got a huge repertoire of creatures, and although they look hollow, they are outlined in blue and white light. Every one of them is amazing, and they can be thinner than fog or harder than steel."

"So, both of you use magic?" Wayne sounded completely captivated by these facts. But before Bray and Woofa could even answer him, he spun around and faced James and Willie. "Do you guys have super powers, too?"

They both lightly chuckled.

"Well," James admitted cheerfully, "My preferred weapon of choice is my handgun, or sometimes I use a rifle." He patted his holstered firearm against his right thigh. "But, Willie likes to hit with his fists whenever he can. Don't you, sexy bear?"

To prove James's point, Willie held up his furry fists nice and high, smiling as he shook both ever so slightly. They were impressive in size *and* thickness. I imagined he could pound the living day lights out of anybody, regardless of their size.

High around the bridge were mounted speakers, and some soothing dreamlike instrumental music began to lightly play as James stepped up to the huge main doors. I guessed the Devil Bunnies and Dean like to listen to their favorite tunes, while working on stuff or monitoring situations. It was nice to hear.

The main doors opened. The four of us followed our captain and his boyfriend as they led the way to the elevator.

"You mentioned past lives," Wayne asked, right before we reached the elevator. "Is that the case for everyone? Do Adam and I have past lives?"

The elevator doors opened, and we all stepped inside one at a time. James hit a couple of holographic buttons along the control panel inside, and after the doors closed we began to descend through the ship.

"Everyone has past lives," Bray informed us. She made eye contact with me and Wayne. Her long auburn hair flowed over her shoulders in subtle curls. "We are a combination of physical, mixed with an extraordinary, supernatural energy. After our bodies are no more, the energy moves on and is capable of joining with a variety of different physical structures. Plus, it remembers all of its former lives, and *that* is how the art of spirit calling is possible. I summon my former selves from an immortal memory."

Woofa reached up, and rubbed his hand over Bray's back in a show of affection. It made his girlfriend smile. She gazed down at him with love in her eyes.

The elevator came to a stop, and the doors opened. We stepped out into a large shuttle bay which was different from the one we had originally arrived in. Recessed bright lights shined from above, and the room was a mix of white and gray colors on the walls. The floors were polished and showed hints of reflections upon them.

All six of us stepped out of the elevator. We followed Willie over to an impressive ship that resembled a sort of lengthy and rounded sub sandwich, only without the meat and veggies. A front window lined its cockpit, and along its sides, near the rear, were small extensions that resembled wings. It was silvery gray, with a few dull red lines running horizontally along its length.

Far to our right, a workroom lay positioned beyond a thick glass wall, along with two workstations that sat fairly close to the shuttle. I assumed they were some kind of secondary controls for maneuvering the craft, or controlling the bay.

James stepped up to the ship where he tapped a few buttons along a control panel which unlocked its main door. It opened with a minor hiss, and then slowly lowered. There were six metal steps lining the inside of the door, and we each walked up them, making our way into his spacious shuttle.

"Everybody get comfortable, and buckle up." James pointed at two long rows of cushioned seats lining the sides of the shuttles interior. "Willie and I will fly us down to their city."

I sat on a cushioned seat beside Wayne on one side of the shuttle, while Bray and Woofa sat across from us. Each of us raised our seatbelts, then secured them around our waists. James and Willie had already gone into the cockpit area. They started the engines after closing the hatch and sealing it.

"Look at that," I told Wayne. I pointed toward the front window where we could see the cargo bay doors had risen. The shuttle then lifted a few feet into the air before moving forward out into space.

A nearby view of the planets beautiful blue and white atmosphere, and surrounding rings could be seen as we veered to the left and traveled toward it. One of our pilots hit the gas, and soon we began diving through clouds and moving beneath its evening skies toward our destination.

"I guess Dean relayed our coordinates to James?" Wayne asked.

"He sent them to the shuttle," Woofa answered. "It'll basically pilot itself. James and Willie just need to make sure everything runs smoothly."

Wayne and I sat staring at the massive city we descended toward. It looked even more impressive than New York or Los Angeles would have, although, I've never been to either. Tall skyscrapers reached toward the heavens, and many of them resembled trees. But, instead of having canopies made of branches, they were made of steel and glass, showcasing what appeared to be very spacious areas for offices, or personal living. Clearly this race was technologically advanced and diverse. Their architecture proved that much.

I could feel gravity taking hold as the shuttle veered and tilted from side to side a bit, while we maneuvered into position to land. We all had jiggled slightly in our seats.

"Pretty smooth ride," Wayne pointed out. He reached over and patted my hand. He shot me a smile too.

Bright spotlights moved all around us. They shined in through the front windshield. I had to squint several times because they were so intense. Wayne squeezed my hand. He and I were both sort of nervous.

"I'm sure they're simply taking precautions," Bray mentioned. I could tell from her relaxed tone, she tried to calm both of us as best as she could. She and Woofa were very nice people.

I nodded, then gave her a quick and confirming smile.

"We're about to land," Willie announced from the cockpit.

I felt the shuttle come to a stop, and we hovered for a short moment before slowly descending toward the landing spot. We moved down through the bright city, along towers of steel beneath a starry night sky above us.

We landed with a few mild bumps, then James and Willie walked to the back of the shuttlecraft where our captain stared directly at me and Wayne.

"Now, if you see any bad stuff, don't get all freaked out," James told us. He took a few seconds to adjust his holstered gun while he spoke. "The rogue agents hit them hard, based upon the reports still coming in through their news media. These people need our help, and that's what we're going to do."

"Will we be able to understand them?" Wayne had brought up a good point.

James shrugged with an indifferent look on his face. "Our pdPhones will be able to translate their language after a few minutes of hearing it. But, when we step outside, we'll just have to settle in and wait for that to happen."

"What's a pdPhone?" Wayne couldn't resist asking.

James, Willie, Bray, and Woofa all pulled out a variety of mechanical devices from their pants pockets, and then aimed them all right at Wayne's face. Each one resembled a cellular phone, only in different sizes, shapes, and colors.

A loud knock sounded against the outside of the ship.

"I guess they're anxious to meet us," Woofa pointed out about the inhabitants.

Willie stepped toward the control panel, where he stood for a moment. He then received an approving nod from James to open the shuttle's door. The hatch locks released with a hiss, and the door leaned outward, showcasing their race and their world to each one of us.

Wayne and I stood up so we could stare outside at the atrocities. We gasped in shock, completely caught off guard and horrified by all the devastation.

3

Each of the alien citizens ranged in height from three to four feet, and all had short fuzzy fur in shades of gray, dark brown and light brown. Unfortunately, I couldn't tell which were males or females. However, the few who had knocked on the shuttle's door now stood near its hatch, and they sounded mostly male. They shouted out to us in their language, with outstretched arms and inviting hands. Most of which I assumed were pleas for help, because their faces looked terrified.

Further out among the city streets, I watched as huddled masses and dozens of individuals scurried around parked vehicles and store fronts. Many acted panicked and frightened from the attacks, and to my surprise, their streets looked similar to any that would have appeared throughout a highly populated city on Earth. Their automobiles did, too. I saw SUVs, trucks, and sports cars. Although, the majority of them were much smaller is size and shape than any human would have driven.

James and his companions tapped their pdPhones to start the translation process with their handheld devices. Three of their race gathered enough nerve and then hurried into our shuttle, where they stood right in front of us. All of them spoke quickly, nervously shaking as they stood. They lifted their furry arms up high, raising their stumpy paws with alarmed and confused expressions.

Their clothing resembled shorts and T-shirts much like Wayne and I had on. They even wore a variety of footwear, ranging from small leather boots to colorful sneakers, which surprised me. I hadn't expected sneakers to be so universal, especially being so many light years away from Earth. And, just like I had seen in the holographic representation, each of them had short snouts with noticeable thick whiskers. Small pink ears and large dark eyes completed their facial appearances.

"What are they saying?" Wayne was eager to understand and help.

He had such a generous and caring heart beneath his rough and tough exterior.

I rested my hand against the back of his shoulder to convey my complete and utter support. I would always be there for Wayne no matter the circumstances. He completed me in so many ways.

James held up his hand to try and stop the three alien creatures from talking. They paused as he showed them his phone, and then flipped his index finger back and forth a few times between himself and them, indicating he would be able to translate soon.

But they were all freaked out and kept jabbering away. They stared at each other and at us with wide-opened eyes. Minor booms and unexpected crashes came from down the street, which caused each of them to jump. From the intrigued expressions on their faces, I could tell they were absolutely amazed by Willie's enormous size. Maybe even sort of startled and intimidated, which only added to their nervousness, I assumed. A dozen of them would barely cover Willie's broad chest.

All three elshons reached out for our hands in an attempt to lure us out of the shuttle. Willie boldly walked ahead and moved right through their group. He showed no fear as he stepped out first, ducking his head as he made his way through the hatch and down the steps, until he stood on the street beside many more of these gopher people.

The rest of us slowly followed, as Willie and his three furry acquaintances led the way. The minute I stepped out and stood upon the pavement, I gasped in horror at the sight I saw behind our shuttlecraft.

Even though it was late evening, the sky was lit up with roaring fires and tall clouds of thick, dark billowing smoke. A horrible odor filled the air. It gagged me for a moment. From what I could see an entire avenue of shops, and what looked like apartments, had been destroyed by these rogue agents.

The gopher people scrambled to help their fallen friends, but from the looks of it, many had been killed by whatever blast demolished the buildings. I saw several dead bodies lying along the sidewalks, each of them had been burned and mangled. Some still smoldered from having been consumed by flames, which was likely what I smelled in the air.

All their burned flesh and fur had been charred to black ashes, leaving only singed remains of who they once were.

Wayne grabbed hold of my hand and squeezed it hard. I could tell he was pissed from seeing all the devastation and mass murders. The angry look on his face said enough. In his science fiction and horror movie brain, I imagined he was thinking about seeking revenge upon the people who had committed these senseless tragedies. After all, that was how the plot unfolded in all of his favorite films.

My tough guy tried to walk forward, but I held him back. "What's wrong?" He had turned around to face me, shrugging and shaking his head with a confused expression.

"Are you sure you want to go over and stand in front of all that?" I was concerned for his wellbeing more than mine. I didn't want to see him consumed by this tragedy.

Wayne pointed at the rest of our team as they headed over to the aftermath. "Everyone else is going over there," he said to me in a mild tone. "We need to follow them, Adam." He gently pulled me closer as he held my hand. "Come on, silly. I won't let anything happen to you. We'll be fine."

His kindness always warmed my heart. I only hoped he wouldn't get too upset after seeing everything up close. Wayne could develop a serious temper at times over mundane situations, but he had only done so with me a few times. He preferred to show me ample amounts of love and support after we had an issue. But what *would* set him off were the usual headaches life tosses at you, like a flattened tire on the highway when you were on a deadline. I've seen him completely lose his temper over stuff like that, so I was certain he would get pissed about what had happened here to our gopher friends.

Fortunately, I knew exactly how to calm him down in stressful situations. Some hugs and kisses always put a smile on both of our faces. Wayne was without a doubt the best lover I had ever been with. He knew exactly how to pleasure me, and I knew how to please him even more. Nothing made him more relaxed and soothed than my light touch and affection. I enjoyed tracing my finger tips as gently and slowly as possible over his body, softly touching his sea of hairs. It tended to give him pleasurable shivers, all of which he enjoyed immensely.

But, such simple pleasures would have to wait. We needed to focus on the moment, on the individuals who needed our help.

While Wayne and I held hands, we followed our shipmates and the three alien friends over to the sidewalks. My stomach had begun to churn with sickness. Pools of blood and bodies littered the pavements. A few tears filled my eyes. Glass from doors and windows had been shattered and covered the wide avenues, along with tons of bricks and stones from the demolished buildings.

Steel and wooden rooftops had fallen down upon the streets, most of which had killed individuals who were merely out for a stroll. Many of the elshons lay crushed beneath the rubble with their blood covered limbs and fur sticking out along the edges. All of it lay matted to the pavement with bodily fluids.

Wayne leaned closer against me, then whispered. "This is seriously fucked up. Who would do something so fucking crazy?"

"The rogue agents have no morals," Bray reminded us. She had been standing beside us, so she clearly heard his comments. "They have zero respect for people. All they care about is power and control. Never forget that." She patted each of us on our backs. I could sense a lot of care coming from her, and a lot of passion to make things better for these people.

From all the jabbering by our tiny alien friends, everyone's pdPhone started to translate what they said. James let his device begin, and it talked in a human voice as it conveyed what was said. In addition, all of our words were translated into their language. Each of their phones was a remarkable piece of technology.

Both Willie and James took a few moments to explain the attack. They gave reasons and intentions to help clarify what had happened.

"But why?" one of the gophers asked. He sounded more male than the others, even though all their voices were kind of high-pitched.

"We did nothing wrong," another added. "We welcomed them to our world and *this* is the payback we get! Many of our people are now dead!"

Both sounded and acted incredibly pissed. They tossed their furry paws into the air. Copious amounts of tears fell from their dark eyes and ran down their furry faces.

"That's why we're here," James explained. "We're going to stop them and pay them back for what they did to your race. Trust me, we will."

Wayne and I couldn't stop staring at the dead bodies, or the looks of agony covering all of their faces. Those who had survived stood over their fallen friends, each crying terribly while mourning for such needless loss.

Our group stopped and stood motionless. I think all of us were feeling a shit ton of emotions, including hatred, confusion, and anger.

James used his pdPhone to make a call. From his conversation, I could tell he had contacted Dean back on the ship. "Okay," James said into his phone. "I'm not asking you, Dean, I'm telling you. Find those rogue ships. I don't care what tricks you have to use. Pinpoint their location so we can find them, and then blow their fucking heads off. You got me?"

James quickly ended his call then slipped his phone back into his pants pocket, while Wayne and I watched as Woofa cast his minimal healing spell.

Woofa cupped his hands and held them directly in front of his chest, as if he were holding some kind of huge invisible ball. Bray informed the elshons in regard to what he was doing, and I stood amazed as Woofa generated his magic. A glowing, bright blue sphere appeared between his hands.

The magical orb was large and full of swirling energy, which made it shine like a beacon in the night. It illuminated Woofa's furry chest, his chin, and cheeks. After a brief moment, he stepped forward. He took slow strides while focusing on his task, and little by little, he swirled his cupped hands around the outside of the glowing sphere that floated before him.

As he stepped along the avenue, small points of shimmering blue light raced out of the main orb and merged with the survivors. Each tiny light penetrated the furry aliens and joined with them upon contact.

Their entire bodies momentarily burst forth with an aura of blue color before they absorbed Woofa's magical gifts.

It was hard to look away, but I took a moment to glance at Wayne. He was utterly captivated by Woofa's healing spell. In fact, I saw the beginning of joyful tears growing in his eyes. I rubbed my hand down the length of his arm, knowing he felt more relieved and calm.

Word must have spread quickly among the gopher people, because dozens of them came rushing out to grab some of Woofa's healing spell. Three or sometimes four points of light raced out from his main sphere, and they illuminated every furry individual, which restored their health, their vigor, and repaired minor injuries instantly. The smallest cuts and scraps disappeared from their faces, leaving them refreshed and restored.

"How can we ever repay you for the help you've provided," one of them asked.

Bray held her phone out and allowed it to translate for us. "There is no need for payback," she said. "We are here to help, and that is what we will do for your people."

I noticed several older elshons moving over the streets, and I saw they had caught Bray's attention. Before I could say anything, she lifted her arms, moved her hands fluidly through the air, and then summoned her spirits from within her immortal memory. She called forth her past lives, her former selves to help these individuals.

From along the streets, a dozen or more small spirit creatures crawled out from below the cobblestone and assisted the older individuals, acting as support for them to lean against or hold onto while trying to get off the avenues. Each of Bray's spirits resembled large dogs. All were four legged, but without long tails. All had long snouts and very tall ears, and around their necks they had what looked liked fins that flapped and moved as they did. Each of her creatures appeared transparent but they were outlined in blue and white shimmering light, which showcased their detailed fur, muscles, and shapes.

This was definitely not a type of animal I was familiar with. But, regardless of how they appeared or how they shined and glowed, Bray's pets helped these people to stand and walk with ease, and I couldn't have been more proud of her and Woofa for casting their magic.

Unfortunately, the crushed victims would not be resuscitated, and there were many of them. The rooftops that had fallen killed quite a few individuals. It was all such a senseless act. Why punish people for not wanting to be a part of your group? Everyone has the right to be who they want to be, to think however they want to, and go through life with their own beliefs and opinions. Violence like this has always confused me, and I knew it seriously pissed off Wayne. We had many discussions about similar incidents on Earth toward gay people. None of it made sense to either of us.

"Are you doing okay?" I gently nudged Wayne's arm with mine.

He nodded and took hold of my hand. "Yeah," he said. "I'm good. I'd be happier if we were blasting the shit out of those rogue agents though. All of this is fucking sick."

I smiled a bit from his comment as I imagined Wayne pounding several dudes right in their faces. He didn't take a lot of crap from people, especially those who seriously aggravated him. He had no hesitation toward expressing his opinion, either verbally or physically.

James's phone rang and he quickly pulled it out of his pocket. "Yeah, Dean, go ahead," he answered.

"I hope you two aren't turned off by all of this," Bray said to me and Wayne. "There is so much more beauty in life than what we see here today. I only wish everyone could see *and* feel the vastness of existence the way I do. They would certainly see life differently."

Bray was so beautiful and kind. The subtle red color of her skin seemed darker in the night and so did her auburn hair. I assumed she liked to wear red clothes. That must have been her favorite color.

"We're okay," Wayne explained, although he still sounded tense. "We understand how fucked up people can be, and these rogues sound like they need a serious smackdown. I hope you guys are going to take care of them." Wayne raised his hand, shaped it like a gun, and then pointed it directly at his head for a moment to demonstrate the best way to deal with our enemies.

Bray slowly nodded as she understood and agreed with him completely. Her summoned spirits were still helping older people move along the streets. They used them for support, placing their hand along each ones ethereal back. She had called about two dozen of her dog creatures. Woofa finished up with his healing, too. He had walked down one side of the street, changed sides, and then continued up the other, where he revitalized all who he had passed while stepping around the rubble.

James moved over to us after he hung up with Dean. Willie followed him.

"Was Dean able to figure anything out?" Bray asked.

Our captain let out a miserable and frustrated sounding sigh. His huge boyfriend had rested his furry hand on James's shoulder, showing care and comfort in this terrible moment.

"Dean said he would need to actually scan one of their ships," James explained. "But, after doing so, we would be able to track its location no matter where it went."

"So how do we find one of their ships?" Wayne sounded determined. "They can't be too far away from us."

"You think they'll come back here to the planet?" I wanted to help out in any way I could, and that was the first question I thought of.

"They might," Willie noted, as Woofa walked over and stood beside our small group. "Knowing their desire to control others, we probably can wait and they'll show up here sooner or later."

"But, do we have that much time to spare?" Bray asked. "They also have shifting engines, so who knows where they will strike next. It could even be Earth."

James shook his head. I could tell he was seriously aggravated with our situation. However, Willie kept rubbing his boyfriend's shoulder and neck in a comforting and soothing manner. With his huge hands, the pressure he applied probably went right through James's black leather jacket, and I'm sure it felt relaxing.

"Don't let this bother you so much," Willie said tenderly to James. "We'll find them. You know they're going to come back here, since they can't resist being the center of attention and stirring up trouble."

Willie's comment made James smile in an appreciative way.

"We should head back to the ship and wait around for a while." James seemed lost in the moment. He appeared sort of stress-free, as if a rush of calmness had washed over him. From the look on his face, he was definitely enjoying all the massaging from his tall boyfriend.

"Sounds like a good plan," Willie answered.

But, right after Willie's kind words, both of their expressions changed to sadness. Elshon versions of police officers showed up along with some medical teams. Flashing lights and sirens sounded. We all watched as they jumped out of their vehicles and started to slowly clear the bodies from the streets. They lifted them, covering each with blankets before placing them into the back of what resembled ambulances.

A single furry individual stood next to us. He wore what resembled blue jeans, a T-shirt, and gray sneakers. His fur was light brown and his head came up to my waist.

"Thank you for your help," he said. Bray held her phone in her hand so it could translate for us. He sounded thankful, yet undeniably saddened for his fallen friends. The fur covering his small face was matted to his cheeks from crying so much.

"We need to return to our ship," James explained to the small alien. "There's a strong chance these rogue agents will return to finish what they started, and we want to deal with them before any of that happens. It's for your own protection."

The gopher stepped forward and offered James a handshake. He politely accepted with a broad smile.

"Our global celebration begins in a few days," the gopher man said. "Please come back and join us for it. You and your crew are more than welcome."

Wayne's face lit up after hearing the invitation. In fact, we all smiled a bit.

"Thank you," James said to our alien friend. "We'll contact you before we return."

He nodded his furry head before walking over to join his companions. Their group watched as the paramedics lifted the last few bodies into the trucks.

Willie and James lead the way back to our shuttlecraft, and we all piled inside, taking our exact same seats. After a brief pause (enough time for James and Willie to take the pilot seats), the hatch and stairs closed, then the door sealed with a hiss before we started to rise into the sky. Another terrible view of the massive destruction streamed in front of the windshield.

Wayne and I were seated beside each other and we held hands.

"You okay?" I quietly asked. All of this chaos left me worried about him, because I knew how easily upset he tended to get.

He nodded a few times before glancing into my eyes. "I'm fine, sweetie." He leaned in and gave me a quick kiss on the lips. "I just hope we find these assholes and put an end to their bullshit. Nothing would make me happier. Well, snuggling in bed with you would definitely make me happy."

Right after his comment, Wayne smiled and winked at me. I squeezed his hand then reached over with my other and rubbed his thigh. We both had on fairly long shorts, but I managed to pull the fabric up a bit so I could glide my hand over Wayne's hairy leg. It felt wonderful, and he enjoyed my attention. I loved his body and soul.

James and Willie guided us through the atmosphere, until the cloudy night sky gave way to a field of stars which grew brighter with every passing second. His ship appeared as a small and distorted point of light, but became more apparent the closer we approached it.

"Is that a standard size for spaceships?" Wayne asked Bray and Woofa.

They were seated beside each other, holding hands while enjoying a peaceful moment together.

"Actually there are some that are as long and thick as skyscrapers," Woofa explained. "I'm sure the rogue agents have a few that will leave you both gasping from their enormous size."

Next to James, Woofa was probably the smallest person here. But, as I looked at him, I remembered his impressive spells he had cast, as well as Bray's spirits she had summoned. It still amazed me that magic truly existed. I felt certain when the shit hits the fan, they both would astound us even more with what they could *really* do.

Our approach slowed and the shuttle bay door opened. James maneuvered us inside of his ship. Within less than a minute, we landed with a hint of jiggling in our seats.

The hatch opened and the six of us worked our way outside in the bay area, then inside the elevator where he headed back up to the bridge. A very solemn journey, all of us had kept quiet from all the thoughts and scenarios likely racing around in our heads. I could only imagine what my handsome man was thinking. He was probably ready to punch some faces with his fists, or break a few jaws and give some dudes a bloody nose.

We all stepped out of the spacious elevator, then made our way toward the massive bridge doors that parted down the middle. Woofa and Bray had brought up the rear, with me and Wayne in the middle.

Dean shouted out as soon as he saw us enter. "I've located some," he told James in an excited tone. "Three rogue vessels are in the Metrall system, and it looks like they're lingering around waiting for something to do, or start."

James, Willie, Bray, and Woofa raced over to their workstations. Seconds later, the main holographic image that floated between the decks of the bridge changed to a view of the Metrall system, with a habitable planet standing out in orange and green glowing hues. The display also showed the three rogue vessels Dean had mentioned. All were positioned in a low orbit above the planet, and each ship looked somewhat comparable to James's, although they were shaped a lot longer and they weren't as thick.

"Dean, do you have the coordinates?" A hefty amount of determination came from James's voice. I could only imagine how badly he wanted to deal with these agents and make them pay for what they had done.

"Coordinates are already in the system," Dean explained. "We can go as soon as you give the word."

James looked at him with a glad smile. Even the three Devil Bunnies kept busy pushing buttons and flipping controls.

"Wait a second," Wayne said. He had stepped forward and sounded a bit anxious and nervous. "Does your ship have shields? I mean, we're taking on three ships. Who knows what kind of high-tech, firepower they have. We could get blown apart."

I stood behind Wayne and patted him on his shoulder, proud of my man for being so involved and asking appropriate questions.

Willie laughed. "We do have defensive shields, and mounted weapons that we can personally aim and fire. Would you like to use one?"

Wayne's mouth fell open with excitement, but then James intervened before my sexy man could say anything.

"Willie," James stated. "I don't think those two need to use our guns."

"Why not?" Wayne asked eagerly. All of the bridge crew were still analyzing their readouts or swiping their hands over holographic buttons floating in the air.

James stood straight up then locked his hands around his hips. "First of all," our captain answered. "You don't know how to use our weapons. And secondly, I don't think it'd be appropriate for you to blast one of their ships to pieces. This is our fight, not yours."

"With all due respect," Wayne said. "This *has* become our fight. We don't want to see the elshon race suffer anymore than you do. Show us how your weapons work." He massaged his hand over my shoulder. "Trust me. Adam will pick up on how to use them almost as fast as I will."

Wayne turned around, then shot me a pleasing smile. He reached out and cradled my face and jaw so he could feel what little bit of scruff I had for a beard. He looked so pleased with me after what he had said.

"I think they deserve to fire off some shots," Willie pointed out.

"I agree," Bray said from across the bridge. "Wayne and Adam have come this far, why not show them everything."

James let out a long sigh before tapping a few holographic buttons on the top of his wide workstation. He then stood straight up and cracked his knuckles, using his other hand to bend each of his fingers.

"Plus," Mortenna mentioned, "We have our attack ships docked on board. It wouldn't be one ship against three. We'd have them outnumbered *and* outgunned." She brushed her purple hand through her long black hair. All three of the Devil Bunnies stared at James with eager looks and anxious views.

The expression on James's face changed. He no longer seemed

overly concerned. He now showed quiet wonder as he contemplated her suggestion. "Bray, Woofa," James said after a long moment. "Take Wayne and Adam to the mounted weapons. Mortenna, Skiss, and Neese, get to your ships and prepare to strike. But, let's plan on disabling each rogue vessel so we can grab a few of those assholes and get some answers. Okay?"

"Looks like all three ships are maintaining a low orbit above the planet," Dean announced. He was hunched over and intricately observing several displays. "I think we have some time to get ready."

"Perfect," James said. "Hopefully, we'll find out what they're up to and put a stop to them."

Wayne and I followed Bray and Woofa out the bay doors, then down the white hallway toward the elevator. The four of us stepped inside and the door slid shut.

"Weapons corridors," Bray stated, and then the elevator began to move down.

"I'm guessing neither of you have ever fired a gigantic gun before?" Woofa asked.

We both shrugged and shook our heads, and then Wayne did something so cute that it put a great big smile on my face. My handsome man raised his hands, joined them together in the shape of a pistol, and then pretended to fire it at the sides of the elevator.

"Just show me where to aim," Wayne stated out loud, "And I'll take care of the rest."

He was definitely living his dream of being in a science-fiction world.

4

Right after the elevator stopped and the doors opened, we followed Bray and Woofa through a lengthy white corridor that had hallways on either side of it, about every thirty feet. Recessed lighting shined through steel grating overhead, and thick armored plates lined the rounded entrances of each additional corridor. All seemed heavily fortified and more than capable of withstanding attacks.

"Are we on top of the ship or below it?" Wayne sounded utterly amazed. The look on his face lasted for minutes as we walked through the hallways.

Woofa slowed down and gave Wayne a friendly pat along his arm. "We're actually positioned around the outer edges of the ship," our furry magician explained. "Each hallway we're passing has a large, powerful canon mounted at its end, along with reinforced shields and structural supports. Any of the guns can fire at targets above or below the ships position."

"This is incredible," Wayne said. He kept curiously glancing down each corridor, likely imagining how huge and powerful the guns were.

Bray stopped near one of the entrances, stood to the side, and then happily gestured for us to proceed down the corridor. "After you," she said with a smile.

The three of us followed Woofa down one of the hallways. It slowly turned and occasionally descended, then rose a few feet as we made our way to the end, where the mounted gun sat. All of it was brightly lit and spacious from side to side. At the center of the room, sat a swivel chair positioned in front of a wide workstation that had a digital screen with lots of holographic buttons and displays.

I nudged Wayne against the side of his arm. "Go ahead," I told my handsome man. "Take a seat. You deserve it."

Woofa stepped aside as Bray and I watched Wayne slowly make his way toward the chair. He laid his hand along its leather back, and looked absolutely mesmerized while he stared.

The four of us had plenty of room to stand without bumping against each other. In fact, towering big Willie could have stood in here and had plenty of headroom.

A floating wide screen showed an outside view of space, and after Wayne sat down in the moveable chair the console came to life, lighting up with a variety of colors. Several holographic displays appeared above the workstations polished surface, along with details about the gun and targeting options.

Red and green streams of data scrolled in front of Wayne, with several controls appearing right beside his hands. There was a steering wheel which I assumed was used to aim the gun. A visual display to his left showed the layout of the mounted gun. They had double barrels and were about as wide as the room we stood in.

Woofa stepped right up and started teaching Wayne how to use the system.

I turned to face Bray. "Thank you for showing him how to operate this," I told her. "I know he's in heaven."

Bray moved forward and gave me a warm hug. She patted my back. "It's not hard to see how captivated he is by all of this technology," she pointed out. "He seems to be enjoying it all so much."

I laughed and took a step back, then noticed that Wayne never once took his eyes away from what Woofa was showing him.

"Yeah," I confessed to Bray. "He's living his dream, that's for sure."

She and I watched as Wayne moved his hands and fingers over the multitude of controls, tapping buttons to adjust the firing range or repositioning the guns to a pretend target he had input.

I approached my tough guy and rested my hand over his shoulder, where I gave him a mild massage. It grabbed his attention and he turned his head to the side to gaze in my eyes.

"You got the hang of it?" I asked.

He laughed, sporting a wide smile. "Oh, yeah," he answered. "This will be a piece of cake."

Woofa backed away after brushing his hand along Wayne's arm. "Well, it seems like you understand all the controls. I'm sure you'll fire off some great shots. Maybe even disable some of their ships."

Wayne suddenly gripped the steering wheel and quickly spun it back and forth, acting like he was firing the guns. He even made popping noises and bangs with his lips and mouth as if he were firing off blasts of energy at the enemy.

I giggled at him and so did Bray and Woofa. "You're a goofball," I told Wayne.

He kept pretending, consumed by his love of such things.

"Of course," Bray explained, "When you actually sit and operate it for real, you will have to wear a harness suit."

"What's that?" Wayne paused for a moment so he could listen to her answer.

"It's a leather harness you wear," Bray told us. "It has the ability to generate a black bodysuit that covers you, along with boots."

"And you'll give both of us a harness suit?" Wayne sounded even more excited.

Bray nodded happily. "We have them stored on the bridge. They sort of resemble the suits the Devil Bunnies wear, but yours will be a little different since its covering a male form."

Woofa's phone rang and he pulled it out of his pocket. He answered it and then ended the call after a brief moment. "It was James," he informed us, "More rogue ships appeared around the planet. He wants us back on the bridge."

The news grabbed Wayne's attention and he and I both sighed. His sounded more eager to attack the rouge agents, where as mine came from being somewhat infuriated by all their bullshit.

The four of us made our way back to the bridge. Bray and Woofa assumed their positions at their workstations. The Devil Bunnies and Dean had welcomed us with smiles, while James and Willie kept working on the main workstation, which sat at the base of the large holographic display at the center of the room.

"Did you pick up some good tips for using the weapons?" Willie asked. He glanced toward Wayne while still pushing a few controls.

Wayne held my hand for a short moment. I could feel the satisfaction coursing through him from his touch. "Definitely," he answered. "Woofa's a fast and meticulous teacher. He showed me all sorts of tips and tricks."

I watched as Bray gave her furry man a quick yet comforting hug, along with a kiss on his cheek. He stood shorter than her, but the love between them showed abundantly.

"I called you four back up here because I'd like some suggestions on how to approach these agents," James said.

"Five more ships have appeared above the planet," Dean added. He then showed us a digital layout of their location and sizes on the main display. "And that one," he said while pointing his blue finger at the images. "That one is *absolutely* huge!"

Dean was right. One of the rogue ships was easily the size of a towering office building turned on its side. In comparison, the smaller ships resembled tiny fingers next to a massive arm. I wasn't sure how we were going to deal with a vessel of that magnitude. It probably had weapons to match its formidable size.

"Do we have enough firepower to take them all out?" Wayne asked. His short training session with the ship's guns probably encouraged him to fight more than anything else.

Willie and James both shook their heads.

"I doubt we could challenge them all without getting out butts kicked," James said.

"Maybe we could shift to a distant location and then scan their ships," Dean added. "Then we could track them down one by one and kick their asses individually."

I watched James take a few seconds as he considered Dean's proposal. His brow narrowed while thinking. It sounded like a good idea to me, but I didn't know how durable his ship was. I had seen how hateful the rogue agents were to the gopher race. I could only imagine how vile they would be to James and his crew, knowing who they were and what they were here to do.

"I'm not sure that idea will work," James mentioned. He kept pushing buttons or swiping his hand over controls atop his workstation.

"If we can scan them then they can scan us too. And, after they grab hold of our signatures, they'll keep coming after us wherever we go."

"Dean, can't you create some sort of dampening field so they won't be able to grab hold of our signatures?" Willie had come up with a cleaver idea. James looked impressed after hearing his boyfriend's suggestion. He reached over and rubbed his hand up and down Willie's furry, black arm.

Dean immediately got to work pushing buttons atop his console.

"Considering their shifting system is nowhere near as advanced as ours," Dean explained. "I think I could hack into their computers while projecting some sort of interference effect. If the MST could do it, then I should be able to. We wouldn't be able to use our shifting abilities while applying the disruption field, but I could certainly screw up their systems enough so they couldn't scan us *or* use their engines again."

"Then we could eliminate them once and for all." Wayne sounded and looked so determined.

I reached behind him to rub my hand over his back. He meant the world to me. I loved the look on his face when he got serious. He could be so manly, yet handsome.

"Dean, how long will it take you to get all of that together?" James shot him a serious stare straight into his eyes.

"I can probably have it set and ready to project in about twenty minutes," Dean answered. He sounded confident, and he looked adorable in his tight-fitting jeans and blue sneakers.

"Where's the nearest bathroom?" I had to seriously pee.

"Would you like me to show you to a private room?" Willie said. "You two can hangout and make use of it while on the ship. It has a roomy bathroom with a shower."

I nodded happily. "That would be great. Thanks."

James didn't seem to mind Willie's offer. In fact, he briefly slipped his arm around Willie's waist and gave his tall boyfriend an affectionate hug. Willie returned the favor, adding a kiss on top of our captain's head. It was so nice to see them affectionate while in front of us.

He and James were such a cute, yet diverse couple. The size difference was always amusing to watch. Willie was gigantic in comparisons to James.

Willie headed toward the wide bridge doors and gestured for me and Wayne to follow him. "This way," he said.

After we stepped out into the hallway, I glanced back toward the bridge while following Willie with Wayne beside me. Everyone was diligently working on the task at hand, making sure everything would be ready to go. They were all devoted crew members.

We took another ride in the elevator at the far end of the corridor, only this time it moved sideways and then up and over again, taking us to a new location inside the ship. When the doors opened we emerged into a similar white corridor with overhead lighting, and it wasn't a far walk before Willie stood to the left of a doorway.

He tapped his furry fingers along a flat screen positioned beside the door. It was about ten inches long with a smooth black surface, similar to glass. The pocket door split open and vanished inside the walls surrounding it.

"Here you guys go." Willie gestured with his huge arm and hand for us to enter before he did.

Wayne and I stepped inside the room and immediately the lights turned on. A few overhead ones shined down through steel grates. But, around the room, a few lamps had activated and also a workstation sat near a wall with framed artwork hanging behind it. There were lots of framed images mounted around the room. Most of which were space scenes, nebulas, galaxies, and an occasional shot of a mountain range or flowing river from some unknown planet.

I thought it seemed sort of unusual to see such fancy pictures, especially on a spaceship. But, it definitely added appeal to the room. Maybe James enjoyed dressing up his vessel. I would probably do the same if I were in charge. I'm sure it made guests feel more welcomed.

"This is really nice!" Wayne took hold of my hand and together we walked around the room, which was shaped and arranged much like a studio apartment. It was completely carpeted too, having a dark beige color to it.

A king size bed sat beneath a long narrow window that gave a great view of outer space. Two dark wooden tables (with lamps having decorative glass shades), bordered both sides of the headboard, and the covers and pillow cases were a silver colored fabric with subtle shapes of golden vines and leaves printed on them.

A large mahogany wardrobe stood against one of the dark gray walls, and a spacious living room sat at the center of the room, complete with a long sofa, a smaller couch, and two roomy recliners positioned in front of a coffee table, which was made of metal with a glass top. Every cushion was covered in a dark brown fabric, and every piece looked comfortable.

Wayne turned around and we stared at the small kitchen. A bar sat along one side of it with stools, along with a double sided sink, a refrigerator, and plenty of cabinets to store food or other items. The door to the bathroom had been left opened, and I could see a toilet beside a tall sink. The floor was tiled but had a carpeted mat lying over it. A spacious shower with a tub was in there too.

"So, how long have you and James been together?" Wayne asked our bear friend.

Willie gave that some thought for a few seconds. "It's been a little over a year, I think. James has two brothers, they're triplets, and we meet after I was assigned to his vessel to help deal with the MST back in our universe." Willie laughed a bit. "We really hit if off fast. It wasn't long before James expressed to me how much he wanted to be my boyfriend. I know he seems course and rigid on the outside, but in bed he's so affectionate. He's a sweetheart. I love him so much."

"Sounds a lot like Wayne," I said with a smile.

He laughed before nudging the side of my arm.

"Well, I'll give you two some privacy time." Willie smiled and winked before he stepped back toward the door and headed out into the hallway. As soon as he did the pocket doors closed, leaving me and Wayne alone together.

My sexy man loosely wrapped his arms around me, then leaned in with some passionate kisses. "Oh, Adam," he whispered tenderly as he moved gently from side to side while massaging my butt. "Making love to you on that bed would feel so good, sweetie."

A faint though enjoyable laugh slipped out of me. "I would love that, but I really need to pee. Plus, we're going to have to be back on the bridge pretty soon."

Wayne smiled and bounced his eyebrows a couple of times. "We can wait for later," he said happily. "That way, I can save up my load so I can fill you up with a huge and hot one later on, then we can work in a ton of cuddling."

I leaned in to kiss him again. Sex with Wayne was the best I had ever had in my life. He really knew how to work his manhood deep inside me, pumping me full of sweet and tender love. And, afterward, he always held me in his arms, caring for me, being affectionate with slow kisses while rubbing his hands over my naked body. I would always melt against him, it felt so wonderful.

"Sounds good," I told him. I then headed to the bathroom.

I didn't bother closing the door since back at home we often used the bathroom at the same time. We often peed together in a toilet, or playfully soaped each other up in the shower.

The toilet flushed just like ours back at home, and afterward I pulled up my underwear and shorts, washed my hands, and then came out to stand beside Wayne. He had never stopped marveling at the room and how beautiful it looked in this subtle lighting. He even gazed through the long window, captivated by the bright stars shining outside in the distance.

"You know, we could ask to stay on the ship and join their crew," Wayne said to me. "Can you imagine how cool it would be to live on a spaceship and travel throughout different galaxies and dimensions?"

I stood behind him then slid my arms around his torso, before rubbing my hands over his wonderful stomach. I kissed the side and back of his neck, his shoulders too. "As great as that sounds, would we quit our jobs and never see our families again." I tried not to sound negative, but I thought I had brought up some good points.

"With the ships shifting engines, we could always go back home to visit people," Wayne told me. "It wouldn't be that difficult. At least, I imagine it wouldn't."

I reached up and cradle his chin with my right hand then turned his face a bit so I could give him a kiss on his cheek. I loved feeling his thick beard.

"Nothing would make me happier," I answered. "But, we don't know if James would even let us live here. Who knows what life is like in their universe. Plus, we could always invite them to come and visit us at our house. Can you imagine seeing Willie in our living room?"

Wayne let out a long and pitiful sounding sigh. He sounded disappointed after hearing my suggestion.

"I know our jobs suck and we could be doing so much more in life," I told him. "I guess it wouldn't hurt to ask James or Willie. Maybe they'll say yes."

My revised plan perked up Wayne's emotional state. He spun around and locked his hands around my waist, then gave me a deep kiss with a few pokes of his tongue in my mouth. "I love you so much, Adam," he whispered.

"I love you too. Life is so good with you beside me. I never want this to end."

We exchanged a few more kisses, then Wayne massaged the sides of my hips with a firm grip. He had such strong hands. His attention got me excited and it left me hard. He then took the opportunity to massage my crotch, where he felt my stiff manhood with every gentle squeeze from his hand.

"We should probably make our way back to the bridge," he mentioned between kisses.

"I wonder if Willie waited out in the hallway for us." I assumed he probably did.

Wayne smiled as he gazed into my eyes. "Let's go find out."

The doors opened as soon as we stepped close to them, and sure enough, Willie had been waiting patiently out in the white corridor for us to come back out.

"All better?" Willie asked. He stared at me with a teasing smirk on his face. He probably assumed we shared some brief intimacy.

"In many ways," I replied cheerfully. I slid my hand behind Wayne then rubbed it along his shapely ass a few times, gliding it back and forth over his silky smooth shorts. My admiration put a happy grin on

Wayne's face as we followed Willie over to the elevator then headed back up to the bridge.

I sensed some growing tension in the air the second after we stepped back on the bridge. Something had taken a turn for the worse, I suspected.

Willie stopped beside James who had never taken his attention away from his terminal. "What's going on?" Willie tenderly rested his large furry hand on James's shoulder for a brief moment, in an attempt to comfort his lover.

James seemed frustrated. He shook his head, sighing with an angry scowl on his face.

"Two more ships showed up with the others," Dean explained. "Plus, we've detected a small craft in a distant orbit around the gopher's home world."

"They're probably preparing to strike again," Mortenna mentioned. "We need to intervene."

"Then we should go and kick their asses right now!" Wayne said. Both of his hands were shaped in to fists. He was more than ready to pound the living daylights out of someone.

James stared outward across the bridge. I could tell he was lost in thought, contemplating how to handle the situation in the best way possible, concerned for his crew and his half-bear boyfriend.

"The dispersion field is ready," Dean announced. "We can easily disrupt their scanning and shifting engines. I can start to project it before we shift to their location."

"We should probably strike before they kill anymore of the gophers," Bray said. She sounded eager and looked as ready as Wayne did. Woofa rubbed his hand along her back as they stood with their eyes fixed on James while waiting for his command.

Willie leaned down and whispered beside James's ear. I imagined he said something to perk up his boyfriend or some kind of tender phrase to help ease his decision. It could have been something loveable too.

As soon as Willie stood up James spoke. "Okay," our captain said. "Let's go do it. Dean, input the coordinates. Mortenna, you, Neese, and

Skiss all head to your warships. We're going to need as much firepower as we can muster."

"Should we man the guns down below?" Wayne asked.

James thought about his offer for a moment and then nodded. "Do it," he added in a positive tone.

"Do you think we could shift into the planet's atmosphere," Dean suggested. "We could still project the disruption field while the Devil Bunnies blast them to pieces."

James face lit up. I could tell he liked Dean's proposal. "That's a good idea. Make it happen."

Bray stepped over to a steel cabinet and pulled out two leather harnesses for me and Wayne. She then approached us.

"Just slip them on over your shirts," she explained. "Once you lock the center ring together, it will activate the suit and boots with a tap of your hand."

We both took a harness and then helped each other slip them on, sliding our arms through the large openings, over our shoulders, and then securing the straps over our chests after locking their ends into the small center metal ring. Each harness then automatically tightened, and fit perfectly to our bodies.

Wayne wasted no time. He tapped the center ring and immediately his harness generated a black bodysuit which appeared piece by piece, emerging outward from the center ring until he was covered from neck to toes in armored leather. Thin gray lines ran along his legs and sides. Both black boots had completely covered his sneakers, and they were over the calf in height with thick soles and dark metal clasps decorating their outer edges. The bodysuit itself was reinforced with protective armor, all of which was layered along Wayne's thighs, calves, arms, and shoulders. It even had heavy gloves, which covered his hands. A large and thick, dark metal collar lay around his neck. All together the suit looked very futuristic, very worthy of a spaceman.

"It can generate a mask too," Bray explained. "And, its communication system will transfer any calls to the ship or to our pdPhones. However you direct it."

I reached up and tapped my center ring which covered me in the exact same suit as Wayne had on. Right after that, I noticed Wayne kept staring at my boots. We both had a thing for feet and footwear, so I was certain they were turning him on a bit.

"How do you turn on the helmet?" Wayne asked.

Bray demonstrated by pretending she wore a suit. She tapped her hand where a metal collar would have been if she had been wearing one.

Wayne followed her lead, and the second he tapped his collar, it generated a black metal helmet which entirely covered his head. A reflective screen covered his eyes and its face. It resembled a mouth and nose. However, they were sealed shut.

"The suit generates an atmosphere in the helmet so you can breath," Bray explained. "You'll be fine in the outermost reaches of space, or deep beneath an ocean. Oh, and the boots can generate an antigravity effect with boosters. The field will engulf your entire body, and you'll be able to levitate above the ground."

I didn't bother to turn on my helmet, and it wasn't long before Wayne tapped his collar again to deactivate his. From the marveled look on his face, I could tell he was anxious to go for a short flight in his suit.

"These are awesome," he told Bray. "Thank you for giving them to us."

"My pleasure," she said, and then gave both of us a pat on our padded shoulders.

"And they can withstand a vast majority of gunshots, too," James added. "But, I seriously hope neither of you end up getting shot at."

He and Willie let out some minor laughs. In fact, all of the bridge crew did, including the Devil Bunnies. Dean kept smiling for a long time. He seemed pleased with having us on the ship.

Wayne took hold of my hand and we walked over to the bridge doors. They opened, and we then made our way back toward the elevator with Willie racing close behind us. The doors closed and Wayne (of all people), pushed the proper buttons to take us to the weapons corridors.

"How will we know when to fire the guns?" Wayne asked.

"You'll see a notification pop up on your screen," Willie answered.

"It'll let you know we're in battle. Either that, or you'll feel the ship shaking beneath your big black boots when they start shooting at us."

We laughed at Willie's comment. Wayne slipped his arm around my waist and pressed our body suits together. He turned his face to give me a kiss on the side of my cheek.

"I'm going to protect you no matter what it takes," he whispered beside my ear.

I couldn't resist. I had to give him a sweet kiss on his lips. He dearly touched my heart.

"I love you so much, Wayne." I gave him another kiss on the lips. Good thing we dressed in these armored bodysuits on or Willie would have easily seen my firm erection through the fabric of my shorts.

5

The minute we stepped out of the elevator, Wayne took the lead. He walked fast and stood up straight with pride. Willie and I followed him down the weapons corridor, where he headed straight for the same area that Bray and Woofa had taken us to.

As soon as we all walked into the gun room, Wayne turned the chair around, sat down in it, and then spun around where he placed his hands on the control panel and activated the weapons console. He was such a quick learner.

The large floating screen came to life. It lit up with a detailed display of our location and everything that was outside of the ship, most of which were only stars right now. He gripped the steering wheel with both hands.

Willie let out an amused chuckle while patting Wayne on his shoulder. "Looks like you got the hang of this really well."

"Woofa showed him everything," I explained. "Plus, he's got a passion for this kind of stuff."

"I sure do," Wayne admitted in an excited tone.

He kept moving his fingers back and forth over the control panel, tapping buttons, pulling up readouts, and swiping his hands through holographic displays. A few vertical, semi-transparent panels had appeared, upon which tons of data scrolled from top to bottom in bold colors of green and blue.

Willie stared straight into my eyes with a questioning gaze. "Woofa didn't show you how to operate the guns?"

I shook my head, but gave him a pleasing smile. "I'm happy enough standing beside Wayne and watching him enjoy all of this. Trust me. He's probably a hundred times better at controlling these guns than I'd ever be."

Willie then nodded with a crooked smile. He seemed content with my answer.

"Well," our big bear friend added, "I'm going to go down to another corridor and operate a different gun on the opposite side of the ship." He started to walk away, but I stopped him with a compliment.

"Thanks, Willie," I said. "You and James are really great guys."

He smiled while taking a few steps closer to me. He wrapped me up in a warm embrace, though I couldn't even get my arms around his waist. He was incredibly hairy, and built like a brick shithouse. I could only imagine how strong of a punch he had. Probably enough to send some rogue agent flying across the room.

I savored this moment while being held by him. I pressed the side of my face against his shirt, feeling his hard yet plush body against my face, his gigantic arms holding me tightly. His fur had a woodsy fragrance to it, similar to the trees and bushes in the park behind our house back on Earth. I found his aroma comforting and relaxing. It sparked many memories of being with Wayne, while we walked around the lake and enjoyed each other's company. I missed those times. Nothing felt better than being with my tough guy.

Some beeps and noises came from Wayne's station. Willie let go of me so he could stare at the screens and decipher what the sounds meant.

"It looks like we're about to shift to the planet," Willie said. "I guess I better get my furry butt over to the other guns, so we can take care of those bastards." Willie let out a loud laugh. "I don't need James bending me over with some disciplinary spanking." He pursed his lips and gave his comment some thought for a short moment. "Or that might actually feel good," he said, with an amused look.

I stood a couple of feet behind Wayne's chair. Willie rushed out of our room, then raced down the corridor to man another gun.

"You think you can handle all of this?" I patted my beautiful man on his shoulder.

"Definitely," he said, and then pointed up at the large screen floating near the wall. "You can see Dean just sent the coordinates to the shifting engines. We'll be in the planet's atmosphere real fast."

I locked my hands around my waist, and closely watched as Wayne worked the weapon's controls. I was amazed at how fast he had caught on, and how well he understood all the readouts and streaming data. He was so smart.

"You never fail to impress me." I moved forward so I could give him a kiss on top of his bald head.

I had to laugh when he turned his face to the side and pointed at his lips. I leaned down and gave him a sloppy kiss, exactly how he liked them. I slipped my tongue in his mouth. I even took the opportunity to reach down and massage his armored crotch. It felt good beneath all that leather, very shapely and prominent.

Another alert sounded, and we both glanced at the workstation and then the screen.

Wayne tapped a flashing green button. "I guess we've shifted into the planets atmosphere. And look at this," he pointed at a holographic image of James's crab-shape ship and several distortion fields that were emanating from it. "Dean is projecting the disruption fields."

"Awesome." I patted Wayne on his chest before I stood up and resumed my spot behind his chair. I didn't want to get in his way if he had to spin the steering wheel a lot. "Hopefully, the bridge crew can scan their ships quick and then get us the hell out of here."

Wayne stayed busy tapping controls on the workstation. But, as I took a moment to glance between the console and his face, he had narrowed his brow and looked concerned about something.

"What's going on?" I asked him.

"It looks like a few of the rouge ships are moving toward us." Wayne pointed at the huge screen positioned in front of us. "I guess those are the Devil Bunnies racing out from the docking bays."

On the main display, I watched as three small arrowhead-shape crafts assumed a position around James's ship. They were all much smaller, with jagged tips at their fronts, and each one appeared much thicker at their rear. I hoped each of their vessels had some powerful guns to fight these rogues.

Honestly, I felt nervous. My stomach started to ache. I raised my hand and wiped a few beads of sweat that had dripped down my forehead.

"Here they come!" Wayne shouted out. He tapped a few buttons, and then firmly gripped the steering wheel with both hands. A simplified digital display appeared directly behind the wheel. It showed a detailed map of enemy targets. A focused and determined look showed on Wayne's face.

On the viewscreen, I saw a representation of four smaller rogue ships making their way toward us. I imagined they were pissed about the dampening field Dean had projected. Who wouldn't be? From everything Bray, Woofa, James, and Willie had told us about them, I'm sure they were out for blood in many ways.

"Are our shields activated?" I asked in a panicked voice. The thought of getting the shit shot out of us was starting to freak me out.

"As far as I can tell," Wayne answered. "I guess we'll know for sure in a few seconds."

The Devil Bunnies hit the gas and flew off like rockets toward the rogue ships, while James's ship veered to the right. I assumed they were repositioning it to get the best shots possible. A couple blasts from a rogue vessel hit our ship and damn near knocked me over on my butt.

"Holy shit!" I grabbed the back of Wayne's chair in a panic, and held on for dear life.

"I've got this," he said out loud, reassuring me as he rotated the wheel and positioned the mounted guns to fire, which they did. Several glowing white blasts of energy shot away on the screen, hitting the nearest rogue vessel. I could also tell Willie's guns were firing from different directions.

"There's no way in *hell* we're going to survive against all of those ships!" I seriously didn't see how we could make it. I thought about that huge rogue vessel Dean pointed out earlier. I was sure that one would shoot the shit out of us!

More intense weapons fire hit the ship, shaking our room like crazy. Wayne spun the wheel, aiming and firing. "You okay back there?"

"I'm fine, just freaking out from all of this crap. I think James should get the hell out of here! We can find another way to deal with them."

On the main screen, I could tell we were surrounded by rogue ships. Four of them had moved in and several alerts sounded off, warning us that we were being targeted. Several powerful shots hit our side of the ship. The room shook terribly, and some sparks shot out of Wayne's workstation. Luckily, he had raised his arm to shield his face from them.

"Did you hear that?" I stared at the floor and walls, feeling terrified. "It sounded like the ship is ripping apart."

And, before Wayne could even react or answer me, a huge section of the wall right next to us ripped away, exposing us to a field of clouds, rogue vessels, the Devil Bunnies ships, and a view of mountains and land several miles below us. A strong wind gusted into the room, and I squinted from the sudden bright daylight.

The main screen had quit working, and Wayne's terminal was flashing like mad as it started to malfunction. Our ship then suddenly dropped to the side, and since Wayne wasn't wearing a seatbelt of any kind, both of us tumbled toward the large opening where we fell over each other, slamming our bodies together, and kicking each other as we attempted to grab hold of the steel floor, but ended up falling outside into the sky.

I shouted and screamed as we fell and spun around through the air. My heart pounded in my chest like mad. An overwhelming fear grabbed hold of me, and I swore I was about to have a heart attack.

But, my sci-fi boyfriend was quick to react. He grabbed hold of my gloved hand, tapped his collar to activate his helmet, and somehow he engaged the suits antigravity field, along with the rocket boots.

In midair, Wayne paused. He held me, hand in hand, as I dangled from his strong grip in the blue sky.

"Turn on your helmet, Adam!" he shouted at me.

But, the sight of watching the rogue vessels continually firing at James's ship had consumed me. I felt certain they would shoot at us, too.

"Adam! Listen to me! Activate your fucking helmet!"

I could hear Wayne's voice as clear as day coming through his helmet. I quickly reached up and tapped the metal collar around my neck. The helmet quickly formed around my head, generating itself bit by bit, until I saw a crisp and clear digital readout before my eyes.

Instantly my suits antigravity field activated, and my rocket boots started up, which stabilized me in midair. Both of us hovered side by side, holding our gloved hands together. And, considering the circumstances, it wasn't difficult at all to use our suits flying abilities. It was much easier than I anticipated, but I was still scared shitless, especially seeing the land miles beneath us.

Unfortunately, James's ship moved a considerable distance away as they fired back at the rogue vessels. I guess Willie's area wasn't hit. His mounted cannons never stopped shooting off their blinding beams of energy.

"What do we do?" I know I sounded terrified.

"We fly back to the ship!" Wayne told me, with abundant amounts of determination.

Plenty of visual controls appeared inside my helmet, and all I did was focus on a particular button which activated the specified feature.

Wayne leveled out, and I did too after a few quick attempts. Holding hands, covered from head to toe in our bodysuits, we shot across the sky on a course straight for the hole along the side of James's ship.

Yes, we did swerve a few times. We twisted and turned a lot with our arms stretched out, until my wonderful man got flying under control. It didn't take him long. He led me and kept me close beside him. I'm sure we looked like two oversized black crows racing through the clouds, only with rocket boots. How cool were those? I was thankful Bray had given us these suits.

Right before we reached the opening, a huge blast from a rogue vessel hit James's ship, and sent it *and* us veering off course. The last thing I remembered was turning toward Wayne and positioning ourselves upright, while gazing at the Devil Bunnies arrowhead ships attacking a nearby rogue vessel. Several enemy shots raced by us, and then one actually grazed the two of us which knocked me out cold.

When I woke up in a startled state, Wayne was holding me. He was behind me, both of us lying down with his back against a brick wall.

"You're okay, you're okay," he reassured me, before adding a few kisses on my head.

"Were the fuck are we?" I was shaking. It was cold, and I felt a bit confused.

"The rogue agents must have grabbed us after that blast hit the ship," Wayne explained. "We're in some kind of prison cell."

I gazed around. I still felt dizzy from getting knocked out.

We were seated on the rocky, cold ground of what resembled a large prison, along with huddled gopher people and several dead bodies from races I was unfamiliar with. Our high-tech suits Bray gave us had been taken away. Both leather harnesses were gone. We were dressed in our shirts, shorts, socks, and sneakers.

I could smell the stench of the dead bodies. They were lying together, somewhat piled up near the far side of the cell. All of them were rotted, with bugs flying back and forth between their bashed in skulls or ripped open stomachs.

The metal bars of the cell walls were rusted and thick, and each section was tall. There were no makeshift beds or any comforts, whatsoever. I didn't even see a toilet or a sink in here. I cringed as I tried to move and stand up, but Wayne tightened his arms around my body even more than before. He wasn't about to let me go anywhere.

"You think James and his crew survived?" I suddenly became worried about them and us. I hoped Mortenna and her companions made it.

Wayne kissed the top of my head, then tenderly squeezed me. I was lying back against his chest. "I hope so, sweetie," he said. "Both of us were knocked out cold. I'm sure with Dean's resources and skills they were able to get away."

"But, what's going to happen to *us*?" I started shaking from fear, from uncertainty and I imagined being locked up in this cell until we starved to death, and looked like those corpses lying across the room.

He rested the side of his bearded face against mine, and then gently swayed us back and forth, soothing me with some gentle massages along my arms and chest. I felt more comforted being held by my wonderful man, but lots of terrible thoughts and ideas kept racing around inside my head. How were we going to survive? What if James's ship had been destroyed and the entire crew along with it? Wayne and I would never get back home. What would our families think after both of us simply disappeared without any explanation?

"We're going to make it, Adam." He leaned in and kissed me on my cheek. "You know I'll take care of you and keep you safe. None of those bastards are going to lay a hand on you, sweetie. You got my word."

One of the gopher people struggled to stand up, and then he slowly walked toward us, grabbing our attention. I assumed it was a male. He was barefoot and wore only a pair of cutoff khaki colored shorts. His light brown fur was caked with mud and dirt. It covered his furry arms and face. As he came closer, I noticed he was missing his whiskers along his short snout. He looked exhausted and worn-out, hunched over and weary. I assumed he had been put through hell.

He lifted his upturned paws in a sort of friendly offering, then uttered something in his language, but we had no way of understanding him without the use of a pdPhone. He stood no taller than four feet, and he stared straight at us with his saddened face and big brown eyes.

"We don't understand what you're trying to say," Wayne explained politely.

I shook my head with a shrug, expressing exactly what Wayne said. But, the small gopher man stepped closer with a pleading look on his face. I got the impression he needed something from us. But, what could we offer, I had no clue. Especially, since all of us were in the same boat.

He stopped right near the side of my outstretched leg, bent over a bit, and then brushed his furry paw along my skin. He pointed at his gopher companions, and gently nudged my leg several times as if he were trying to bring something to our attention, something of importance.

Wayne and I both turned our heads toward his friends. Another gopher had stood up and was holding some mechanical parts in his paws. He then hurried over to me and Wayne, and presented the pieces to us. They resembled a mound of explosive paste along with a digital charger.

"Is that what I think it is?" I asked.

I could feel Wayne nodding his head with growing excitement. "It looks like our way out of this prison cell," my man said. He pulled his arms from around me, and together we wiggled apart so we could stand up and get a better understanding of what our gopher friend was offering.

Wayne picked up the two pieces. He held them in his hands, while I stared at him and our gopher friends with a questioning gaze. The one who had brought it over then pointed at the cell door, at the lock to be specific. He seemed eager for something to take place.

"How did you get this stuff?" Right after I asked my question I realized they wouldn't understand me.

"So, I'm guessing we use this to blow the door open?" Wayne asked.

I shrugged. "It looks like explosives. I just don't understand why they would have waited so long to use it. That's kind of odd, especially with those dead bodies in here. You'd think they'd want the hell out of here as fast as possible."

Wayne stared at me with a raised brow. "Well, think about it, Adam. If there's any rogue agents outside in the hallway, these little gopher folks wouldn't be able to fight them off. You and I, on the other hand, will be able to beat the shit out of them. How's that sound?"

"That sounds pretty fucking good," I told him. "But, I don't think I'll hit them as hard as you can. *You're* the tough guy. I'm better at snuggling and romance, and enjoying all the flowers you bring me every Sunday."

He laughed a bit at my comment. "Let's get this show on the road then, so I can get some snuggle time from you later on."

We quietly walked over to the cell door, and listened for any guards or agents outside. We never heard anyone. The gopher people had followed us. There were six of them, but they all looked exhausted and worn out. Wayne and I were in much better condition.

"And, let me guess," I said to Wayne, "From all the movies you've seen, you know exactly how to use these explosives."

He chuckled while reaching his hands through the bars and shoving the mound of paste into the lock. "Of course I do. I've seen this a million times in movies."

Wayne separated the wires, then inserted both ends into the gray mound of paste. He tapped the screen of the small control device, and a digital image of a timer appeared. It started counting down from sixty seconds.

"Okay, okay, let's all back away." Wayne took hold of my hand, and our group huddled together along the opposite side of the cell.

We waited and waited until the deafening sound of the explosion blew the entire lock away. I actually jumped a little, but Wayne was quick to slip his arm around me.

A cloud of thick gray smoke hovered in the air, and the cell door had opened all the way. It banged loudly against the other steel bars after it hit them.

Immediately we heard the sound of boots running over the ground. Wayne had heard it too, and he raced over to the door, stepped outside of our tiny prison cell, and ran right into a rogue agent, who reached for his holstered handgun along his thigh.

The agent wore no helmet. In fact, he was dressed in gray cargo pants, with old work boots and a black T-shirt. Wayne quickly and powerfully punched the guy right in his jaw, which sent him falling back against the wall outside of our cell. My tough guy then jumped down and straddled this dude, locking his knees and thighs around his torso, where he then pounded the living daylights out of him.

The agent tried to squirm and push Wayne off of him. He shouted in some foreign language, probably cursing. But, Wayne hit him in the face with all his strength, bashing him over and over again. It didn't take long before the guy passed out.

My tough guy quickly stood up. His fists were covered in blood, and the guy's face was covered in a lot more. In fact, blood was all you saw. He had no face anymore. His nose looked completely smashed, and his mouth was twisted to the side.

"Come on!" Wayne shouted at us. His face was all scrunched up, and he was ready to pound the shit out of more assholes. "Let's get the fuck out of here!"

I ran over to the cell door with the six gopher people behind me. Wayne knelt down and wiped the blood off his hands using the agent's shirt. My handsome man then stood and held his index finger straight up against his lips, signaling that we all should keep quiet.

Slowly we walked down the old wooden hallway. The dusty and dirty floors creaked at times, because Wayne and I were heavier than the gopher people. The walls had cracks in them and we saw an occasional large hole, almost as if a sledgehammer had been slammed through them.

"This place is a filthy piece of shit," I pointed out.

Wayne chuckled. "Well, from what James and Willie had told us, these rogue agents probably don't have a lot of resources. They take whatever they can."

The front room was a complete mess. Two dilapidated wooden desks sat in here, each next to windows with old broken shutters covering them. The floors were made of rotten two-by-fours, with some gaps and holes here and there. The ceiling was in worse shape. Part of it had collapsed and fallen onto the floor, which exposed bigger beams above it.

Luckily, there were no more agents inside, so Wayne proceeded to the front door and slowly opened it. He listened for any sounds outside. We heard nothing.

It was a beautiful sunny day outside, and the four other buildings lining the street all appeared as if they were from some old western film. There were horizontal posts for horses to be tied up along them, and old wooden rocking chairs on their decaying front porches. All had angled roofs and windows, with thick and heavy glass that you could barely see through.

"What the hell kind of world is this?" I'm sure I was just as surprised and confused as Wayne was.

"I'm not sure." He stood staring at the dirty street and buildings. "But we should probably get as far away from here as we can." He turned his head and gazed into my eyes.

"Let's do it," I answered.

To my surprise one of the gopher guys reached up and tapped my hand so he could grab my attention. It seemed like they knew where to go. Three of them hurried out the door, and then down the stairs on the old wooden porch. Each flapped their paws, signaling for me and Wayne to follow them, which we did.

A gorgeous range of mountains lined the horizon to our left. Each was covered in snow with steep sides. Smaller hills and valleys lay nearby, which is where our friends led the way. All the gopher people kept close together, chatting in their language and occasionally glancing at me or Wayne.

"I wish we could understand what they're saying," I said.

Wayne nodded in agreement. I wanted to hold his hand, but I could still see some blood on it, especially between his fingers and along his wrist. I'm sure we'd come across a creek or river soon enough, and he could get them cleaned.

We walked through fields of knee-high grass, lined by tall trees with wide and full green canopies. We followed old dusty paths, packed with bushes and shrubs, all in a variety of colors with bold blooming flowers that were absolutely gorgeous. It reminded me of many times when Wayne and I would explore the paths around Spanish Lake Park behind our house back on Earth.

Day turned into night. The beautiful blue sky and puffy clouds gave way to a blanket of stars. I couldn't even begin to guess how many miles we had walked. I could have pulled out my cell phone and checked with an app, but both of our batteries were dead because we hadn't recharged them before leaving our home.

It wasn't long before we all came to a stop. We needed to rest and take a break. Our gopher friends were all chatting and keeping busy with preparing what looked like a makeshift campground. They cleared a center area, then dug out a large hole with their paws, that they soon filled with all kinds of dried branches and bites of wood.

Wayne and I sat down with our backs against a large tree.

"I guess we're camping here tonight," I mentioned.

"Looks like it." Wayne faced me, then leaned in with a kiss.

I felt proud of him for dealing with that rogue agent back at the prison. I reached over and rubbed his hairy leg, and he closed his eyes for a moment, enjoying the feel of my sensual touch.

Somehow, the gophers managed to light the wood on fire with some sort of rocks they found in the woods. They banged them together, releasing a bunch of sparks, which ignited the leaves and dried grass. A roaring blaze soon formed, and the heat felt good since the air had turned chilly.

"Don't you think they shouldn't sit so close to the fire?" I asked Wayne. Each of them sat down around the burning wood, and I was only concerned because they were all covered in fur.

"They'll be okay," Wayne reassured me. "I'm sure they've sat around plenty of fires before."

It wasn't long before both of us started to get sleepy. Wayne and I made ourselves comfortable on the ground. We stretched out our bodies and legs. He positioned himself behind me, using his right arm as a pillow for me to rest my head against. He wrapped his left arm around me, holding me close and secure.

"Sweet dreams, Adam." He slowly and sweetly kissed the side of my neck.

"You too." I wiggled myself closer against his body, leaving no gaps.

It wasn't long before I heard him lightly snoring, and soon I was out, too.

6

Bright morning sunlight hit my face. It woke me up with a wide yawn. It must have stirred Wayne also, because it wasn't long before he snuggled his beard against the side of my neck with some kisses.

"Good morning, babe," he said. "Did you sleep okay?"

"Yeah," I answered with a minor chuckle. "I was out cold."

Speaking of cold, the air felt damp and much cooler than last night. All six gopher people were up and moving around, gathering more dried branches, leaves, and twigs to build another fire, which they soon did. Within minutes it was blazing.

The intense heat felt good. If only our companions could have whipped up some coffee or a nice breakfast. That would have seriously perked me up. Wayne sat up and gave me a playful tap across my thigh. He then stood and walked over to a large bush, where he stopped to pee. I got up and moved beside him so I could do the same.

"You think we'll ever see James and his crew again?" My stomach churned with worries and fears. I shook my wiener, then tucked it back down inside my shorts.

Wayne rubbed his hand along my back, and then moved it lower so he could massage my butt. "Like I said, sweetie, I doubt the ship got destroyed. They most likely shifted away from the battle. That's what I would have done." He turned his head and aimed a sweet smile right at me. "James knows his shit. He's a smart guy. He wouldn't let his crew go down in some fucked up fight like that."

In the distance, I noticed one of the gopher dudes taking a dump. He had pulled down his pants, squatted beside a different type of bush, and then did his thing. I wondered if the hair on their butts got all messy from pooping. Of course, that wasn't the most important question I needed an answer for. I was just curious.

It tickled me to see such similarities between races. But, like a famous book said, everybody poops.

I was caught off guard by some increasing noises coming from further inside the woods. All of our gopher friends noticed it too. They didn't seem surprised. But, they did pause for a long moment to stop, stand, and listen. We needed to be cautious considering the rogue agent Wayne beat the shit out of back in that dilapidated prison. He could have called for backup, and several troops could be stalking us while standing here.

Wayne pulled the front of his shorts up over his private parts. He wasn't wearing underwear like I was. He nudged the side of my arm with his hand, then tilted his head a few times to the right, indicating he and I should take a walk and see what the hell was making all this noise.

It sounded like a herd of cows were walking through leaves and grass as they got closer. I heard some bellowing, snorting, and grunting. How unusual on an alien planet? But, through the trees, around their trunks, Wayne pointed as he squatted.

"Holy shit!" he said. "Look at those buffalo creatures!"

In a clearing beyond the trees, maybe two hundred feet from us, we saw what looked like large black and brown buffalos, complete with massive horns on their heads. But, what really intrigued me was that each one had gigantic wings growing out of their shoulders, which looked similar to an eagle's. Each wing was completely covered in feathers that matched the animal's body color.

"What the hell are those things?" I quietly asked.

"I think the more important question," Wayne said, "Is who are those people walking with them?"

I hadn't noticed any of the people moving throughout the herd. I was too fascinated by the buffalos. But, each of these people had dressed in similar styled clothing of brown shorts and matching shirts. All of them were covered in light brown colored skin, with much darker colored, cropped hair. There were short haired males (some were bald), and females with long flowing locks. The first question that came to my mind, was whether or not these people were going to be nice to us or hostile?

I wasn't sure we should even make contact with them. But, without hesitation two of the gopher dudes started making a ruckus and quickly ran over to these people with their furry arms waving in the air.

"Son of a bitch." Wayne sounded annoyed. "What the hell are they trying to do?"

While squatting, we peaked over the top of the bushes and watched what looked like friendly introductions between the gophers and this other race.

The buffalo creatures came to a stop and started grazing, while one of the individuals raised his hands and produced some type of magical effect that looked similar to Woofa's healing spell.

A bright blue light had appeared directly overhead of each gopher, and then it spread out into a glowing cloud shape. Slowly it drifted down to engulf our furry friends. After the cloud was absorbed by their bodies, each one seemed like they stood taller and appeared suddenly refreshed.

"I'll take that as a friendly gesture," Wayne said.

"I think you're right."

Wayne glanced into my eyes with a shrug and a humble grin. We then watched as the other four gopher folks followed their friends over to these new people. One of them stopped briefly and waved for us to join them. He shouted out too.

I sighed. Why not, I figured.

We both stood up, and Wayne took hold of my hand as we walked through the forest. We moved around trees and shrubs, until we emerged into the clearing and stood before these people.

There were fifteen of them, with twenty animals in the herd. Two (a male and a female), seemed surprised to see me and Wayne. The looks on their faces proved that much. They quickly came over to stand in front of us, and we got a much better view of their features.

Their skin resembled tree bark. It was gray but with lengthy grooves, dents, and tiny darker dots here and there. Both of them were as tall as us, and from what I could tell, they were about the same age, too. They each wore what looked like Caterpillar work boots, with laces tied, and somewhat stained. Their steel toes appeared worn from so much time in the forest. I guess they were more advanced than I had thought. I don't think a primitive culture would wear steel toed boots.

The male appeared intriguing. He was very fit, yet beefy in a bearish kind of way, and he was totally bald, but had a beard that resembled dark brown moss you would find growing on the sunless side of a tree deep in the woods. The lady was pretty and tall. Her long dark green hair (which resembled long strands of moss), fell in subtle curls over her shoulders. And, surprisingly, she had some curves going on along with a busty chest.

He spoke in his language, with a friendly smile aimed our way. He raised his hands in a welcoming gesture. But, neither of us understood what he had said. I heard Wayne sigh. I'm sure he was feeling frustrated from a continued lack of communication.

"We should have borrowed a pdPhone from Willie or Bray," Wayne mentioned.

The female nodded, then raised her hands. She held both of them right in front of our faces. A small pulse of light appeared from her palms, followed by two bright green orbs that raced toward both of our faces, then disappeared upon contact with our foreheads.

"Now we will be able to understand each other," she said.

Wayne and I both looked at each other, utterly mesmerized by her magical ability.

"We come from the planet Earth," Wayne explained to them. "We got separated from the ship we were on. Some rogue agents abducted us, then locked us up in a prison cell along with our gopher friends."

All six of our furry companions had gathered nearby, and all stood together in a group. The female raised her hands again, and shot out six orbs of light that hit each gopher right between their eyes. After that, all of us could understand each other's language.

"My name is Sireth, and this is Duluth," she explained. "Our race is called shaybohan. We are magical beings, and are in touch with the spirit of all life around us."

Wayne and I introduced ourselves to them as more of their kind walked over to greet us.

"Thank you for helping us," one of the gophers said. "We greatly appreciate it."

"We are familiar with these agents you speak of," Duluth said. He had a deep voice. The bark like textures on his skin captivated me. I couldn't stop staring at him. Both of them were unique and intriguing. "They have tried to infiltrate our society many times before, but we always sense aggressive and hostile intentions coming from them, along with ample lies. They are not welcomed here. We're a peaceful people. However, strike us and we *will* strike back."

"Have you fought with them before?" Wayne sounded curious to know more.

"We have," Sireth answered. Her voice was soft and smooth, and their faces matched the skin along their arms. "They have tried to attack our city a few times. But, so far, we have always managed to crush their forces."

"Well, we appreciate any help you can give us," Wayne added. "Some food would be good, too."

Our new friends laughed at his comment. My handsome man loved to eat. And, I'm sure his tummy was growling.

"We will be happy to take you to our city where you can rest and fill your stomachs with some delicious meals." The man sounded more than happy to accommodate all of us.

"Where's your city?" Wayne asked.

The male pointed toward a distant mountain range. He had muscular arms and thick hands. All of their shirts were sleeveless, giving a great view of their bark-like arms and shoulders.

"Our city is just beyond the Carex Mountains," he said. "I think you'll enjoy the trip and the site of it."

"How are we going to climb those mountains?" a gopher asked.

Our new friends laughed again. "There is no need to climb," Duluth said. "We can all fly on the backs of our bomtars"

Now it made sense. I finally understood why these massive buffalo creatures had wings. Although, the thought of sitting on their backs without any type of saddle started to freak me out. I could only imagine falling off of one and then hitting the side of the mountains. We didn't need anymore problems.

"You'll be completely safe," Sireth reassured us, with a smile on her face. "They fly easily and gracefully."

I looked at Wayne with a considerable amount of doubt. He shrugged. "You can always grab hold of their long hair," my tough guy told me.

I raised my eyebrows with a twisted grin, and nodded as I considered his suggestion. Each buffalo had plenty of hair along their necks and backs to hold on to. It was worth a try.

"Let me show you how to ride our pets," Sireth said. She was very intriguing to look at. All of them were so unique and different.

Our new friends helped our gopher companions up on the backs of two buffalos. It was three gophers per bomtar, sitting rather high upon their winged mounts. Duluth petted the forehead of one and then led it over to me. The top of its head was about ten inches taller than mine. They were absolutely huge.

"Here you go, Adam," he said. "Just hold on to its back and you can put your foot in my hand so I can help you up."

I took a deep breath, and then did what he said. As soon as I grabbed the thick black hair on the bomtar's back, Duluth squatted so I could rest my foot in his hand, and he then lifted me up so I could swing my other leg over the buffalo's back.

I could smell plenty of odors pouring off of this hefty beast. It was a combination of outdoors, animal hide, its breath, and maybe it's stinky behind. I knew it was a male, because I got a good view of its balls dangling between its legs before I jumped on its back.

Duluth helped Wayne get on the back of a female bomtar, and he looked like he was in heaven. I could only imagine how excited he was to ride one of these creatures, flying through the sky, through unending puffy clouds and over mountains. I winked at him, and he returned the same to me with a smile.

Duluth stepped away, and then climbed on one of the animals. As soon as he did, all the buffalos took off at full speed, racing toward the mountain range on their legs.

I about shit in my shorts! With both hands, I grabbed hold of a huge amount of hair along the back of this beast and held on for dear life. Before I could even fully prepare myself, all their wings opened, each began to flap like mad, and before I knew it we were climbing high into the air, the green ground below us getting further and further away with each passing second.

I took a deep breath in an attempt to calm myself, but it barely made a difference. We moved closer to the clouds, high above the valley yet kept climbing since the mountains were so incredibly tall. But, what really surprised me while hanging on to its hair, was that all the buffalos formed a V-shape flight pattern, just like cranes or geese would have done. I shook my head and felt utterly in awe of such a fantastic experience. How many people can say they've gotten to fly on the back of a buffalo?

Some of them grunted loudly while in flight, opening their mouths wide. They turned their heads, gazing and viewing their course with each of their thick pointed horns tilting left then right. The thought of falling hadn't freaked me out too much, because I figured with these peoples magical powers they could easily save me before I hit the ground. At least I hoped so.

"Are you enjoying this?" Wayne shouted out to me. He sounded absolutely thrilled, and the look on his face matched.

My first instinct was to give him a thumbs up, but I wasn't about to let go of my buffalo's hair. "Yeah," I answered him. "A little scary, but overall it's pretty cool!"

Wayne and I were positioned halfway down the V-shape of the buffalos. There were nine in our party, and all together they had formed three different groups. As we got closer to the mountains, they began to climb even higher in the sky until we rose above each puffy cloud and soared along their cotton ball tops. Pockets of moist and warm air tickled my body. Overhead, I gazed at an unending stretch of beautiful blue skies. I wished I could have been sitting behind Wayne, holding my arms around him, loving him during such an amazing moment. He would have enjoyed my company.

The rush of warmer air against my face and body felt good. These buffalo creatures soared through the sky super fast. I figured we flew for about thirty minutes before Wayne grabbed my attention.

"Adam," he shouted out while pointing. "Look at that!"

I hadn't noticed anything far in the distance. But, straight ahead, beyond the clouds hovered a massive chuck of mountain floating in the sky. It defied gravity, and was easily twenty miles in width and probably two miles thick. The closer we got I started to see the outline of a city built upon it, stretching from one side to the other. Rooftops and towers outlined its silhouette.

How remarkable. "Is that your city?" I had turned to face Duluth and stared straight into his eyes with wonder. "How does that huge chunk of land float in the sky?"

He briefly laughed and smiled. "With magic," he explained, while lifting his hands into the air. "Our city has been there for over four thousand years and has gone through many restorations and headaches."

Headaches? I wondered what he was talking about. I gave him a questioning stare as I shrugged.

"Many people have tried to overtake our city," he explained. "Outsiders are always drawn to our magical abilities, and they feel the need to control us. But we are *not* weak!"

From what Duluth had said earlier, I imagined the rogue agents had already tried and failed. But, after hearing stories from James and Willie, I figured it wouldn't be long before they came back for another round. Those troops were total dipshits.

Through puffy white clouds we soared, rising and diving at times, turning and gliding through the beautiful sky, until we got closer to their city and the buffalos slowed down.

I was astonished at the sight of the buildings and avenues, and I knew for a fact that Wayne was even more captivated than me from the look on his face. His mouth had fallen open.

Their city was a wonderful blend of styles. Modern skyscrapers and commercial districts occupied its left side. Ancient towns and villages, with homes covered in thatched roofs lay to its right side. I saw streets built from cobblestone and lined with old wooden storefronts. There were also plenty of green fields. Some of which looked like recreational parks, and others resembled farmland. The edge of the island was rocky, coarse, and thick. A few lakes caught my attention, along with flowing creeks and streams.

Our winged mounts suddenly took a step dive, which scared the crap out of me, but I had never let go of my rides full tuft of hair. Each buffalo quickly leveled off after a few seconds, and appeared to be heading straight for a farm, where more of their kind kept grazing in a pasture.

A modern looking, two-story farmhouse sat on the property, complete with three enormous barns and farming equipment neatly placed around the perimeters.

I shook my head, amazed at how different cultures could share such similarities. I then wondered if our paths throughout life were more universal than different. They could be.

Our group separated, leaving me and Wayne with Duluth. Sireth waved goodbye to us as our three rides quickly leveled out. Each buffalo rapidly flapped their wings in order to land in the field. Everyone else had kept flying, heading to some other location beyond the farmhouse. The buffalos carrying our gopher friends followed them too. None of them landed.

As soon as our rides made contact with the ground, each one shook their heads, tossing slobber and spit into the air. I scrunched up my face and turned my head to the side so none of it got on me or in my mouth. I would have gagged.

Wayne quickly hopped off his ride after Duluth did. My strong man came over and offered me his hand to help me jump down easily, although I probably could have done it by myself.

"Thanks, sweetie," I said to him, and then gave him a kiss while Duluth watched us.

"You two are a couple?" he asked.

I nodded while slipping my arm around Wayne's waist. "We've been together for three years," I told him.

"That's wonderful," Duluth said. "My husband is inside the house if you both would like to meet him. We pretty much run this farm by ourselves."

So our bearish friend was gay after all. Something told me he was.

He has a deep and scruffy voice like Wayne, but there was something about his demeanor that gave me a hint.

Duluth tapped the butt of a buffalo, and all three beasts walked off to go and join their fellow animals out grazing through the grass. Together we walked side by side toward the house. It was beautiful and well decorated. A nice long porch wrapped around its front and sides complete with plenty of rocking chairs, a handrail, and large ceramic urns filled with flowering plants.

The doors and windows looked exactly like a home on Earth. There was a wind chime hanging near the screen at the front door. The second story windows formed a peak at their tops, and I could see decorative drapes hanging in front of each pane of glass.

"This is a beautiful home you've got," Wayne told Duluth. "It looks very cozy."

"Thank you," he said. "Ramsey and I have lived here for about twenty years."

The time frame surprised both me and Wayne. We stared at each other with curious grins.

"You really don't look that old," I told him.

Duluth smiled at us then wiggled his fingers in the air. "We use magic to keep us young. Everybody does."

"Ah, okay," Wayne nodded with a smile. "That makes sense."

A garden of flowering shrubs lined our path, and I could smell the sweet scent of each colorful bloom. It didn't take long before we reached the few steps leading up to the front porch. His husband, Ramsey, came out and greeted us. He was about the same height and build as Duluth. Both were fit, yet kind of stocky, bald, but with mossy beards and body hair, and Ramsey's skin also resembled tree bark.

What amazing guys. I felt relaxed being here on their farm. I looked back and saw a huge lake about a mile from their house. It seemed inviting, and I was certain they probably owned a boat of some kind.

However, in the back of my mind, I was still worried about James and his crew. I hoped they had shifted away before things got out of control. I didn't want to see any of them hurt or suffering. They were all good people.

"This is Wayne and Adam." Duluth introduced us to his husband.

"Nice to meet you both." Ramsey offered both of us a handshake.

Wayne took a moment to explain our situation and how we ended up here.

Ramsey seemed concerned and worried for both of us after hearing our story. "Well, we can always use our magic to help locate your friends," he explained. "We can project an image of you to them on the bridge of their ship, and you'll be able to speak to them."

"You mentioned food," Duluth reminded us. "We can fix you something inside, and then relax for a while, if that's okay."

Wayne tenderly rubbed his hand over my back. "That sounds perfect. I think we're both pretty hungry."

We followed Ramsey into their house while Duluth politely held the door open. Again, I was surprised by the similarities. They had a large cushiony couch and two recliners sitting on top of a wide decorative rug. It was beige, but had green ivy and leaves printed on it. Something that looked like a television hung on one of the walls, and there was a fireplace with a mantle, along with plenty of short wooden tables to sit a drink on.

While holding each others hand, Ramsey and Duluth led us into their kitchen which was spacious and well decorated. The first thing I noticed were the framed paintings hanging on the walls. They were of battle scenes, involving huge beasts engaged against a single warrior, and others were of gorgeous scenes of mountains blanketed with an orange and red sunset.

"Nice kitchen," I told them. And, it was.

An oven sat in the corner with a stove built upon it, and there was a large table at the center of the room with enough chairs to seat six people comfortably. A wide and tall window lined with sheer drapes gave us a great view of their backyard, and they had plenty of cabinets to store things in. A refrigerator, a toaster, and a microwave sat in here, too. Electricity didn't seem to be a problem for them. Or, it could have been magic powering these devices? I wasn't sure, but I assumed it probably was.

Ramsey pulled out two chairs and gestured for me and Wayne to sit in them. He had on khaki shorts and a sleeveless T-shirt. He was barefoot, too. I stared at his incredible feet several times. "You guys relax," he said. "My hubby and I will whip up something real tasty for all of us!"

Wayne and I sat at the table, watching while those two gathered vegetables, cheese, some sausages, and different bags of bread crumbs. Whatever they were sautéing it smelled heavenly. My stomach started to growl, and I even heard Wayne's doing the same thing.

"After we eat, would you two like to take a dip in our hot tub?" Duluth sounded excited.

"You have one?" Wayne asked. Again, the similarities surprised me.

Duluth pointed out the wide kitchen window. "Right there. It's roomy enough for all of us. But only if you guys want to."

"Are you kidding," Wayne blurted out. "We'd be happy to jump in it. We've always thought about getting a hot tub for our home back on Earth."

Wayne rubbed my shoulder with joy before he leaned in and gave me a sweet kiss. We gazed into each other's eyes, happy and content in the moment. But, in the back of my mind, I sincerely hoped we would be able to get back home to our cozy house in Spanish Lake. Nothing pleased me more than knowing I could come home after a long days work and enjoy Wayne's company, or his touch, and his tender care for me.

It wasn't long before they brought a few casserole size dishes over, and offered us a huge amount of food. They handed us napkins, plates, and utensils.

"What would you two like to drink?" Ramsey asked. "We've got water, some fruit flavored beverages, and if you'd like to have an alcoholic drink we have those too."

"A fruit beverage sounds good," Wayne said.

"Same here," I told them.

They handed us two bottles and grabbed some for themselves, before they sat down and dished out generous portions on our plates.

"Thanks guys." I shot them both a delighted smile. "It smells really good!"

The first bite I took melted in my mouth. I was in heaven with such a delicious blend of everything they had pulled out of the fridge and cabinets. All of it had been mixed with a wonderful cheese. Wayne kept busy shoveling forkfuls in his mouth. He was gobbling up everything.

After everyone cleaned their plates, both of our hosts did the dishes quickly, and then turned around staring at us while they dried their tree bark looking hands with a towel.

"We have some trunks if you'd like to wear those in the hot tub," Ramsey offered.

But, Wayne shook his head with a scrunched up expression. He even dismissed their suggestion with a flap of his hand. "We can go in naked. Not a problem." Neither of us tended to be shy when it came to showing off our bodies.

"Perfect," Duluth said. "Then let's go out there and take a dip!"

Ramsey opened their refrigerator and pulled out some more of the fruit flavored drinks. They were delicious. I selected one that had a similar taste to apples. Wayne did the same.

Their backyard patio amazed me. Hardwood panels were under our feet, and the hot tub itself was made of vertical wooden slates which were all held together with two thick steel straps that wrapped around the tubs sides.

Ramsey hit some buttons on a small control panel mounted along its edge, and the jets started to rapidly churn the water. Right after that, our hosts stripped out of their clothing and stood naked before me and Wayne.

I have to say, their tree bark textured skin proved amazing to look at. Every strand of hair on their bodies, even their pubes, looked exactly like a dark brown moss. They were both so fascinating.

"Feel free to ditch your clothes," Ramsey told us with a friendly smile.

The tub sat lower along the edge of the deck, so they both sat down and then slid into the water. I could tell it was warm because small amounts of steam were rising up from its swirling surface.

Wayne and I got naked, then sat down just like they had before we jumped in the tub. Ramsey placed the drinks next to the edge, so we all could easily reach them.

The water was up to our necks, and I sat in front of Wayne so he could slip his arms around me. He gave me a few kisses along my neck. Ramsey and Duluth did the same, but Duluth was the one sitting behind his husband. I assumed he was the top in their relationship.

"So, how can you use magic to contact our friends?" Wayne asked. He was always curious about such things. "And, what other kinds of magic can you guys do? Destruction spells, or can you conjure fire?"

"We can access your memories," Ramsey explained. "Then, we get an impression of your friends which allows us to send them a message. It will appear beside them, like a waking dream, and you'll be able to talk to them through it."

Duluth nodded a few times. "We can do all sorts of magic, including destruction spells."

"So when can you help us contact James or Willie?" I was anxious to let our bridge crew know that Wayne and I were alright.

"We can do it right now, if you'd like." Ramsey gave both of us a warm smile, and Duluth pushed him forward a bit, moving his husband closer to me.

I scooted forward a few inches and patiently waited for him to do his stuff. Wayne kept lightly brushing his fingertips over my back. He sure knew how to make me feel relaxed *and* loved.

"Are you ready?" Ramsey asked me.

I nodded happily, giving him a friendly smile.

Ramsey raised his arms so he could cradle my face with his palms, and as soon as he started to stare into my eyes, I could feel his magic taking hold of me. I could also feel the rough texture of his manly hands. I guess their tree bark looking skin did indeed feel like a tree.

I focused on his beard, staring into his brown eyes as I tried to relax.

I could feel his spell penetrating and coursing throughout my entire body. I guess that was his way of accessing my memories. As I glanced down a bit, I noticed his hands were glowing with a radiant blue light. His eyes seemed to sparkle with a touch of the same hue.

"I see them," he said. "I see your friends, James and Willie, and I also see some devilish females and a guy with blue skin."

Wayne and I both laughed.

"Those are the Devil Bunnies and Dean," Wayne explained. "They're very nice ladies, and Dean is a friendly, smart guy."

Ramsey nodded. He understood. "I'm going to project an image of you and Wayne to the bridge of their ship. You both will appear as you are right here, right now, sitting in this hot tub. You will be able to talk to them, and let them know where you are."

Right in front of my face, a round and small, screen-size portal of magic appeared which showed a lengthy image of the bridge. I could see the main holographic display, surrounded by all the workstations. It was as clear as a television screen, and I could hear James, Willie, and everyone else's voices perfectly.

The magical projection caught Dean's attention right away. "Look!" He shouted out while pointing at me and Wayne. Everyone came running over to the image of us. All of them stopped and stared at us with delighted smiles.

"We're safe and on a planet with some magical friends," I explained. Wayne partially leaned around me and waved to James and his crew. "They're projecting this image so we can communicate with you."

"I'm just glad to see that you two are okay," James said. "I was worried. We took some damage to the ship, which Kurt and his team are trying to repair. We did manage to destroy two of their smaller ships."

"They weren't able to track you guys down were they?" Wayne sounded concerned about the rogue agents shifting scanners.

"No," Dean told us. "My dispersion field never stopped working. They weren't able to scan any of us or the ship. But, they did punch a few holes in the hull."

"Which is why we're sitting low for a while and trying to get things fixed," James explained.

"I'm glad you two are okay," Willie told us with a smile. He stood with his arms crossed over his powerful chest with a glad look on his face.

"Me, too," Bray added. She was standing beside Woofa and they looked delighted to see us.

"Give us about a day or so before we can come and pick you up," Willie said. "Will you guys be alright on the planet where you are?"

I smiled with a lot of nodding. "Definitely," I told them all. "We've met some really nice friends here. They're magical, and they live on a farm." My comment left the bridge crew laughing.

"Okay, we have your signatures stored in the system," James informed us. "We'll see you in about thirty hours, or so. Okay?"

"Sounds great. Thank you all so much!" I waved goodbye to them and so did Wayne. Seconds later, the image of the bridge disappeared and Ramsey lowered his cupped hands away from my face. He leaned back against Duluth, who wrapped him up with some sweet, tender hugs and kisses along his mossy shoulders.

"So, are you guys related to trees in some kind of way?" Wayne couldn't resist learning more about them. He had slipped his arms around me, and we both leaned back against our side of the tub. I could feel his growing erection pulsing against my lower back and butt. Sitting naked in this warm water was definitely turning him on.

"Ages ago, there was another race living on our world," Ramsey explained. "They were tree beings, but they were aware of us and able to loosely interact with other life forms. One day, unexpectedly, some kind of disease infected them. We tried our best using magic to cure them, but it never worked."

"All of them ended up dying," Duluth added. "The only way to preserve their heritage was to fuse some of their genetics with ours. We were more than happy to do that for them, considering how respectful we are toward nature and our planet. So, we appear today as we have always been since that moment."

"Your beard and body hair is similar to brown moss?" Wayne nuzzled his face against my shoulders after he asked his question.

They both chuckled with wide smiles. "Yes," Ramsey answered. "Our body hair disappeared after the fusion, and now we grow a type of moss. Some males have darker or lighter shades of it, but overall, it is similar to what you would find in a forest covering rocks or the sides of trees."

"That's amazing," Wayne uttered. "I never expected to see such incredible things."

Duluth reached over and grabbed some bottles of fruit beverages then handed one to each of us.

"Your race doesn't use any sort of magic?" Ramsey asked.

Wayne and I chuckled at his question. "I wish," he said. "Our race is good at making weapons, which we use to kill each other."

"That's not a good way to live." Ramsey sounded disturbed by Wayne's comment. "Your people should be united and work toward a better future for everyone."

I laughed out loud. "Well, most of our kind does do that. But, there's always a few who like to stir up some trouble every now and then." They both nodded and understood while taking a drink from their bottles.

We sat in the hot tub until it started to get dark. A few times, Wayne and I had to jump out to go take a pee over by some bushes. Ramsey and Duluth did the same.

But, what really impressed me the most, was all the moons that started to appear after the sun set. Six showed in the sky, all at different distances and sizes. One actually had what looked like an atmosphere. It was blue, with swirls of puffy white clouds.

Later on, after the stars came out, along the horizon I could see what resembled the Northern Lights back on Earth. They shimmered and danced in beautiful green and orange colors, filling the sky with their brilliance. Wayne appeared awestruck as he stared into the night sky and admired all the gorgeous colors and moons.

The four of us eventually got out of the hot tub, and our two friends closed it down, turning off any lights that had been on. We put our clothes back on, carried our socks and sneakers, and then headed back into the house, where Ramsey showed us to a room we could sleep in. Both of them were so generous and kind.

Our guest room upstairs was quaint and cozy. A queen size bed sat above a large area rug beside a long window. There was a bathroom, a table with two chairs, and plenty of wardrobes to hang clothes in. All of the furniture had an aged yet appealing look. Overall, I'd say the room had a country theme to it.

"You two have a good night," he told us, then stepped out of the room and slowly closed the door as we wished him the same.

"You look tired," I said to Wayne.

"I am." He moved closer to give me some kisses. "How about we hold off on sex for now, and just clean ourselves up a bit before cuddling in the sack."

I smiled then laughed while I massaged his crotch. "That sounds perfect."

We pulled off our shirts and dropped our shorts, then laid them on top of a dresser before we took a shower together in the bathroom. We took turns dropping down on our knees to fill our mouths with some sensual appreciation of each other. Wayne ended up getting hard as a rock, and both of us finally got off in each other's mouth.

While on my knees, I sucked him slowly while rubbing my hands over his hairy stomach, down his thighs, and over his shapely ass. He had such wonderful calves and feet. And, let me tell you, my handsome man could really blow out a huge amount of liquid love. I think he shot four times in my mouth, and I did the same to him. But, I enjoyed pleasing him and making him feel good. It warmed my heart knowing he was happy. Getting off had relaxed both of us.

After the shower, we dried off, turned off the lamps, and then snuggled together in bed. Some sparkling colors from the Northern Lights shined in our room through the window.

Wayne preferred to lie behind me so he could enjoy my hairy shoulders and back. His plentiful kisses and adoration always made me happy. It felt good having his strong arms wrapped around me, holding me close, his beard against my skin, and his lengthy wiener positioned right along the crack of my butt. I couldn't have asked for a better man in my life.

"Love you, sweetie," I whispered.

"Love you too." He gave me a warm hug.

7

A loud knock on the bedroom door woke us up. It was morning. Sunlight poured in through the window. It illuminated the sheer drapes along its edges.

Without any warning, Ramsey opened the door and leaned in. "Sorry to wake you up," he apologized.

"No, you're fine," I told him. Wayne woke up, too, and we both stared at Ramsey.

"We were just contacted by some friends of ours," he explained. "Apparently more rogue agents are stirring up some trouble along the outskirts of our city. Duluth and I were asked to patrol the surrounding lands, and make sure none of them are sneaking around. I just wanted to let you both know."

Wayne and I quickly sat up in the bed after hearing his news. Ramsey stared at both of us with wonder plastered on his face. I guess our hair and bodies were intriguing to him.

"Well, let us get dressed and we'll come with you," Wayne offered. "Would that be okay with you two?"

"Sure," Ramsey said, with delight in his voice. "You're more than welcome to join us. We'll be ready to leave in about twenty minutes." He stepped back out into the hallway and quietly closed the bedroom door.

"How the fuck are we going to help them?" I gave Wayne a kiss on his prominent, hairy shoulder.

Wayne mildly chuckled. "After they knock them on their asses, I'll be happy to pound their faces to pulp." He held up his fist and shook it in front of the hateful look on his face. "You can hit them too, Adam. Don't hold back."

I laughed while giving him another kiss on his shoulder. All the hairs against my lips felt heavenly. "I think I'm more of a lover than a fighter. I'll leave the ass kicking to you and your sexy butt."

Wayne turned his head and gave me some sweet kisses. He reached up with his hand and used it to grip my chin, holding my face in a sensual way while showing me ample amounts of love.

"You turn me on so much," he whispered. "Nothing would make me happier than shoving my dick in your sweet ass right now."

I smiled. "Well, he did say we have about twenty minutes."

Wayne smiled and then pushed away all the blankets. I hopped on my back and he raised my legs while kneeling down so he could lick me down there, getting me nice and sloppy so he could shove his meaty mammoth inside of me.

Wayne was usually very gentle when it came to having sex, but this morning he didn't waste anytime. He squatted on his knees, grabbed hold of my ankles, and raised my legs up high. He was an expert at the hitting the target, and he rammed his dick inside me really fast.

"Oh, fuck," I said out loud. "Damn, that feels good."

He kept working it inside me really fast, pumping me while holding my ankles. He sniffed the bottoms of my feet and ran his tongue along them, too. Then, he sucked on my big toes, taking turns between each foot until his face scrunched up and he shot a whopping huge load of love inside me.

"Oh, man. That felt incredible," he said. "Now let me sample some of your deliciousness."

Wayne loved giving me a blowjob. He had a special knack while doing it, which felt amazing. He lowered my legs, moved back a bit, and then started his special treat. He always kept a tight suction around my dick, and swirled his mouth while doing it.

"Wow," I said. "You do that so fucking good."

He kept working fast, since we didn't have a lot of time. It didn't take me long to get off, and my tough guy swallowed every drop I gave him.

"How was that?" He sat up, facing me while wiping his lips.

"You are truly the master blaster at giving head," I told him.

He laughed and gave me a sweet smile. "I guess we need to get going."

We both jumped out of bed and put our clothes on. We pulled up our socks over our feet, and then slipped on our sneakers. We stepped into the bathroom to straighten ourselves up a bit. Both of us peed, and then picked up some toothbrushes that were laying out for guests. Both stood in a cup along the sink, so we each used one along with a squirt of toothpaste.

Since our cell phone batteries were dead, we had no idea how long it had been, so we hurried downstairs to a wonderful aroma that filled the entire house. We found Ramsey and Duluth in the kitchen standing beside the table, which was covered with tons of tasty treats for us to eat.

"You guys are so sweet," I told them, after Wayne and I walked over to the table.

"Well, it might be a long journey," Ramsey explained. "We didn't want you guys to get hungry."

"Help yourselves!" Duluth handed each of us a plate, and we both filled them up fast.

There were sausage links, scrambled eggs with bacon bits, biscuits and gravy, something that tasted like orange juice, a variety of fruit slices, and even some chocolate coated crunchy bites which were really tasty.

"Thank you." I shoved some eggs with bacon in my mouth. "This tastes incredible!"

"It sure does," Wayne added. He kept busy with the sausage links and gravy, dipping each one of them in it before gobbling them up.

"Several smaller rogue vessels have been spotted above the city," Ramsey told us. "There's an alert issued for all citizens to be on the watch."

"More fucking shit from those assholes," Wayne stated with a bitter tone. "Well, we'd be happy to join you and make sure this area is safe."

"And, just to make sure you two are armed," Ramsey said. "We have the ability to temporarily gift you with some magical attacks. They won't be as powerful or plentiful as ours, but, they will help you if we get outnumbered."

Wayne's face lit up like I had never seen before. His mouth dropped open and he seemed utterly fascinated by the offer. "What will we be able to do?" he asked in an excited tone.

"Project some minor shielding," Ramsey explained. "And, cast some repulsive spells which will launch people away from you and send them flying through the air."

Wayne's face showed sheer bliss. "Can we have these powers now?"

Our magical friends smiled happily, then looked at each other and shrugged. "Sure," Ramsey told us. "We can show you how to use them too."

Duluth approached me while Ramsey headed toward Wayne. Both of them raised their hands, then cradled our faces with their magical, glowing touch.

His hands generated warmth. More than I expected. I felt a tingling sensation penetrating me, coursing throughout my body, giving me shivers as I stared into his eyes. Again, I saw the blue light emanating from his hands, and the same sparkle radiated within his eyes.

I felt as if I had slipped into a dreamlike state. All of nature and the planet itself had connected with me. I understood this place, our friends, and their gifts. The entire universe welcomed me. It wished me well, and imbued me with its wonders. Distant voices sang to me in a soothing harmony. I understood existence. Everything made sense. My purpose became clear.

The glowing light faded, and they simultaneously lowered their hands from our faces. I turned to look at Wayne. He seemed as mesmerized as me.

"Are you guys okay?" Ramsey asked. He seemed concerned, yet anxious to hear our response.

We nodded.

Duluth headed over to the counter by the sink, where he took a drink from a bottle of that fruit flavored beverage. Ramsey backed away and demonstrated. Quickly, he brought the back of one hand close to his chest while holding out his other, which faced us. A huge glowing aura appeared right in front of him. It distorted his appearance, shrouding him in a protective sphere.

"Try it," he said to us.

Wayne did exactly as Ramsey had done, and sure enough he produced a shield just like our friend had done. I followed his lead and mine appeared as soon as I positioned my hands.

"That's so fucking cool!" Wayne shouted out. "And, you said we can toss them through the air too?"

Ramsey and Duluth laughed. "We'll show you how to do that outside," Ramsey told us.

"Yeah, we don't want to destroy the house," Duluth added.

We were ready to go, so Wayne and I followed them outside through the back door, walking along the porch and then down the steps into the yard. All of us stopped and stood together, as Ramsey stretched out his arms to project a distorted wave of green and yellow colors toward an old wooden barrel. It flipped over fast and then rolled several times until he stopped his magic.

"Try it," he told us with an excited smile.

Wayne mimicked his movements, and instantly shot out a colorful effect that hit the barrel with considerable force, launching it high into the air.

"Very nice!" Duluth shouted out. "You've definitely got the hang of it."

I did exactly as Wayne had done, and I hit the barrel, tipping it over a few times. Unfortunately, my effect was no where near as powerful as my sexy man's had been. A little more practice, and I was sure I'd get the hang of it.

Ramsey stuck his thumb and index finger in his mouth and blew out a few whistles. Six of the buffalos came running over to him, with their wings slightly opened and drool dripping from their mouths, along with snot dangling from their noses. Four of them were black and two were brown. "Let's ride!" he said in a positive voice.

Wayne helped me climb on ones back, and I wrapped my hand around its thick tufts of hair. He then expertly climbed on the back of his, while Ramsey and Duluth sat on theirs waiting patiently for us to follow them.

"We'll scout out the area from above," Duluth informed us.

Ramsey whistled again, and right after he did all the buffalos raced forward like bats out of hell. They opened their wings, and before I knew it we were flying up into the sky, soaring over the plentiful treetops where I got a nice view of the lake in the distance. Unfortunately, we were headed in the opposite direction. It would have been nice to see the relaxing water.

The morning breeze felt good. It had turned out to be a warm, yet mild day. Birds were chirping, and I could see faint images of the moons high above us in the morning sky. I should have asked how many they actually had orbiting their planet. I was surprised Wayne hadn't been eager to ask, since he loved stargazing.

Ramsey shouted out to us. "There!" He pointed at a small rogue vessel, which had landed within a clearing at the center of a dense section of woods. His buffalo took a steep dive and the rest of them quickly followed, until we landed with a thud in a field of grass. We were about two hundred feet from the rogue agents.

Ten of them stood around their shuttlecraft. All aliens, no humans. There were seven males and three females. All but one wore black bodysuits similar to the ones Bray had given me and Wayne. Some carried rifles, and others had holstered handguns strapped around their thighs. Some had green skin with dark hair, and others resembled red colored demons with horns on their heads.

One in particular (the leader of their pack, I assumed), was a tall and muscular male, probably at least eight feet tall. He looked like a cross between a human, a rhinoceros, and a bodybuilder on steroids. Two spiraled, dark brown horns jutted out from above his temples. His skin was dark gray with short hair on his head, and a partial beard. He was the one without a bodysuit. He wore jeans, brown square-toed boots, and a red flannel shirt with its sleeves cut off.

All of them stopped and stared at us. I figured they knew who Ramsey and Duluth were from previous encounters, but Wayne and I were most likely a surprise for them. I'm sure they didn't expect to see humans.

I hiked my right leg over the back of my buffalo, and took the liberty to jump down. Wayne followed my lead along with Ramsey and Duluth. Our herd slowly scattered to feed on the nearby grass. The agents eyeballed us from across the field. They all stood watching, scrutinizing, and quietly chatting to each other.

The huge horned guy walked forward with his crew following him. Each one had gripped their rifles or pulled out their handguns, ready to shoot us.

Wayne quickly used his magical gifts. He stuck out his left arm, held his right one close to his chest, and then projected a glowing energy that raced across the field and lifted two of the agents high into the air. It launched them back toward the shuttlecraft, where they landed against it with a loud thud. Both looked knockout.

Several of the agents aimed their weapons at us, but the tall horned guy held up his hand and stopped them from firing.

"A most impressive display," the horned guy said. He had a deep voice which was blended with a lot of arrogance and pride. "I haven't seen a human use magic in a long time."

"Maybe we're not human," Wayne shouted out in a detestable tone.

The horned guy laughed then scrunched up his face in a suspicious manner. "I can tell you're human, because I'm very familiar with your race. You're kind has altered the universe we come from. And, unfortunately, it will never return to the way it was. My name is Korath, and I would ask that you refrain from attacking us so we can talk about your future."

"There's nothing to talk about," Wayne told him. "We know about your organization and how power hungry you are, how much you want to control everyone. Why are you all here on their planet? What do you intend to do with it?"

Korath sighed and shook his head with a roll of his eyes. "It sounds like you're been talking to the wrong people. *We* are here to offer advancement to any race that would be willing to join us."

"Join you," Wayne blurted out. "I've heard all you're interested in is controlling people, and subjecting them to your will."

The two agents who hit the shuttlecraft finally stood up. Both had recovered. They shook their heads, obviously dazed from Wayne's impressive magical whacking. Our herd of flying buffalos had moved away to graze on better grasses, which left us to stand before our new acquaintances.

"I can see someone has already filled your heads with bullshit lies," Korath said. "That's too bad. I think both of you would have been excellent additions to our forces."

The horned guy wore a holstered handgun strapped around his beefy thigh. He rapidly pulled it out and fired off a shot directly at Wayne. But, my handsome man had clearly anticipated the attack. He raised his hands and arms just like Ramsey had shown him, and generated a protective barrier that deflected the shot entirely.

The other agents aimed their weapons and blanketed the four of us with blinding blasts of energy. Wayne, me, Ramsey, and Duluth had all generated our magical shields. There was no way their shots would hit us.

Ramsey then produced some sort of swirling orange and black mass right above the agents, which began dropping gigantic balls of fire at them the size of a dumpster. They jumped out of the way or ran like cowering fiends. The fire balls hit the grassy field where they erupted and scorched the land, leaving it a sizzling, smoking mess.

Some agents had fallen on the ground as they jumped out of the way, but all kept firing their rifles and guns at us. Duluth projected a huge defensive barrier, so the rest of us could focus on hitting them with our spells.

Wayne impressed me so much. He used his magic to grab two and sometimes three of the agents at once. He would launch them through the air, back toward the woods, or bang their bodies against the shuttlecraft which left them in a dizzy state.

I managed to hit Korath with my spell, and it sent him flying backward where he landed right on his shapely ass. His jeans were tight and clearly showed off his musculature. But, just as he stood up and aimed his gun at me, a loud clap of thunder came from directly overhead. I recognized the sound without any doubt in my mind.

James's ship had appeared right above us. Ramsey and Duluth freaked out as the crab shaped shadow covered the land, and blocked out the all morning sunshine.

"It's okay!" I told them. "That's our ship with our friends onboard!"

Both of them looked relieved. I'm sure they thought more rogue agents had suddenly shown up.

Every agent fled back to their shuttle, even Korath ran like a frightened child. They all piled inside before the hatch door lowered, and they sped away into the sky, flying over the treetops toward the city. In comparison, James's ship vastly outsized their small craft. I'm sure with a single shot they could have destroyed the rogue shuttle.

James's ship veered to the side, and it looked like they were slowly following the rogue agents. I figured they were heading toward the city to stir up more trouble.

"Should we follow them?" I asked.

Ramsey nodded, and then whistled for our rides to come back over to us. We all jumped on the backs of our buffalos and each one took off running. They flapped their gigantic feathery wings, taking us into the sky, where we moved above the tall green trees of the forest. I got an incredible view of the lake in the distance, and felt a second warm rush of air against my face.

From this height, I saw a couple of thin columns of smoke rising up from the city. I could only imagine what the rogue agents were doing. We kept behind James's ship which moved considerably faster than the four of us. Then, from the corner of my eyes, I saw three small rogue vessels appear along the horizon. Each one headed straight for us.

All were shaped like long loafs of garlic bread, the kind you'd cut in half and then bake in your oven. Before each enemy ship could fire off a shot, the crew onboard James's ship attacked them. From out of the forward pinchers of his crab ship, several brilliant blue shots of energy raced through the sky, hitting each rogue vessel, and completely destroying them within a loud and fiery explosion.

I watched as pieces of burning metal fell toward the land. Each impact tossed dirt and grass in the air, and I imagined how many agents had been killed. But, it was to save our magical friends and their home, so I felt zero remorse for what James's crew had done. Actions give way to responses. And, every agent I had seen so far was a complete and utter smartass, desiring only to control everyone. Who wants to live like that?

We flew over farmlands and houses while following James's ship. We soon crossed over suburban neighborhoods and the modern outskirts of the city.

His ship came to a stop and our buffalos flew around it, where we got a great view of its design. It was such a remarkable vessel, thicker in its rounded center and thinner along its sides and rear. I felt thankful that Wayne and I were allowed to partake in such an amazing adventure.

Our flying buffalos circled around his ship, and then hovered in the air for a moment as we watched several rogue vessels flee from the city. Many were shaped like loaves of bread, and they shot out from its downtown area, passing along the towering silver skyscrapers as they ran like cowards from these people's magical attacks.

One of the larger cargo bay doors opened along the side of James's ship, and the maintenance team of Kurt, Reese, and Amp waved at me and Wayne, signaling for us to come and land in the bay.

I pulled on one side of my buffalo's hair, and he turned toward the bay. Ramsey sounded off a different type of whistle, and soon all our rides headed toward the opened doors, where we landed along the edge and each of our mounts hurried inside. We stood beside some of our smaller shuttlecrafts and the maintenance team.

Kurt reached up and petted the top of my rides furry head. "Nice to see you both again," he said to me and Wayne in his course voice. "Looks like you made some new friends."

They were all dressed in dark brown work boots, worn jeans, and T-shirts. Kurt had a bit of a tummy in comparison to Amp and Reese, so his shirt stuck out further. But, overall, he still looked good. A burly yet muscular guy, they were all so nice and friendly.

Wayne and I immediately jumped down and gave each one of Kurt's team a warm hug. "This is Ramsey and Duluth," I told them. "You may not understand them until they touch you with some magic."

Without hesitation, Ramsey raised his arms and sent colorful blue orbs racing toward all three of them, so they could communicate without any problems or their pdPhones. Each colorful orb had disappeared between their eyes.

"Welcome, welcome," Amp said happily. He had opened his rust colored, reptilian arms in the air, inviting our magical friends to hop off their buffalos and join our group, which they both did right away.

They all shook hands. Ramsey and Duluth kept glancing at Amp with amazed looks on their faces. I wasn't sure if they had ever seen someone before from his race. Amp was definitely an interesting person to encounter. He was the tallest of us all.

"Those rogue bastards giving you a lot of headaches?" Kurt was blunt but polite with his question. I picked up on his bluntness when Wayne and I first met the maintenance team.

"They're very persistent about trying to infiltrate our city," Ramsey explained. "Luckily, none of our citizens have been killed our abducted. I know our magic keeps us safe and turns them away."

"It sure does," I added. "You're spells are amazing!"

"Thank you," Ramsey said. He and Duluth smiled.

"Hopefully those three ships we just destroyed will send them running with their tails between their legs," Reese added. He was so young and cute, yet he showed a passionate desire to succeed and help out as much as he could.

"Would you two like to meet James, Willie, and the rest of the bridge crew?" I figured I'd offer to introduce Ramsey and Duluth to everyone else.

"You'll like the bridge," Wayne added. "He's got an impressive ship."

"Only if it's okay," Duluth said. "We don't want to get in the way of anything."

Wayne and I both batted our hands through the air. "Its fine," I told them both. "James absolutely hates the rogue agents, so all of us will get along wonderfully."

Ramsey and Duluth followed me and Wayne over to the pocket doors covering the bay entrance. They parted, and then the four of us stepped out into the white corridor. Our guests kept looking around, gazing at everything, every doorway, the recessed lights above us, and our reflections along the polished steel floors.

We led them right to the elevator. Its doors opened and they followed us inside. Wayne knew exactly what buttons to push on the holographic control panel, so he did his thing and we immediately started to move up through the ship.

"You're really going to like the crew," I told them.

"I just hope the buffalos don't crap all over your cargo bay," Duluth mentioned.

We all laughed at his comment. "Well, if they do take some dumps," Wayne said cheerfully, "We'll just hang on to it and cram that shit down the throats of any agents who we come across."

I reached behind my blunt man and gently massaged his butt. His silky shorts felt great against his toned cheeks. He surprised me by leaning in and giving me a lengthy kiss. It was nice to see Ramsey and Duluth do the same thing. They were both such sweet and caring guys.

The elevator doors opened and we proceeded to the bridge, climbing the slightly slanted hallway until we reached the huge doors that parted and slid inside the walls. Wayne and I took a few steps in the bridge and then introduced our friends. Everyone, including the Devil Bunnies, had smiles and excited looks on their faces.

"Everyone," I said out loud. "This is Ramsey, and his husband, Duluth. Don't get all freaked out if he drops some magic on you. It's their way of translating our languages."

The entire bridge crew came over to greet our two magical friends. They shook hands and patted each other on their shoulders. Bray and Woofa seemed particularly intrigued by Ramsey and Duluth, probably because of the magic I had mentioned.

Wayne and I explained what happened to us, along with the gopher friends we met in the prison cell out in the middle of the woods. They all seemed shocked, yet grateful we made it out okay. Bray seemed upset about losing our harness suits, but she explained there were more in storage.

Ramsey raised his hands and projected his magical translation orbs toward everyone. He even applied some to me and Wayne again. All the glowing balls hit us right between our eyes.

With a smile on her face, Bray demonstrated her spirit calling skills. She may have wanted to show off. I wasn't sure. But, she summoned about three dozen oversized butterflies that hovered around us, all in ghostly hues of blue and white light. They were vague at times, translucent and hollow, except for their outlined shapes.

How beautiful. I wished Wayne or I could have summoned creatures from our past lives. Think how cool it would be to walk the trails near our home, with bunches of spirit critters following us around. Everyone who passed us would be completely captivated.

"It's great to see you guys," Willie said. He swooped in with furry hugs for me and Wayne.

Our magical friends looked intrigued by Willie. In fact, all of the bridge crew seemed delighted from the expressions on their faces.

James wasted no time bringing us up to speed on the situation. "We were able to scan the rogue troops during the battle, and we also got signatures for the freaks who were trying to kill you down near the woods."

"We'll be able to shift to any of their locations," Dean happily added.

"A surprise attack will teach those fuckers," Wayne said.

I nudged the side of his arm, giving him a smile as we made eye contact. He stroked the side of my hand with his fingertips, showing his appreciation and love.

"How long have they been attacking your city?" James asked our friends.

"A little over a year," Ramsey answered.

"We've always been able to push them away with our magic," Duluth explained. "There are so few of them, I doubt they will ever be able to decimate our city."

"Still though," Willie said. "We want to make sure they are taken care of so they don't stir up anymore issues throughout your universe."

"You all are welcome to come and visit our city," Duluth told us. "We can have lunch at one of the swanky clubs downtown."

Wayne and everyone else's faces brighten up considerably.

"I think that's a fantastic idea!" Willie blurted out. He patted his tummy. "I could use a good amount of food right about now."

James smiled as he shook his head. He then reached over and brushed his hand along Willie's furry arm in a tender yet loving way.

"Let's do it!" our captain announced.

Everyone was invited to come and have some lunch, including the ship's maintenance team. Using the main holographic display, Bray and Woofa directed us toward a docking port which sat atop a large section of a building in the downtown area. Ramsey contacted several people by means of magic, and explained to them that we were no threat to their city.

After we landed, our group met with Kurt, Reese, and Amp down in one of the cargo bays. The wide doors opened, showcasing a beautiful afternoon sky above a remarkable city filled with shiny skyscrapers and a variety of designs. A staircase was mounted along the edge of the doors, so we were able to walk down to the top of the docking port where we got a much better view of the city streets.

It didn't look different from a city on Earth, except for a few flying vehicles and several absolutely gigantic wooden ships that resembled something pirates would have sailed on across the sea. They literally floated in the skies all around the city, drifting and hovering near the tops of skyscrapers, without making any kind of noise from engines.

Wayne pointed at one of the ships. "You guys use magic to keep them in the air?"

Ramsey nodded. "It's a tribute to our way of life from long ago. They're free to ride if you guys would like to take a trip around the city. They can dock right here along the edge of the landing area."

Wayne and I both stared at each other with excitement on our faces. Willie nudged James's shoulder a few times with a smile on his face. I think he wanted to jump on the ship as much as we did.

"Sure, we'd be happy to take a ride," James told them.

"After lunch, though," Willie added. He raised his arm and flexed his whopping big bicep. "I need some food to keep all this looking good."

Everyone laughed at Willie's wisecrack. Ramsey raised his left arm high above his head, and shot off a magical symbol shaped like a gigantic shield that must have grabbed the attention of the pilot on one of the airships. It quickly changed direction, and started heading right for our group.

I stood amazed while gawking at the airship. I couldn't believe how much it looked like a pirate ship, only without the tall sails. There weren't many people riding it, and as it got closer, I could hear music playing which left me staring curiously.

"A band plays on each ship," Duluth explained to us. "It's just another way to make everyone happy during their ride."

Once the ship got closer, I could see a small gathering of musically talented individuals seated along its right side. Probably six or seven hundred feet in length, it docked right beside the edge of the roof, and extended a wide wooden plank for us to cross. I could smell the scent of wood riding on the breeze, and there were several crewmen (both males and females), ready to assist us with anything we needed.

Wayne held my hand as we climbed the floorboard, and then passed the thick yet decorative wooden frames standing vertically along the ships edge. Within seconds we stood on its main deck and stopped to take in this breathtaking moment.

"Amazing," Wayne said.

"Yes it is." I pulled him further along while the rest of our friends walked around admiring this amazing craft.

A large section of offices sat at the rear of the ship, with a covered command center above them. I noticed small birds hanging out and jumping around along the edges of its roof. At the front section was a multitier viewport, with plenty of levels that lined the area and provided different heights where people could stand and admire all the breathtaking views. The band had never quit playing their lively tunes. It sounded like something from a video game, or a mix of upbeat classical music. It wasn't loud at all. They played at a quiet level, similar to background music you'd hear in a retail store.

Wayne and I stood along the edge of the ship. We leaned over its thick hardwood rail and gawked at the city streets far below. He slipped his arm around me, then leaned close to my side where he nuzzled his beard and lips against my neck.

"I love you so much, Adam," he whispered. "I can't tell you how grateful I am to be here with you."

"Me too. You mean the world to me, Wayne."

After the ships stairway receded, the huge vessel pulled away from the edge of the rooftop and took a direct course toward the heart of city. We flew beside incredibly tall buildings, each with glass windows where we could see inside of them. We got a great view of tree-bark-looking people working at their jobs. Some of them noticed and waved at us. We happily waved back.

"So you're sure you still don't want to live in a place like this?" Wayne asked me.

I turned to face him, then gave him a kiss on his lips and then his cheek. I worked one across the tip of his nose too. "As long as I'm with you, we can live wherever you want."

A wide smile stretched across his face before he gave me a passionate sloppy kiss. He shoved his delicious tongue in my mouth several times while pressing our lips together.

"We're almost there." Ramsey pointed at our destination. It was a rooftop cafe that looked fairly busy. He and Duluth were holding hands. So were James and Willie, Bray and Woofa. Dean was hanging out with the Devil Bunnies, and also with Kurt, Reese, and Amp. They were all laughing, and I figured they were making sexually slanted jokes about each other.

"Can you smell that?" I said to Wayne as we got closer to the cafe. "They must be cooking a ton of tasty food down there."

He confirmed my assumption with a few nods, a delighted smile, and wide open eyes. I could tell he was enjoying our flight. We both were.

The airship veered to the side and slowly maneuvered its way toward the rooftop restaurant. Wayne and I leaned further over the chest-high edge of the ship, so we could glance down at the streets. Several flying vehicles zoomed by underneath us, while dozens of other ones moved along narrow avenues or over wide roads while making their way through the city.

Our gigantic wooden ship slowed and then parked along a section of the building designed for docking and guest departures. Ramsey and Duluth led the way down to the cafe, as our diverse group followed them. We got a lot of looks and stares, but overall, everyone seemed intrigued by our presence. They were a hospitable race.

A male waiter showed us to a long table with plenty of chairs for all of us to sit down and enjoy each other's company. The menus were in their language, so Duluth translated for us.

"Steak for me," Wayne announced. "Maybe we need some beer, too."

I completely agreed with him, but felt confused a bit. I guess some of their race ate meat while others respected their animal friends. Their planet was starting to sound more and more like Earth, all of them having a wide diversity of interests.

We joked around with each other, sharing stories, compliments, and getting a better feel for our new friends until the food came. There were a wide range of pasta dishes, steaks, potatoes, lots of vegetables, tea and beer, and barbequed appetizers with cheese sticks added on the side.

"So you intend on tracking down these rogues with your shifting technology?" Ramsey asked.

James swallowed his mouthful of food. "Yes," he said. "After we're done here I'll have Dean begin the process. We should be able to locate them and figure out where their bases are, or at least where they're located."

"Then kick the shit out of them!" Willie added loudly. He had ordered a considerable amount of food, about four steaks with a huge bowl of grilled, seasoned potato slices, which he kept gobbling up.

"We won't be coming with you, if that's alright," Duluth said. "We need to stay here and protect our farm and our people."

"That's fine," I told them. "James has an awesome crew. We'll take care of them."

"Did you guys get all the repairs done?" Wayne asked.

All of the maintenance team laughed. "Piece of cake," Amp said. He batted his scaled hand through the air. "The holes weren't a problem, and there were only a couple of major repairs we needed to make to the ship's systems." He was also eating some steak. I guess reptiles loved meat just as much as the rest of us did.

"We managed to increase our shielding, too," Kurt added. "We'll be able to deflect a lot more of their weapons fire."

Reese raised his glass toward Kurt, and they bumped their beers together in a celebratory salute to their awesomeness. Amp did the same. All three of them smiled at each other, proud of their accomplishments.

James then raised his drink and held it in midair above the table. "Well, I would just like to say that *all* of you are a great team, and I couldn't ask for a better crew. I'm thankful for having you all, and for everything you do."

Everyone raised their glasses toward James, including Ramsey and Duluth, followed by thankful nods and warm smiles around the entire table. After about an hour, we all had finished filling our bellies.

"We need to get back home and check up on stuff," Ramsey said, "And, make sure none of those freaks are messing around with our place."

Duluth leaned back in his chair then rubbed his boyfriends shoulder. It pleased me to see them in love. I wished them the best in life. Who knew if we would even see them again? I certainly hoped we would.

Slowly we made our way back to the airship, which took us back to James's spaceship. As far as the bill for our dinner, Ramsey and Duluth took care of it.

"Thank you for a great meal," I told them both.

They both gave me and Wayne friendly hugs.

"You're welcome," Ramsey said, with a wide smile. "It has been a pleasure to meet both of you. You're really great guys."

"So are you!" Wayne slipped in some more hugs for our magical friends. We all gave each other pats on the back. Good times.

Wayne and I led our friends back to the cargo bay on our ship, while the bridge crew had maneuvered it back to their farm. And, yes, a few of the buffalos had pooped in the bay, but it looked solid and fairly easy to clean up.

"We've reached the farm," Dean announced over the bay's intercom.

I took a moment to push some buttons in order to raise the cargo door, and let some afternoon sunshine fill the room with its brilliance. It was a beautiful day, with wonderful blue skies and small, cotton ball clouds.

"Best of luck to you both," Ramsey told us. Duluth stood beside him smiling at us.

"And to you," I told them.

"Thanks for everything," Wayne said. "We appreciate all your help and the magical spells you gave us."

We exchanged another round of warm hugs before they both jumped on the back of two buffalos. The ship had slowed and hovered about sixty or seventy feet above their farm. As I stood near the bay door, I got a great view of their land and house. All of it looked so inviting. I'd miss this place, their world, and especially them.

Ramsey made a loud whistle, then all of the buffalos took off toward the door. Their hooves sounded like iron tapping against the steel floor, and as soon as they reached the outside edge of the bay, they spread their wings and took off into the air, soaring above their beloved farmland and home.

A few tears ran down my cheeks as Wayne and I stood watching them leave. He slipped his arm around me and looked into my eyes. "You okay?"

I nodded while giving him a smile. "Yeah," I told my handsome man. "I'm just feeling a little emotional. We had a great time with them. I hate to see it end. It's so much better than work."

Wayne turned me toward him and hugged me for a long moment. He kissed the side of my face while rubbing his hands over my back. "You're such a sweet and caring man, with such a great heart," he whispered beside my ear.

I rested the side of my face against his left shoulder. My nose and lips touched his thick beard. It felt wonderful against my skin, and it reminded me how much I loved his arms around me. I was in heaven.

Together, we stood and watched as Ramsey and Duluth disappeared into the white clouds in the distance. After that, I closed the cargo bay door, then informed the bridge through one of the workstations that they had left and we could move on.

"I'm giving everyone some time off this afternoon," James replied. "We all deserve a bit of relaxation. Go and take some time for yourselves."

Wayne gave me a mild jiggle after he wrapped his arms around me again. I'm sure he and I were thinking the same thing concerning our time off.

"Would you like to go back to our room, take a shower, and then we can make some sweet love." He smiled at me, eager for some fun in the bed.

I nodded happily. "I'd like that a lot."

Hand in hand, we made our way to the elevator, taking it down a few floors, and then headed straight for our room that Willie had shown us. Wayne activated the pocket doors and allowed me to enter first. He was such a sweetheart. As soon as I stood inside, he followed me and closed the doors.

He stood in front of me, holding his hands around my waist while giving me sweet and tender kisses on my lips, neck, and cheeks.

"I love you more than I can say, Adam." He had reached down and massaged my crotch, caressing the front of my silky shorts. His affection got me hard right away, and it made him smile. "Let me help you out of your clothes."

I stood still while he squatted and untied the laces on my sneakers. He pulled the left one off first, and then held it up to his nose where he took a deep whiff of its scent. After that, he pulled off my sock and shoved it against his face, inhaling their flavorful aroma.

"I haven't washed those for days," I told him.

"They smell great, babe," he said. "You have really sexy feet. They're never stinky."

After he took off my other sneaker and sock, he pulled down my shorts and underwear, knelt on his knees, and then slowly swallowed my erection down his throat.

Wayne gave such good head. He kept sucking me nice and tight, twisting and turning his mouth, treating it with so much care and love. It felt beyond incredible.

I gazed down and watched as he stroked himself. With no underwear on, his meaty mammoth stuck out along the side of his shorts, right along his leg. Easily ten inches in length, it was nice and thick, too.

He slid his hands under my shirt, moving them over my stomach until he reached my hard nipples. He pinched each one (which I enjoyed tremendously), then gripped them tightly while adding a few twist and tugs. I loved when he played rough with my nipples. It turned me on so much.

Wayne stood up, then pulled my shirt up and partially off of me. I raised my arms up high expecting to be fully naked, but as soon as he got my shirt around my forearms, he lowered it behind my back, pulling my arms slightly back behind my head. He shoved his face right into my armpits where he sniffed, kissed, and then licked them for a long moment.

"Oh, you smell so fucking good," he uttered. Both of our pits were hairy, and Wayne made sure he enjoyed every strand of hair I had to offer. He gently tugged on them all with his lips, then ran his tongue firmly across the entire area, savoring the scent and sweatiness.

After a few minutes, he leaned his head back, stared lovingly in my eyes, and then gave me some sloppy kisses. He loved showing his tongue in my mouth. I enjoyed it, too. I could smell the scent of my armpit on his breath.

I wiggled my arms and dropped my shirt from around them, then reached down and pulled Wayne's shirt up and over his head. I tossed it over toward the bed.

He pushed off his sneakers and kicked each one to the side. While still kissing me, he reached down and pulled off his socks, then dropped his shorts.

Our hard dicks touched, and I wrapped my hand around them both, stroking them slowly with a mild twisting motion.

"Oh, fuck that feels so good," he whispered happily. "You have no idea how close I am to getting off."

I laughed. "Well, don't shoot yet. I'd like to feel your warm load inside me."

He nodded with ample amounts of excitement. "Let's go and get cleaned up."

We headed into the bathroom, and turned on the shower to let the water get nice and warm before we stepped inside. There were washcloths and bottled bodywash with a manly fragrance to it. Both of us soaped each other up, then spent some time kissing and stroking each other. The bodywash had made our dicks wonderfully slick. I kept stroking Wayne's. It felt so good in my hand, and it was going to feel even better inside me.

"You'd better stop doing that," he said teasingly, "Or I'm going to shoot all over your tummy."

After some kisses and rubbing our hands over each other's hairy bodies, we rinsed off, turned off the water, and then stepped out where we dried off with two towels.

Wayne almost dragged me toward the bed. I tried to stand beside the mattress, but he pushed me over on it. Stars shined in through the long window along our room. The ship had moved into a low orbit of Duluth's and Ramsey's home world. It was becoming a heavenly moment.

As I lay on my back, Wayne grabbed my ankles, spread my legs wide open, and then dove in with his wet tongue, slurping around my sweet spot, and getting me nice and wet, more than ready for him to do what he did best.

"Oh, that feels great," I said. I had rested my legs over his shoulders while he worked his magic.

He would shove his tongue deep inside me, and then lightly circle it around my hairy hole, teasing me while he massaged the side of my thighs. It felt incredible. Wayne was the best lover I had ever been with. He knew all my favorite spots. But, most of all, he enjoyed making me feel satisfied. And, I did the same to him. We were a perfect match.

He lifted his head, kissed my thighs, then fingered me, making sure I was ready for his love. I spread my legs even further apart, inviting him to put his dick inside me.

He stood up, grabbed hold of my ankles and held them up high. Like a pro, he hit the target and slowly worked his rock hard piece of meat deep within me. My eyes closed as my head fell to the side. I was in heaven, feeling sheer bliss while he pulled it out then shoved it back in over and over again.

"You like that, babe?" he asked.

"You're the best," I reassured him, "Your cock feels amazing."

He sped up, pounding me lightly, with some added twists and turns of his hips. He kissed my calves and then the bottoms of my feet. Wayne was a huge fan of toes, just like me, so he ran his tongue between my little troopers, and then spent some time sucking on my big toe. And, just like giving head, he made sure he kept a tight suction around it the entire time.

"Oh, man," I mumbled. "That feels incredible."

He lowered my left leg, and began to stroke my hard erection. It wasn't going to take much for me to get off. All his lovemaking was plenty to push me over the edge. He let go of my right leg and then lowered himself on top of me, still pumping me full of love while we kissed. I wrapped my legs around his lower body, feeling his shapely ass against my feet which turned me on even more.

We each shoved our tongues in each other's mouth, swirling them around, making sure our lips were wet and moist.

"Oh, babe," he said. "I'm getting really close."

"Do it, sweetie. I want you to fill me up."

Some dirty talk always got Wayne aroused. Right after I spoke, my handsome man shook and jiggled as he pounded me over and over. He filled me up with several warm loads of his love. His forehead fell against my chest, as he panted and caught his breath.

"You're turn," he whispered. He brushed his face through my chest hair.

He didn't bother to pull out of me. In fact, I could still feel his firm erection. I flexed my hole several times around it in a teasing manner, and he smiled. After he stood up, he raised my right leg. He kissed my rounded calves, my foot, and then sucked on my toes. He spit into his right hand and started stroking me with a tight and twisting motion.

That was all it took. "Here it comes," I told him.

He quickly jumped down from the edge of the bed and started

sucking on me, until I filled his mouth with my warm load. One of the best things he always did, though, was after I got off Wayne continued to keep sucking on me, which always felt amazing.

"Wow," he said. He took some time to lick the side of my wiener and make sure he didn't miss a drop. "That was a lot, Adam. I must have really turned you on."

I laughed a little. "You always do, handsome."

He stood and then lowered himself on top of me so we could kiss, and I could taste myself in his mouth. We often took different sides when cuddling, but today, Wayne chose to lay beside me, with the side of his face against my hairy chest.

"How do you think James and Willie have sex?" The thought was still in the back of my mind. "Don't you think Willie is absolutely huge down there?"

Wayne laughed and tickled his fingers across my side. It made me flinch. "Well, I'm sure they figured out some way to deal with it. Maybe James likes getting opened up really wide."

We both giggled at his silly comment. "I think we should get under the covers and do some snuggling?" I wanted to feel his arms around me and lay my face against his muscular chest.

"Sounds good, babe."

We both jumped off the bed then pulled back the sheets. The room lights were dim enough so it wouldn't bother us. I slid in first, turned on my left side, and then Wayne crawled in behind me where he wrapped me up in his wonderful arms, with a few kisses on the top of my head.

"Love you, sweetie," I told him.

"Love you too, sexy man."

9

I woke up with a huge yawn. I still felt tired. Wayne was lightly snoring. He turned on his right side with his hairy back facing me. The sheets were pushed down a bit, and I could see the top of his furry butt crack. I couldn't refuse brushing my fingers along it, showing him some love and enjoying the sensation of touching him.

Outside our bedroom window I saw stars, however, some of the planet's atmosphere showed along the edge of the glass. We were still in orbit. Hopefully, no rogue agents had noticed us. I wasn't sure if the magical people we had met used any kind of space travel. I assumed they probably did, but I wasn't sure.

I turned on my side, edging myself closer against Wayne. He always enjoyed me brushing my fingertips lightly over his back. So, I did. I could never get enough of his shoulders. They weren't as hairy as his chest, but they came close. Everything about him (his body, his personality, his humor), turned me on so much.

"Good morning, babe," Wayne said, "Or good afternoon. I'm not sure which it is." He yawned and then turned over to face me. I smiled while stroking his full beard, and then I moved my hand lower to feel his chest, where I gently tweak his nipples.

"Good morning to you, too." I leaned in and gave him a kiss. "I guess we should get dressed and see what's happening up on the bridge."

Wayne yawned. "Probably a good idea, but first I need some snuggles."

He always made me smile. I scooted closer, and he slid his right arm over me, cradling my body while rubbing my back. It wasn't long before he moved his hand lower to play with my butt. Softly he squeezed my cheeks, then worked a few fingers deeper inside, teasing me. I gave him kisses on his cheeks and along his beard. I lightly pulled on the hairs with my lips, which he loved feeling. It always made him moan delightfully.

Our chests touched. Our tummies did too. It felt wonderful.

A few minutes passed before we hopped out of bed, cleaned ourselves up in the bathroom, peed, put on our tired old shirts and shorts, socks and sneakers, and then headed up to the bridge.

The thick steel doors opened and we stepped inside to see everyone busy at their workstations. An image of the planet floated in the center of the room with exceptional details, including clouds and continents. A swirling mass, I watched as it rotated, and the atmospheric patterns changed right before my eyes.

"About time you two show up." Willie laughed at his own comment. James slightly chuckled.

"Well, Adam wanted me to pound the living daylights out of his ass, so we took our time," Wayne boldly stated.

I nudged the side of his arm with my elbow, then shook my head while rolling my eyes. He tended to be blunt with his jokes, but he always amused me. We walked over to James and Willie at their workstation.

"How is everything?" Wayne asked them.

James shrugged. "We have the signatures of those freaks that attacked you by the woods, and we've collected all of the others who we battled with. Now, all we need to do is find a place and a time to attack them."

Our captain sounded determined to drive them out of our universe.

"Where are they at?" Wayne kept prying, but I wasn't about to hold him back. I agreed with his determination.

"They are orbiting an unpopulated world," Dean answered. "It has a breathable atmosphere, so there's a strong possibility they might construct bases of some kind."

"We don't know that, Dean." James sounded disagreeable.

"But, it could very well happen," Willie added. He reached over and rubbed his gigantic furry hand over James's shoulder. "You know how they like to operate."

James pushed a few holographic buttons floating above his console. He kept busy analyzing readouts and data which poured in. All of it streamed down in green and gold translucent colors that hovered right in front of their faces.

A pleasant smile showed on Bray's face as she walked over to us. She carried two harnesses in her hands, and then handed them to me and Wayne after she stopped and stood in front of us.

"Here you go," she said. "We have plenty, so don't feel bad about losing your original ones."

Wayne humbly took his. "Thanks. Our shorts and shirts are starting to stink. Our socks are too."

I nodded in agreement, but in the back of my mind, I enjoyed smelling Wayne's stinky socks.

Bray chuckled at his remark. "Well, we have machines to clean clothing. They're down a few decks near the kitchen. Trust me, all of it will come out smelling fresh and clean within a few seconds." She leaned closer with a delighted smile and bobbed a single eyebrow. "Even your socks will be sniffable."

Wayne and I glanced at each other before staring at Bray. "Are you and Woofa into feet and socks?" I asked.

She mildly laughed, then whispered. "Woofa loves my feet. He's always telling me to wear my tall boots. He says they get him all excited."

Good to know, I suppose.

In a bold move, Wayne pushed off his sneakers, reached down and pulled off his socks, and then pulled off his shirt before dropping his shorts. He stood entirely naked before me and Bray, and the entire bridge crew.

I noticed a lot of watchful eyes glaring at his hairy body, and prominent manhood which wasn't hard, but it did have some firmness to it.

He stared straight into my eyes. "What? We need to clean our clothes. You should do the same, Adam."

Wayne was bold and couldn't have cared what everyone was thinking. I noticed Bray glancing down at his dick a few times. The Devil Bunnies were leaning over the sides of their consoles to get a better view of my sexy man. I'll admit, he definitely turned me on. I wasn't about to drop my shorts with a semi-erection.

My handsome man slipped on his harness, attached the clasps over his beautiful chest, and then activated his suit. It covered him within a few seconds. And, to my surprise, a holstered handgun had appeared along his right thigh. We both looked at Bray.

"These particular harnesses come with firearms," she explained. "Just in case you two get in anymore trouble." She smiled and winked at us before heading back over to Woofa.

Wayne nudged the side of my arm with his elbow. "Don't be so shy. Everyone here as seen a penis before. Trust me."

After I took a brief moment to calm myself down, I pulled off my shirt and then pushed down my underwear and athletic shorts. Wayne was kind enough to kneel down and help take off my sneakers and socks. He even raised my foot and kissed to top of my toes. He was such a sweet and loving man. I'm sure everyone was staring at my tattoos running down my arms.

He helped me slip on my harness, and together we adjusted it, making sure it was perfectly positioned over my shoulders before attaching the small latches over my chest.

I started to raise my hand to activate my suit, since all his touching was getting me aroused again, but Wayne surprised me. He held my wrist with his left hand before tapping the control button over my chest with his right. Within seconds, I was covered in a black leather padded suit, with gravity boots and a holstered handgun.

Dean headed over to the main doors on the bridge and stood still as they opened. "I can show you where to clean your clothes," he offered happily. "I need to use the bathroom and grab a drink of water."

We nodded, then followed him out of the bridge and down the hall toward the elevator, where he tapped a few buttons after the door closed.

"So are you gay?" Wayne asked Dean.

I shook my head and rolled my eyes. Leave it to my man to ask a direct question.

Dean laughed, but didn't seem surprised. "I've actually been with men and women," he admitted. "But, because I'm such a nerd they usually take what they want and then break up with me."

I patted his shoulder caringly.

"You guys are lucky," Dean told us. "It's nice to see you two, Bray and Woofa, and even Willie and James in love. I'd like to find that some day with either a man, or a woman."

Wayne gave Dean a heartfelt brush along his arm. "Sorry to hear that. I'm sure somebody out there would be happy to have you in their life. You're very cute. What about one of the Devil Bunnies?"

Dean's face scrunched up as he shook his head. "Those girls are too much for my simple tastes. It's okay. My love life will work out eventually. I'm in no rush." He sounded pleased with his decision.

The elevator doors opened and we followed Dean down a short hallway, until he stopped and stood still. "Here's the kitchen." He pointed with his right hand, showing us the roomy dining area.

A wide doorway opened up to a spacious room, which had several rectangular tables inside with four chairs on their sides and two on each end. A long countertop sat along the left side of the room, and there were even two swinging doors that covered the kitchen area. Along the right side of the room, stood a few wide doors positioned near each other, and they looked like they could lift up for a relaxing view of space or a planet.

"You guys ever cook down here?" Wayne kept looking around the room, taking in every detail.

"James used to have a cook, but he's temporarily away on personal business," Dean informed us. "You're more than welcome to use the kitchen and make a meal. There's plenty of stuff in the refrigerators and pantries."

"Sounds nice," I said.

Dean excused himself to go use the bathroom, which was no more than twenty feet down the hallway.

"See," Wayne said to me. "We could live on the ship and cook all kinds of great meals. Wouldn't that be nice?"

I leaned in closer to give him a sweet kiss. "You're determined to move in here, aren't you?"

He smiled with a shrug. "It might be a nice change of pace. Or, we could take a vacation here. I'm sure James would let us stay in the room they gave us."

Dean pulled the bathroom door open and came out. "Let me show you two the area where we clean our clothes."

We followed him to a doorway right beside the kitchen area. It opened, and inside the small space stood two vertical, narrow booths. Both were covered with black glass, and each had several compartments you could open and insert your clothing into.

Dean stepped toward one and opened two compartments. "Put your clothes in there," he said while pointing. "It just takes a few seconds to clean them."

Wayne let me go first. I sat my clothes down in the top section on a shelf, while my sexy man slipped his in the compartment below mine. Dean then closed the two glass doors, and activated the device by pushing a few buttons along its side. Within less than ten seconds, Dean opened the doors.

"All done," he said with a smile.

Wayne reached in and pulled his clothes out first. He held his socks up to his face so he could smell them. "Nice," he said. "It's like they're fresh out of the dryer."

I was amazed at how clean everything was. "How does it wash them so fast?"

Dean waved his fingers high in the air. "It's magic." We both laughed at him and shook our heads. "Actually," Dean added, "It analyzes each piece of clothing then removes whatever isn't part of its design. It then infuses them with a warm and fresh scent. You guys like it?"

"Yeah," I told him. "That's pretty impressive."

Wayne nodded happily. "Can we take them back to our room and then meet you back up on the bridge?"

"Sure," Dean answered. He playfully bobbed his finger in the air at us.

We headed back to the elevator, and Dean dropped us off on the level where our room was located. "See you guys in a few minutes," he said after we stepped out and walked away.

Once inside our quarters, we sat our clothes down on a wooden table and Wayne turned me around to face him. He gently rubbed his hands over my suits armored chest before fondling my crotch.

"Damn, Adam, you look so fucking sexy in this suit and those boots." He leaned in to kiss me while moving his hands all over my body. "You're giving me a huge boner. I bet you'd look even hotter with your tattoos showing."

"Let's see about that." I stepped back and lowered my head until my mouth was near my chest. "Sleeveless," I announced in a commanding voice.

Inch by inch my suit's gloves and sleeves disappeared, until it stopped around my shoulders, which showcased my colorful tattoos Wayne loved so much. He moved his hands down my arms, tracing his fingers around some of my colorful flowers.

"You're so beautiful." He kissed me several times while brushing the back of his fingers over my beard. He tenderly gripped my rear with his other hand, and firmly squeezed my leather-covered rear.

Willie's voice came through the room's intercom. "Wayne, Adam, you two should get up here to the bridge. We've got an issue."

"On our way," Wayne answered in a firm voice. He gave me a few more kisses before we left the room, hopped in the elevator, and then hurried inside the bridge after the doors opened.

"What's happening?" I asked. We stood beside Willie and James, who both had disgusted looks on their faces.

"They're attacking the gophers' world again," Dean explained.

Willie let out a hateful growl, then angrily swiped his fingers over several translucent buttons floating above his workstation. James kept busy right beside his furry boyfriend.

An image of their planet appeared on the huge holographic display centered in the room, along with a bunch of rogue vessels in orbit. Their ships looked different. They were long with pointed ends, yet thick and bulky along their midsections, and all were huddled together with their tips pointed directly at the planet. Smaller rogue ships were flying around them. I wasn't sure how we were going to handle the situation.

"Are they going to destroy the entire planet?" I asked.

"We're not going to let that happen," James added.

"Coordinates are set," Dean said. "We can shift right above their city where we took the shuttlecraft before."

"Are their any agents in the capital city yet?" Wayne looked and sounded irritable. I felt the same way.

"Not from what I can tell," Dean answered. He kept moving his fingers and hands quickly over his console. "But, I'm sure it'll be just a matter of time before they flood the city with troops. They're after whatever resources they can get their hands on."

A sudden burst of purple and white energy appeared near the bridge's main doors. All of us gasped in shock. It was a swirling thick mass, maybe several feet across and twelve feet tall. It churned with various intensities of the colors that blended around and through each other.

The Devil Bunnies pulled out their handguns and aimed them at the glowing effect. Wayne did the same, aiming his gun right at the heart of the phenomenon. Willie had positioned himself in front of James to protect his smaller boyfriend. Woofa raised his arms and stood ready to strike with some sort of magical spell.

To my surprise, Duluth and Ramsey stepped out from the colorful portal. And, right after they stood still on the floor, all the energy disappeared in a snap.

Ramsey smiled and waved to us before raising his hands. He produced his tiny globes of light. Each one raced out and merged with us between our eyes so we could understand them.

"Sorry about the unexpected visit," Duluth explained. "Ramsey sensed some tension building inside Wayne and Adam, so we decided to come on board to see if we could help."

I hurried over and gave each one of our tree-bark looking friends a great big hug. Wayne did the same after he holstered his gun.

Smiles covered our faces. It felt so good to see Duluth and Ramsey again. And, how cool would it be to suddenly move around like they could do. I was amazed.

"Perfect timing," I told them. "The rogue agents are messing with our gopher friends. I'm sure with your magical spells, along with Bray's and Woofa's we'll knock the shit out of them!"

Wayne winked at me while rubbing my shoulder. I could tell he was proud of what I had said. It was written all over his face.

"We'll appreciate any help you can provide," Willie said, with a smile.

Everyone had gone back to their workstations. The Devil Bunnies had put their guns away.

"So you two can move around anywhere by using a portal?" Wayne looked intrigued.

"We need to be familiar with a place in order to travel," Duluth said. "So, once we've been to a location, opening a portal is easy."

"The ships are moving closer to the planet." Dean sounded anxious. "Can I initiate the shifting engines?"

"Do it," James said.

Dean swiped his right hand over some controls that floated in the air, and the main holographic image changed as we shifted above the city. An image of downtown soon appeared at the center of the bridge. Much of the damage from earlier attacks still showed.

"You did notify them that we were coming, didn't you?" Wayne asked.

"Yeah, they know," Willie said.

"We'll stay here with Dean and operate the ship," Mortenna informed everyone. "You guys go and take care of those assholes."

Everyone seemed fine with Mortenna's suggestion. Wayne and I headed to the bridge doors. After they opened, we stood and waited for our four magical friends and our captain with his furry boyfriend. Our group hurried down the hallway, but all eight of us couldn't fit in the elevator at one time, so we ended up taking two trips down to the cargo bay.

Dean had expertly parked our ship near a docking port, so after opening the wide bay doors, we were able to step out and greet our gopher friends. Our magical companions cast their translation spells upon a few dozen of their citizens.

"Those bastards are attacking us again!" A gopher said in an irritable tone. He was dressed in armored clothing and he pointed up at the sky. He wore a black cap with a padded vest, thick boots, and cargo pants.

James shrugged and flipped his hands in the air. "Well, we're here to help. We've got a lot of magical spells we can cast."

I gazed up at the nine rogue vessels that were slowly moving through the atmosphere. Each pointed tip of their ships came closer. I could only imagine what they would do. Was each ship going to puncture the land? Would they generate some kind of global effect and wipe out all the gophers in one shot? My stomach churned with worry.

Wayne grabbed hold of my hand. He could tell I was feeling disgusted by all of this crap. I stared at him and gazed right in his beautiful eyes.

"We're going to take care of them," he whispered to me. "Don't get too upset. We've got this." He winked at me, then nodded his head toward our magical friends while smiling.

My handsome man warmed my heart. But, before I could even respond to Wayne's tender comment, I watched as Bray lifted her arms in the air and summoned seven gigantic spirits, all of which were transparent except for their glowing blue and white outlines. She had dressed in all red, wearing a sleeveless vest over a tank top, with pants tucked inside of knee-high, red boots, which I'm sure Woofa was enjoying on her.

Her huge winged beasts resembled flying serpents, and all had appeared a hundred feet above us. Each had thick lengthy bodies, probably sixty feet long, and all were covered in scales, with shoulders and two muscular arms stretching out far. Each hand had five clawed fingers. They had large armored heads that resembled a snake, and each was topped with three huge horns that curved backward. Their wide mouths were filled with sharp fangs and long tongues. I imagined they could shred the rogue ships apart easily.

Bray brought her arms close to her chest, then quickly jutted them outward which sent her spirit pets flying high in the sky directly toward the rogue ships.

Woofa raised his arms, too, which opened his sleeveless vest and gave us a great view of his dark furry chest. He wore blue jeans over black boots with rounded toes.

He cast his magic, generating a huge swirling mass of red and orange energy some thirty or forty feet above us. From out of it shot gigantic and brilliant glowing balls of fire. It travelled high in the sky at the speed of a rocket, until it hit one of the rogue ships. The impact sounded loud. Woofa's magic jolted the ship, veering it slightly to the side. Sparks and metal debris burst forth and saturated the air with plenty of damage.

"If you keep doing that they're going to crash down on our city and destroy everything!" one of our gopher friends shouted out. He sounded pissed and extremely irritable.

"You're city will survive," Duluth told him. "Ramsey and I can open portals, which will direct the debris elsewhere."

The angry gopher stood with his furry paws locked around his waist. He wore khaki shorts, white socks with grey sneakers, and a dark blue short-sleeved shirt. "And *where* do you plan on sending all of this debris?"

Duluth looked a bit frustrated. "We'll open the other ends far out in space where all the pieces will float around harmlessly."

I gazed skyward and watched as Bray's serpent spirits attacked the rogue ships. They had gotten very close to the planet. Her pets whipped their ghostly tails against each one's hull, or chewed at them with their meter-long fangs. Pieces of metal fell toward the ground.

Duluth and Ramsey projected their portals, twisting their arms and hands in fluid magical motions where they relocated all of the larger chunks out into space. Each portal appeared as a short-lived, round band of energy which hovered above the city, yet showcased outer space within each one's center. Their portals consumed each fragment and moved it far away, just like they had promised.

But the rogue vessels kept coming closer to the planet. They moved slowly down through the evening clouds, despite the attacks from Bray's spirits and Woofa's huge fireballs.

"Maybe this will help!" Willie said. He and James had brought along two long and broad rifles. Both had been tucked away along their backs, in black leather holsters strapped over their shoulders.

Willie reached over his shoulder and pulled his rifle out. He held it with both hands while aiming it at the rogue ships.

James did the same. "It's a Kimoon TC," he informed me and Wayne. "They're powerful weapons made by the Kimoon Corporation. My brother, Doug, owns one back in the Expanse."

Willie fired a blinding shot of blue energy. It raced out from the tip of his rifle with a loud and quick blast, which made me jump a little. Wayne quickly squeezed my hand to comfort me with his presence.

James followed his boyfriend's lead, aiming at different ships. I watched as each shot hit the vessels, blasting holes along their hulls and sending clouds of bright sparks and metal fragments out into the air. But, considering the size of each rogue ship, I doubted their rifles would damage them that much. Bray and Woofa kept hitting them too, but it wasn't having a considerable effect against their fleet. They were still approaching.

But, I forgot about our gopher friends. Before we got here, they had placed mounted guns along the city streets, all of which continually fired powerful blasts of blue, swirling energy at the rogue ships.

Now, those shots made a difference. They hit the enemy hard, which kept Duluth and Ramsey busy casting their portal effects so the city didn't get trashed.

But, just when we thought things were going good, a problem popped up. Small attack crafts poured out from along the sides of every rouge ship. They were no bigger than a comfortable recliner you would sit in while watching television, but there were hundreds of them.

"Look at that!" The angry gopher guy pointed at them.

"Are there pilots in each one of those?" Wayne asked.

"No," Willie answered. "They're all mechanical. And, we're going to shoot the fuck out of each one!"

The attack crafts were round with a flattened top and bottom, but each one also had mounted guns along their sides, and they kept firing at the city streets, trying to knock out the gopher's mounted cannons.

Bray waved her hands through the air again, which summoned her spirits. She called forth swarms of huge insects that were probably larger than my chest. Each was shaped like wasps, with stingers on the tips of their tails, but they also had claws on their six legs and noticeable teeth in their mouths.

I could hear their wings flapping like mad, and their swarms took off toward the mechanized attack crafts, where they surrounded several at a time high above us. They stabbed them with their stingers or ripped them apart with their teeth and claws. Sparks filled the sky over the city, and Bray's ghostly beings shredded each one severely that only small pieces fell down.

James and Willie kept firing non-stop, while Wayne and I ducked a few times because of weapons fire from each robotic flying weapon. My handsome man finally pulled out his handgun and fired off several shots. He actually hit a few of the automated machines, sending them flying off course where they crashed against buildings, or plummeted toward the streets and exploded after hitting the ground.

"Nice job," I yelled to him. The sound of all the shots and shredding metal was extremely loud.

"Use your gun," he told me.

I pulled it out and fired at some of the automated weapons as they flew by us. They kept firing at the streets, at the gophers mounted guns. They actually hit several citizens and wounded them. However, a few looked like they might have been killed. We owned a higher view from atop this docking platform.

Seeing such pointless murder only pissed off Wayne even more. He stood straight up and fired his gun at a few incoming flying robots, and he hit each one until they fell out of the air, where they crashed below us against the front of the building we were on top of. He had really great aim. I had never seen him shot a gun before. I was impressed.

Duluth and Ramsey kept busy with their portals, while Bray and Woofa hit the main rogue ships hard with their magical sprits and spells. James and Willie continually fired their rifles, changing from the main ships to the drone things that kept breezing by real fast. And, every shot from their rifles that hit a drone blasted it into pieces.

Several rounds of shots fired from James's ship. I assumed the Devil

Bunnies must have manned a couple of the guns. I watched as the closest rogue vessel in the sky was damaged severely. So much, in fact, that it backed away and moved up through the atmosphere, fleeing like a coward.

"I guess they're not as tough as they claim to be," I shouted out.

Wayne laughed at my remark while he kept firing his gun. "Yeah, these drone things are pretty shitty as far as construction goes!"

As I watched my handsome man shooting blasts of energy from his handgun, I felt incredibly bad for our gopher friends. No one deserved such hateful attacks against their planet. Was it really for all their resources? I mean, couldn't these agents just start over again somewhere else and *not* destroy people's lives. The more I thought about the situation, I wanted nothing more than to destroy every rogue and their ships, plus that big horned dude who approached us in the woods. He seemed like an arrogant piece of shit.

Between the gopher's mounted guns, our magical attacks, the Devil Bunnies manning the ship's weapons, along with the Kimoon rifles, we started to turn away the rogue ships.

Bray's serpent spirits moved inside each vessel, and I could only imagine the amount of damage and terror they brought. But, before I could even guess as to what they were doing, a huge explosion came from one of the rogue vessels. The blast opened its hull with lots of fire, and thick black smoke poured out of the gapping hole.

"Are they destroying their engines?" I asked.

Bray and Woofa both laughed. "Yes," she answered. "I bet they didn't expect that!"

Woofa launched several more gigantic fireballs at their ships. They must have had some sort of density to them, because every strike damaged the hulls and sent them veering off course.

Between James and Willie, all the drones were quickly getting slaughtered. Less than a fourth of them remained.

A much larger explosion came from another rogue ship, and I watched as Bray's serpents shot out of the blast. Each one of them twirled and twisted with pride. I think that was the indicator for the agents to withdraw, because their ships began to pull back.

"Take that you pieces of shit!" Wayne shouted. He shot at retreating drones that flew by us. He hit a few and destroyed a couple.

I couldn't have been happier seeing them retreat away from the planet. Bray had never stopped her attacks. Her serpents kept relentlessly attacking each of their ships.

"Let's get back onboard and follow them," James said. He and Willie had both hurried over to the cargo bay doors, and the rest of us followed.

"We'll be back," Willie told the military clothed gopher guy who had stood next to us through the attacks.

"Thank you," he said. "We wouldn't have survived without your help."

Wayne and I waved goodbye to him after we stepped inside the cargo bay. After the doors closed, our group hurried back up to the bridge where we found Dean and the three Devil Bunnies already moving the ship.

"Follow them," James ordered, as he and Willie raced over to their workstation.

Dean hit several buttons and I felt the ship move. On the main holographic display, the nine rogue ships had positioned themselves above the planet's atmosphere. They slowly drifted through space while making their way further away.

"I projected a field again," Dean explained. "And, I scanned all of them for signatures. We shouldn't have a problem locating any of them."

The look on James's face was of utter bliss. "Good job," he told Dean. "And, thank you all for manning the guns," he told the Devil Bunnies.

All of them smiled and gave our captain some appreciative shakes of their shoulders and cleavage. James laughed at their silly antics.

On the main holographic display, I watched as Bray's spirits continued to ravage the rouge ships while they fled. It wasn't long before one of them exploded with fires and swirling strands of energy consuming it from top to bottom. Huge pieces of metal impacted the other ships, which damaged each one of them. Bray's serpents kept flying around, breezing through each vessel, until two more of them exploded which must have completely devastated their fleet.

"Holy shit!" Wayne raised his fist in the air. "Take that you heartless bastards."

I assumed the massive explosions must have disrupted Dean's dispersion field, because the remaining rogues shifted away as soon as they could.

"Sorry," Dean said.

James shrugged and shook his head. "No problem. Like you said, we can track them. And that's exactly what we're going to do."

10

James and Willie hit some holographic buttons floating above their workstation, and I watched as the main display changed to a representation of the gopher's world. I assumed they were making sure no more ships were attacking.

"Everything looks alright down there," Willie said in a casual tone.

"I have all of their signatures in our system," Dean informed James.

"Thank you," James replied. "*Now* would probably be a good time to attack them since their ships are damaged."

Willie tenderly massaged James's shoulder, conveying the love he felt for his little man as well as his approval.

"But how do we get on their ships?" Wayne asked. He glanced over at Bray with a smile. "I guess we could use spirits to keep ripping them apart."

Bray and Woofa both giggled. "Oh, we will definitely use more spirits," she said. "They can rip apart metal like professionals."

"Well, I would rather enjoy shooting them in person," Mortenna added. She shaped her hand like a gun and raised it in the air. "They deserve an up-close and personal payback."

Willie gave her a thumbs-up. He looked excited about her suggestion.

"Did they shift back to the planet they were orbiting?" James asked.

Dean nodded. "Yeah, they're in the upper atmosphere. And, from what I can tell, most of their ships are heavily damaged."

"With most of their drones destroyed, we shouldn't have too much of a problem dealing with them." Woofa raised his hand and tenderly massaged Bray's shoulder. She looked in his eyes and smiled with abundant amounts of love.

"So what's the plan?" Wayne asked. "Do we just go at them full-force, or something more subtle. I kind of like Mortenna's idea. Shoot them right through their fucking heads."

"I completely agree," James said. "But, we need to make sure all of them are there at the same time. I'm not leaving any stragglers behind."

"We can always come back and check things out," Willie added. "It's a simple trip from our universe to this one."

Wayne suddenly appeared sad. I guess the mentioning of our shipmates leaving our universe wasn't what he wanted to hear. My loveable stargazer was having such a good time with our new friends. I hated to think about us going back to Earth and living our ordinary lives. But, in the back of my mind, I knew we had to eventually. Wayne and I didn't really have any other choices.

I brushed my hand along his leather covered arm. He didn't wear his suit sleeveless like I had done, but, he looked incredibly sexy in it. I hoped we would get to keep them. Our suits might prove for some interesting love-making later on.

Dean raised his blue index finger in the air with an idea. "Duluth, can't you and Ramsey use some magical ability to scan the signatures I have in our system, and open a portal to the rogue agents?"

Ramsey shrugged while shaking his head. "We've never tried anything like that before. We would actually have to *be* in a location in order to open a portal. How many signatures are there?"

Dean pushed some glowing buttons on his console. "After the battle, there are currently six-hundred and forty-three signatures remaining on their ships."

"Holy shit, that's a lot." I'm sure I sounded surprised. "That'll be a lot of heads for you to shoot." I playfully nudged the side of Wayne's arm with my elbow.

He laughed at me. "Our guns use energy, sweetie. Remember? We won't run out of shots." He leaned closer and gave me a kiss. "I'll be happy to take them all out for you." He could be such a sweet man.

Duluth and Ramsey headed over to Dean's workstation and stood beside him. "How could we get the signatures of their crew?" Ramsey asked Dean.

"I'm not entirely sure," Dean answered. "I can project the signatures of specific individuals on the main display. Maybe you could pick up on them, and then open a portal on their bridge?"

"Hopefully you have Korath's signature," Wayne said. "He's that tall and bulky guy with the horns."

"You forgot to mention he's a smartass," I added. Wayne laughed at me then reached behind my rear and patted my leather clad butt a few times.

Dean displayed a random signature on the main holographic display. It showed a vague representation of an alien individual. She looked similar to the Devil Bunnies, although her horns were much larger and more twisted. Plus, the one on the right side of her head looked chipped on the tip, almost like it had been broken. Perhaps it got that way during our attacks.

"Here you go," Dean told them. "Maybe focus on one signature, and then hopefully you can pick up some others."

Our magical friends walked over to the main display at the center of the bridge. They each raised a single arm, then moved it through the hologram. I wasn't sure if they'd be able to pick up anything from the female demon.

"Can you sense her?" James asked. He never stopped watching while tapping some controls.

"It's very unclear," Duluth told us. "It might take some time before we can actually open a portal and move directly to them."

"Well, we'd appreciate any help you can give us," James said.

"Like we said, we'll be glad to help," Ramsey told our captain.

An alert sounded, and Dean was quick to answer it. "A message from the gopher people is coming in."

"Play it on the main display," James ordered.

Dean hit some buttons, and a clear image of the military gopher guy we had met during the battle appeared at the center of the bridge.

"Thank you for all your help," he said. He was still dressed in his cap and armored vest. "But, if you could, please, we need some additional help with injured people. Some sort of disease came from those drones all of you destroyed. It's some kind of airborne infection. Can you come back and lend a hand to our citizens? We're losing people."

James nodded, although he looked a slightly irritated. "Sure, we'd be happy to come down and help."

"We look forward to seeing you again," the gopher said.

The transmission ended. I could tell our captain wanted to deal with the rogue agents before anything else. His thoughts clearly showed on his face. But, James had a caring heart, which Willie proved many times over to all of us, so we would help our gopher friends first.

"Bray, you and Woofa take Wayne and Adam, along with Duluth and Ramsey down to the planet," James said. "We'll stay up here and monitor all those rogue assholes."

Duluth raised his arms in a circular and fluid manner, which opened a portal to the docking port we had visited earlier. Outlined in a ring of blue and white swirling energy, the portal showed a clear view of the downtown area, with many of our gopher friends standing near it. All of them gawked and stared at his magic. I wondered if they saw us on the other side. They probably could.

Duluth stepped through the portal, and we watched as he stood on the dock near a gathering of gophers. Ramsey courteously gestured for the rest of us to step through before he did. I wondered what our gopher friends thought about their tree-bark looking skin.

I held Wayne's hand as we walked through together. It was no different than stepping through the front door of a house. We appeared on their planet, on the docking port.

We watched as Bray and Woofa came through next, followed by Ramsey. The portal then vanished. It disappeared fast in a flash of blue and white light.

"That was quick and awesome," I told Wayne.

He gave me a wink and sweet smile before squeezing my hand a few times, then letting go. I conveyed my affections with a mild pat across Wayne's shapely ass. A few of the gophers saw what I had done, and they stared at us with wide opened eyes and questioning gazes. They didn't seem shocked or confused, so I assumed they had gay citizens on their planet too, which seemed logical.

Duluth's and Ramsey's magical translation spell was still working on many of the gophers they had imbued it upon. Several stood staring at us, while others were slightly hunched over with obvious stomach issues. Some of them had vomited on the dock. They didn't look like they were dying, but they obviously had something wrong.

"How the hell did they poison all you guys?" Wayne sounded pissed. I was sure he wanted to make all the rogue agents pay for what they had done.

A female of their species stepped toward us. She wore military attire similar to the male gopher we had talked to. Her black cap was slightly tilted to one side. She was light brown and very furry. Her face appeared more distinct to me. I guess from being around their kind, I was finally starting to see differences in each one of them.

"It either came from those drone things, or they saturated our atmosphere with some compound," she concluded. "People are getting sick throughout the entire city, and we have no way of knowing how bad it's going to get."

I heard Duluth sigh in a frustrated tone. He and Ramsey looked a bit overwhelmed by the situation. Bray and Woofa appeared just as confused about what to do.

"Can you take away this disease?" the female gopher asked. She seemed desperate for a confirmation.

"We're going to need some help," Ramsey told her. Quickly he waved his hands through the air about chest high, and similar to what I had seen before, a magical communication window opened so he and Duluth could talk to their friends back on their planet.

"We need to perform a global healing effect on this world," Duluth explained to a woman who had a darker colored skin tone than him. She wore a sleeveless, dark-green vest, and it showcased her arms which were covered with similar looking tree textures. She was bald and the skin on her head stood out with a much bolder appearance of a tree. Her eyebrows were similar to thick green moss, like the body hair on our two friends.

"We can open a portal as soon as you're ready," Ramsey said. He reached up and patted Duluth on his shoulder, comforting his boyfriend in this troubled moment.

"Give us a few minutes, and we'll gather up some others so we can project the spell," the woman said. She sounded pleased and more than happy to help.

They ended their communication spell and most of the gopher people stood staring at us. "You can heal the entire planet?" the military guy asked.

"Yes," Ramsey said, in a positive tone. "We'll shroud your world in a healing energy, one that will cure and restore everyone from whatever these rouges did."

Many of the gophers seemed excited, yet concerned about their comrades who were still hunched over and riddled with this plague.

Woofa began casting his minor healing spell. He projected tiny orbs that raced toward a few individuals, and it covered them in a healing blue light that quickly penetrated their furry bodies.

A few minutes passed before Duluth spoke. "They're ready." I hadn't seen any further communications between their people, so I assumed they must have contacted him by some telepathic means.

Ramsey fluidly moved his arms through the air and opened a portal. It appeared identical to the one we had stepped through. On the other side, I recognized their world and I enjoyed seeing all the lush green hills, nearby trees, knee-high grass, and numerous flowering shrubs. It would be nice to visit their farm again someday. I'm sure Wayne and I would get the opportunity eventually.

Twenty-four people stepped through the portal and stood on the deck around all of us. It got a bit crowded, but they were needed. Males and females had come in a variety of heights, and all were dressed in various clothing which included pants or shorts, T-shirts or jackets. Some of the men were topless and showed off their tree bark skin. Many wore those work boots I had seen before, yet, some had on sandals or sneakers. A few were barefoot.

We could understand every one of them. The woman, who we had seen on the communication spell, stepped up to Duluth and Ramsey. "We should begin," she said in a humble tone.

All the gopher people stared at them with awestruck faces. I wondered if they had ever experienced magic on this type of level before.

Hell, Wayne and I had never seen anything like this before, either. How were they going to heal the entire planet? I had no clue.

A wide staircase lay on the right side of the dock, and Duluth and Ramsey lead their friends down the stairs, then through the streets toward a nearby park which was no more than a block away.

Wayne and I followed, along with Bray and Woofa. Many of our gopher friends kept close behind us. They chatted quietly to each other, likely intrigued by how this was going to take place.

The park had a large, decorative steel gate that had been left open, allowing all of us to enter. We passed along a few tall trees while following our magical friends out in a large field with ankle-high green grass.

All twenty-four of them formed a circle with outstretched arms. They joined hands while Duluth and Ramsey stood in the center of their group. We all watched with fascinated and excited looks.

"Have you ever seen anything like this before, Woofa?" Wayne asked.

Woofa shook his head. "No, this'll be the first time."

Bray kept rubbing her hand over the back of Woofa's sleeveless jacket. She seemed so proud of him for his minor healing he had done, all of which was greatly appreciated.

A bright white light had formed around each of the twenty-four individuals, and it spread slowly from one to the other. It swirled and dipped at times, consuming them all from head to toe, until it shined with the intensity of hundreds of light bulbs.

Duluth and Ramsey faced each other and held each others hands, as the magical white light expanded out from each of their friends and consumed the two of them in the center of the ring.

They both leaned their heads back, eyes closed, and an even more intense white light began to ascend toward the sky, emanating directly from where our magical friends stood. It travelled high in the sky, pulsing and flowing, moving far above the city, beyond the few clouds above us, where it soon expanded and spread out, covering all of the sky overhead.

I faintly heard all of our magical friends chanting as they projected their global spell. Wayne and I tilted our heads back and watched as the sky became a bright and glowing snowstorm of renewing energy.

It wasn't long before their spell spread out and covered all of the downtown area. Their magical effect produced dazzling flecks of light, which slowly rained down as far as I could see. I imagined the entire planet was being covered by them. What were gophers on the opposite side of this world going to think? Would they be amazed or startled? Hopefully, they were notified. I'm sure they were.

Each tiny speck of light passed through our bodies, then moved down beneath the ground.

"Oh man," Wayne said. "They feel so warm. Do you feel them, Adam?"

I nodded while lifting my upturned hands in the air, so I could feel more of the magic flakes. "It's incredible."

Both Bray and Woofa embraced this wonderful gift. They each stood still with their heads back, and welcomed our friends healing moment. Even all the gophers seemed astonished. They all casually walked around through the brilliant rain, making sure they passed through as many points of light as possible.

It wasn't long before James's crab-shaped ship slowly flew along at a low altitude, passing through many of the glowing flakes. I assumed they wanted to make sure they were healed also, in case one of us had been infected. After all, we didn't know if this disease was meant for only the gopher people or others, too.

It was nice to see our captain's ship fly by. It reminded me of when Wayne and I saw it over the lake when we first met James and Willie out in the woods. A great memory I would always cherish.

Wayne took hold of my hand and pulled me closer against him. While standing beside my handsome man, he wrapped his arm around me, holding me in a very loving way. He even added a kiss on the side of my head, as many of the bright flakes passed through us. Several drifted right through my face and chest, my shoulders and arms, looking like confetti tossed out by people during a parade or festival.

I felt refreshed. A surge of revitalizing energy coursed through my body. No worries seemed to matter. The one person I valued most in life stood beside me, and it filled my eyes with glad tears to see he and I got to experience such a remarkable treat.

James's ship soon disappeared after ascending higher in the sky, and Wayne and I stood for about thirty minutes, where we savored their magical healing while our minds had become cleared of all bad thoughts, of all burdens and worries. A tingling sensation filled me with love for Wayne, and I leaned my head to the side where I rested my cheek against his shoulder. I could have gone to sleep standing right here. The soothing flecks of light pacified me and probably everyone else, too. It was like a welcoming melody of sound, and adagio for sleep, so passive and nurturing, calming and rejuvenating. All of time seemed to stand still.

"You mean the world to me, Adam," Wayne whispered.

I kissed his leather covered shoulder. "Being with you is the best feeling on any world."

Wayne turned his head enough so we could share a kiss while within this wonderful shower of lights. After a long moment, we noticed that the bright flakes began to fade and the glowing ring of light, that moved through our twenty-four magical friends, started to disappear. It wasn't long before the healing spell completely vanished, and all of our friends stopped holding hands. They all stood for a moment, watching their magic in the sky before it faded away.

"I wonder what they'll do next," I mentioned.

Wayne casually shook his head. "I'm not sure."

We watched as Duluth and Ramsey went around and happily said goodbye to their friends. Some laughed and smiled, others shook hands and nodded gracefully, more than happy to have helped.

After several minutes, Ramsey opened a portal which showed their wonderful lush and green planet. One by one, our magical friends stepped through the opening. Several of them waved goodbye to me and Wayne, as well as our gopher friends who were standing beside us.

"They all seemed really nice and friendly," I said.

Wayne nodded with a smile. "Now, we just have to figure out how to deal with those rogue bastards."

I gave him another kiss on his shoulder. "Hopefully, Duluth and Ramsey will be able to open a portal and then we can take them all out."

Wayne laughed before he turned around to face me. He seemed delighted by my remark. He locked his hands around my waist and happily swayed a bit from side to side. "Since when did you become such a badass?"

I gazed directly in his eyes with a heartfelt smile. "I guess you're rubbing off on me, tough guy."

Wayne laughed out loud with a roll of his eyes before leaning in to give me a kiss. "I would *love* to fill you up with some more warm love. You turn me on so much, Adam, especially those sexy arms and tattoos."

I raised my arm and twisted it a bit to give him a good show of my colorful flowers and vines. "You would look hot with some of your own."

"Maybe when we get back home," Wayne said.

Duluth and Ramsey had walked over to us after their friends left through the portal. Both of them stood beside me and Wayne. "Your world is healed," Ramsey told the gopher people. "And, now that we have activated portals, we should be able to come back and help you out if any more agents attack you."

The female military gopher smiled with a few tears as she stepped over and gave Duluth and Ramsey hugs. She wasn't very tall, so she ended up hugging their thighs, but they patted her shoulders appreciatively.

"Thank you for being patient," Ramsey told her.

She stared into their eyes. "All of our thanks go to you two, and your friends. We would have died without your help."

Duluth and Ramsey both nodded before she released her furry arms from around Ramsey's thigh, and went back to join her gopher companions.

"We need to inform our world about how it has been healed," she told us. "Thank you again."

Her companions followed her, and the other military gopher guy headed back toward the city streets. I assumed they had some global communications system they would access and inform the rest of the planet.

"I guess we need to get back to the bridge of your ship," Duluth said.

Wayne and I nodded with smiles.

Ramsey opened a portal to the bridge, right next to the main holographic display in the center of the room. We stepped through, with Bray and Woofa following us before Duluth and Ramsey came aboard and closed the magical gateway.

"Everything go okay?" James asked.

"Perfect," I answered. "The gopher citizens were very thankful. I think they were dazzled by the bright lights."

"The spell is called Morning of Light," Ramsey explained. "It is very ancient, and it restores everyone who takes part in it."

"So, all of you should feel refreshed and rejuvenated," Duluth said.

"We do," Willie told him. He was standing beside James, rubbing his boyfriends back with a wide smile on his face. I could tell James was enjoying all the attention.

"Now, we just have to figure out how to sense these signatures," Ramsey mentioned.

"I may have discovered a way for you guys to detect them more easily," Dean said.

Our magical friends seemed surprised in a good way. Dean projected an image of one of the rogue agents on the main display, along with streaming bars of data along each side of her. It was the same female demon we had seen before. Although, this time the details appeared more abundant. Whatever Dean had done, he promoted a very comprehensive signature of this female.

"Do any of you mind if Adam and I take a small break in our quarters?" Wayne asked.

Most of the bridge crew shook their heads. They were all busy at their workstations.

"Sure, that's fine," James said. "Take as much time as you'd like. We're most likely going to be awhile before we figure these signatures out."

While holding hands, Wayne and I headed over to the bridge entrance where the wide doors parted before we stepped out in the hallway, and headed down the corridor to the elevator. He pushed the buttons taking us down to the level where our quarters were.

The door to our room opened, and after we went inside they closed behind us, Wayne immediately deactivated his leather bodysuit and stood before me naked. I gazed at him from head to toe. He had such shapely thighs and calves, plus perfect feet. I absolutely loved to kiss them.

He stood in front of me with his hands around my waist. I could feel his minor tugs as he tried to pull me closer, but our tummies were already pressed together.

"I'm not wanting sex, sweetie," Wayne said. He had tilted his head to the side while staring in my eyes. He looked so adorable and sweet. "I only want to snuggle with you for a while and kiss you, show you how much I love you. You deserve it."

I wasn't about to say no. Both of my hands were behind Wayne's rear. I always enjoyed feeling his hairy butt. I could have done it all day long, but I needed to deactivate my suit. I raised my right arm to my chest, then tapped the front of my suit and it deactivated.

Wayne stepped back a few inches so we could both take off our harnesses. He slowly moved his hands over my chest, cupping my pecs, sliding his fingers through all the hairs, feeling my beard, my chin.

"You're in a very affectionate mood," I said happily. Wayne always made my heart melt in many wonderful ways.

He leaned in and pressed his lips along the side of my neck, kissing me sweetly and tenderly several times. I could feel his manhood getting hard. It was poking against me, rubbing along my own erection.

"Let's go lay in bed," Wayne whispered beside my ear.

He held my hand and led me over to our bed, then pulled back the comforter so we both could lie down. Wayne loved to snuggle behind me, so I turned on my right side and let him do his thing.

My handsome man spread my butt cheeks and then slid his hard dick between them. His intentions weren't to go inside me, he just wanted some minor pleasure, some teasing which he enjoyed, and I was more than happy to let him have.

He slipped his left arm around me, and I held his hand against my chest as he kissed my hairy shoulders, and gently pulled on a bunch of hairs with his lips. Slowly he kept thrusting his hips so he could playfully poke at me down there. We mingled our feet and legs together, taking turns brushing our toes over the top of each others, which got me hard fast.

"You feel so good, sweetie," he whispered between kisses. "You're the greatest man in my entire world, Adam."

I moved my left arm behind my leg so I could feel Wayne's hairy thigh, and then I reached around further to adore his shapely butt. "You mean the same to me, too." I mildly patted his rear before returning my hand back to his, where I held it against my chest. "You're such a sweetheart, and I love how you cuddle and kiss me. It feels so good." I lifted his hand to my mouth and kissed the back of it.

He brushed his beard across my back. I felt its fullness against my skin. He then pressed the side of his face between my shoulders, along the center of my back, adding some kisses from the side of his mouth. It felt incredible to be cradled in his strong arms and loved so intensely.

I wiggled my body, pressing myself closer against Wayne's chest, stomach, and legs. He never stopped sliding his erection between my cheeks. Every poke and pull felt wonderful. I occasionally flexed my ass just to give him some added tight fun.

We cuddled together for an hour before James's voice came over our room's intercom.

"Sorry to bother you guys," James said, "But we could use you two up on the bridge."

"We'll be right there," Wayne replied.

I had fallen asleep a few times. The bed was comfortable, and snuggling with Wayne tended to wash away all my worries and fears. His arm was still around me. I brushed my lips over his hairy forearm.

Wayne kissed the side of my neck. "I guess we need to get going, sweetie."

I casually nodded while holding his hand closer against my chest. "It feels so good laying here with you. I miss this."

"I know you do, babe." He tenderly rubbed his beard against the back of my head. "We'll have plenty of time once we help James and his crew. Trust me, I'm gonna snuggle you so much you're going to get drunk on my love."

I chuckled. "I'm looking forward to that."

After several more kisses on my shoulders and back, we got out of our bed and slipped our harness suits back on. They must have some kind of memory storage in them, because when I activated my suit it was still sleeveless.

"I guess their programmable," I told Wayne.

His suit covered him from neck to toe in armored leather and high-quality boots. Our footwear appealed to me a lot. They had thick soles and stood tall, covering our calves. I took a few seconds to admire them by turning my heels to the side a few times.

"Having sex with you in these suits is going to be so damn hot and intense," Wayne said. He kept massaging his crotch as he stared at me. A huge and anxious smile stretched across his face.

I smiled back at him while stepping closer, until I stood in front of him. I placed my hands around his waist, and gave him a few tender squeezes while staring in his eyes. "And, I'll be able to deactivate it around my hips while leaving the rest of it on," I mentioned.

Wayne seemed suddenly more intrigued and aroused. He cradled my face with his hands and then kissed me, slipping his tongue in my mouth a few times. We gave each other a round of hugs then rubbed our hands over each others leather clad backs.

"Let's get going," Wayne whispered beside my ear.

I slipped in one final kiss on his cheek and felt the edge of his beard against my lips. I could have stood there all day and showed him love, but duty called.

We left our room, hopped in the elevator, and headed to the bridge where everyone was still working at their workstation. Duluth and Ramsey were standing beside the main holographic display at the center of the room, with Dean beside them.

After the main doors closed, Wayne and I walked over to our friends. "Did you figure out how to get on their ships?" Wayne sounded anxious.

Dean shrugged. "We're a few steps closer. We just need to fine-tune the scanners so we can get a precise location where they can open a portal, unless you all want to appear right in front of a rouge agent with a gun in your hand."

Wayne nodded happily with his eyes opened wide. "That's not a bad idea."

Willie laughed as he came over to stand with the five of us. "Did you two have a nice and relaxing time," Willie asked us.

"Yeah," Wayne answered. "We just needed some cuddle time, nothing major."

Willie chuckled and raised his black furry arm so he could pat Wayne against his back.

Another rouge agent's image had appeared on the main holographic screen. It was an alien male with a mix of dark and light brown skin. His skin resembled rocks and he looked rough and tough. A bulky guy, he was slightly overweight with short black hair and a minor beard.

"Dean, are you figuring anything out yet?" James asked. He stood in front of his workstation with his arms crossed over his chest. I'm sure everyone wondered the same thing while waiting for Dean to solve this dilemma.

"Here we go," Dean said in a satisfied voice. He kept busy flipping switches and pushing holographic buttons in the air. "I didn't realize I could promote the signatures as a readable display *and* as an actual physical mass. This should solve our problem."

Duluth raised his hand and slipped it inside of the representation of the alien man. He focused on touching the man's image, instead of the technical readouts and schematics that scrolled through the air. "I've got this guys signature," Duluth said. "Opening a portal near him should be relatively easy now."

"Relatively," James uttered. "So, your portal will only open next to one of their agents?"

Our magical friends both nodded. "Exactly," Ramsey confirmed. "We'll have to open a gateway near someone who is alone. Otherwise, we could be facing a serious showdown."

Willie nodded before he walked back over to stand beside James. He rubbed his boyfriend's shoulder. I could tell our captain had been getting frustrated with so much waiting. James was the kind of person who wanted to resolve issues immediately, instead of later. I could see that much in his attitude and demeanor.

"I'm on it," Dean said. "I can pinpoint a single agent so we can open a portal near them. We just have to wait for someone to go to the bathroom, or go to their quarters alone, and *then* we can jump on their ship."

The main display changed to a detailed schematic of a huge rouge ship, one that had tried to attack the gopher's planet. It showed the outlined structure of its massive size, with tons of red dots sprinkled throughout its many floors and rooms, which represented each rogue agent.

"Well that sucks," Dean mumbled. "There's no one alone right now." He kept staring at the display while letting out a few frustrated sighs.

"Give them a few minutes, then we can try," James said. He sounded hopeful, and a bit anxious to use a portal so we could jump on their ship. He held up his handgun and fiddled with it before placing it back in his holster.

Willie walked over to a metal storage closet on the far side of the bridge, opened its doors, and then pulled out one of their precious rifles, a Kimoon TC. He held it in his huge hands, staring at its length and thickness. He seemed ready to fight.

"So, what's the game plan?" I asked. "Do we just eliminate everyone, or should we try and blow up their ships?"

"Once we get onboard," Bray said, "I'll summon spirits to shred their ships to pieces. You guys can handle the rest."

Willie held up his long rifle and cocked it in midair. "Adam, I think you know *exactly* what we're planning. They need to be eliminated. No exceptions."

I understood their goal. After what the agents tried with the gophers' world, why not wipe them all out. I just hoped we could accomplish our task without any further headaches. I didn't want to see anyone get injured or shot, especially Wayne. I remembered the force fields Duluth and Ramsey had gifted me and Wayne with, so that made me feel better about sneaking on board their ship. I had my handgun also, so I wasn't about to let any agent shout out for help.

I reached over and took hold of Wayne's hand. He faced me, smiling, and then lifted my hand and gave me a kiss on the back of it.

"We'll be fine, sweetie," he promised me. "Plus, we can't let our gopher friends suffer anymore. That wouldn't be fair in any universe."

I leaned in and rested the side of face along his shoulder and arm, then added a single kiss against his leather suit. Wayne always made me feel good. He imbued me with confidence. He had such a strong will. It gave me strength during many moments.

"Here we go, here we go," Dean shouted out. "It looks like an agent is going off by their self."

"Pull up their signature," James told him.

Dean magnified the holographic image of the rogue vessel, and focused on the single individual noted by the red dot that was moving down some kind of corridor. The ship showed in outlines of green and blue with the red dot moving along slowly. I could see various sized rooms and much larger areas on the map. The details were impressive. Dean must have scanned their ships methodically.

"Let's wait until the red dot is completely alone," James said.

"Do you think they'll detect us once we show up?" Wayne asked.

James and Willie both shook their heads. "I doubt it," Willie said. "With all the damage Bray's spirits put them through, they're systems probably aren't working at a hundred percent right now."

"Can we see who this agent is?" Willie asked. He had been keeping a close watch on the main display, scrutinizing every detail.

After Dean pushed some buttons and pulled up a small image of this person down in the corner of the display, it turned out to be the bulky guy whose skin looked like dark brown rocks.

"Where's he headed to?" Wayne seemed as intrigued as Willie.

"His quarters, or a bathroom, if I had to guess," Dean said, with a slight laugh.

"So we could appear while he's taking a dump," I mentioned.

Wayne nudged the side of my arm with his. "That'd be the perfect time to appear and surprise that piece of shit. No pun intended."

I shook my head, rolling my eyes with a smile after my tough guy's joke.

"Now, when we open the portal, Ramsey and I will go through first," Duluth informed us. "That way, we can knock him out and then get ready to purge the vessel with our forces."

Willie picked up his rifle and cocked it again. I wasn't sure why an energy weapon would need to be pumped like that, but I assumed it might be some customary habit or something related to an "old school" gun.

Bray and Woofa gathered around us. Everyone was waiting for Dean to give the word so we could hop through the gateway.

"I think he's in a bathroom," Dean said. "It looks like a small room. Would you guys like to wait a minute so he can finish?"

Everyone laughed and giggled.

"Like Wayne mentioned," Willie said, "Now would be the perfect time." He held his rifle in his furry hand, ready to fire.

Ramsey swiped his arm through the air and created a portal outlined in glowing swirls of white and blue light. Within it, I could see the bathroom on the rouge vessel. It looked similar to a restroom in a store or mall.

Duluth held Ramsey's hand as they hurried through the portal. Willie followed them with Bray, Woofa, Wayne, and I bringing up the rear. My handsome man had already pulled out his handgun. I did the same as soon as we were on the ship.

"Is somebody there?" the agent asked from inside the stall. He didn't sound nervous, just curious after hearing our footsteps and Willie's loud stomps with his oversized boots. "I just needed to use the toilet. I'll be back up on the command deck after I'm done."

Duluth nudged the side of Willie's furry arm, and then pointed at the door to the stall where the rogue agent was sitting. Ramsey produced a glowing green light that consumed his hand, right before Willie raised his leg and kicked the door open to reveal our chunky target.

"Who the *hell* are you freaks!" the guy said. He quickly reached for his pdPhone, but Ramsey shot off his magical green light which hit the agent right in the center of this chest, knocking him out cold.

The overweight guy slid off the toilet and fell toward the left side of the stall, where he lay unconscious with his pants down around his ankles. We could see his manhood and his whopping belly, and we got an even better view of his skin. Every inch resembled course stone.

"How long is he going to be out?" Willie asked.

"Hours," Ramsey said with a satisfied look.

"James, do you copy?" Willie said.

"Yeah, you're coming through loud and clear, big bear," James answered via their phone's speakers. "It looks like most of the red dots are above and below your current location. Can you guys get to them?"

"We will," Willie answered. "Please keep monitoring them."

"You got it, fur ball." James sounded delighted knowing Willie was here with us, and Willie smiled after James's playful names for him.

The bathroom was no larger than one you'd find in a restaurant. There were four stalls and three sinks with hand dryers mounted on the walls near the main door.

Duluth slowly opened the bathroom door and stepped out in the bright corridor. Its appearance resembled James's ship with the overhead lights and white walls, only they were much wider than his hallways. Ramsey followed his boyfriend, with the rest of us keeping close behind them.

"Should we split up or stick together?" Wayne asked.

Woofa gave him a mild shove along his shoulder. "I think it'd be best if we deal with them as a group. We don't need to get caught in a deadly showdown."

"Okay, okay," Wayne said happily. "I wasn't sure about our attack plan."

"We shoot anyone we come across," Willie stated. "*That's* our plan. Then Bray and Woofa can rip this ship apart."

"Hey, don't forget about us. We can rip ships apart too," Ramsey said with gusto.

Willie patted Ramsey's shoulder, silently apologizing for his oversight. They both exchanged a pleasant and understanding smile, paired with a wink.

The seven of us moved quietly down the corridor and Duluth

checked around corners before moving ahead. Willie kept his huge rifle aimed forward. It was easily a few inches above my head. He stood incredibly tall.

Further ahead down the corridor, a room's doors opened and two agents stepped in the hallway and freaked out as soon as they saw us. They were both wearing leather armored suits similar to the ones Wayne and I wore, but before they could even pull their handguns from their holsters, Willie shot them both with two blinding bursts of blue energy. He hit them both in their chest and they collapsed on the ground. I wasn't sure if they were dead or unconscious. Both were lying with their legs folded under their bodies, and they each had dropped their handguns.

"Take that you assholes," Willie uttered in a hateful tone.

"Are they dead?" I asked.

Willie nodded and then scratched the side of his beard with his fingertip. "That's what we came here to do, Adam. I'm not playing games with these bastards after all the destruction and abuse I've seen them do over the years. They put my race through hell for many years."

Wayne gently rubbed my shoulder, comforting me as best he could. He could tell I was uncomfortable seeing death or watching people get shot right in front of me. I felt like we were inside one of his horror movies, where everyone gets slaughtered until the big bad guy comes out near the end.

We cautiously moved further down the corridor, making sure our boots tapped against the steel floor as quietly as possible. Soon, we came to a wide flight of stairs, the kind you would see in an apartment building. They went up and down to higher and lower levels of the ship.

"Should we follow them?" Wayne asked.

Willie nodded. "James," he whispered, "Is there more red dots below or above us?"

"Above you," James answered over the phone.

"Okay. Then we're going down," Willie said.

One by one we headed down the stairs, taking our time while trying to be quiet. After a few flights, we came to another long corridor where Willie led the way. He aimed his rifle as we passed several doors.

"Hey, big bear," James said over Willie's phone. "You guys must have alerted someone, because a lot of red dots are swarming toward your location. Do you copy?"

"Yeah, we copy," Willie said in an aggravated voice. He shook his head.

"Maybe some spirits might help us out." Bray fluidly waved her arms through the air, and summoned two smaller versions of her serpents that had ripped apart those rogue ships earlier. Each one covered the corridor behind us and in front of us, and both were probably thirty feet long with scaled bodies and long fangs.

Two dozen rogue agents swarmed the hallway on both sides, and immediately started firing their rifles and handguns at us.

"Die you fucking scum!" one of the agents shouted while firing at us. He was a demon male with horns and red skin, and he wore an armored leather suit.

Bray's spirits blocked all the gun fire, and she quickly swirled both arms through the air commanding her pets to attack the agents. They hit the rogue troops hard, knocking them to ground while rapidly slithering all over them. A few shots got through and we all ducked to avoid getting hit, but one blast of energy from a rifle hit Wayne in his left shoulder, and I saw a glob of blood spurt into the air.

My handsome man fell back against a wall, and then dropped down where he lay on his back writhing in pain as he held his hand over the wound.

Bray quickly commanded her spirits to pound the rogue troops with their massive bodies, and Woofa used his magic, summoning what resembled a stormy cloud above the agents from which huge chunks of ice fell from its swirling blue and white mass. Each chunk crushed the agents, and each piece was so cold the air around them had changed to mist that rolled off of each piece. The steel ground was now littered with bits of ice and pools of blood.

My heart about jumped out of my chest. I freaked out and fell on my knees beside Wayne while pushing my hands over his wound, which was oozing a lot of blood. I honestly thought the suits would have protected us more than that. Whatever rifle had shot him, it must have been pretty powerful.

"Oh, that fucking hurts," Wayne cried out. He kept squirming and twisting his body in agony, pushing at my hands or grabbing my wrist.

"Holy shit, you're losing a lot of blood." I kept my hands over his shoulder, but it was doing very little to prevent him from bleeding. I slipped into panic mode.

Ramsey opened a portal back to the bridge of our ship, and he helped me quickly pick up Wayne so the three of us could step through to safety on the other side. Duluth kept busy projecting force fields in front of everyone, while Willie kept randomly firing his rifle.

"Are you kidding me," James said after we appeared at the center of the bridge. He and Dean hurried over to the three of us.

"It looks bad," I told James. "He's losing a lot of blood."

The Devil Bunnies hurried over and stood beside us. There really wasn't much for them to do, they only watched with terrified looks.

Ramsey kneeled beside Wayne, then stroked the back of his tree-branch colored hand down his face. "You're going to be okay," he said to Wayne. "I'll heal you."

11

Wayne was lying flat on his back with Ramsey beside him. Our magical friend held his hand over Wayne's shoulder and released a continual flow of bright white light that penetrated my handsome man's tissue. It healed him completely before my eyes.

Wayne's skin looked just the way I remembered it. Every tiny hair had been rejuvenated and restored. I cried happy tears while staring, and then as soon as Ramsey stood, I gave him a firm hug, holding him close against my body with my arms wrapped around him.

He patted my back. "There's no need to cry. Wayne will be as good as his old self."

I leaned back and stared straight in his eyes. "From the bottom of my heart, thank you."

Ramsey nodded with a smile, and before I knew it Wayne sat up on his rear end. I reached down and lent him a helping hand so he could stand up. He then gave Ramsey a nice warm hug, too.

James reached over and gave Wayne a tender pat on his shoulder, followed by Dean. Proud smiles were on all of the Devil Bunnies faces.

Wayne turned to face James. "I promise, I'm going to destroy every last one of those assholes."

"Don't do this from a sense of vengeance. Do it because it's the right thing to do," James told him. "Protect our gopher friends, and eliminate the rogue threat forever. That's why we're here. That's what we're going to do."

A wave of calmness washed over Wayne's face, and he nodded a few times, agreeing with our captain.

Another portal opened right next to us. It was a clear image or our friends surrounded by a swirling mix of energy around its perimeter.

Willie stuck his head halfway through. "I was going to ask if Wayne was okay, but I can already see that he is."

"Can we come back through?" Wayne sounded eager to get back to the fight.

"Sure," Willie said. "We've taken care of all the agents who came down here to kill us."

I was certain they had killed all of them. As soon as Willie backed away from the portal Ramsey stepped through it, with Wayne and I following him before it vanished.

Dead troops lay everywhere. They were crushed beneath Woofa's icy chunks or had been torn apart by Bray's serpents, which left body parts scattered all over the ground. Several had been shot by Willie's rifle. Pools of blood covered the steel floor.

"Geez," I mumbled in shock. I wasn't use to seeing stuff like this in real life, only in movies.

Wayne held my hand in an attempt to comfort me. "Like James said, sweetie, we need to make sure our gopher friends will be safe. There's no other way."

"I know," I replied with a nod. "It's just disturbing."

Willie turned around to face us with a welcoming smile. "Glad to see you're okay."

"Thanks," Wayne said. He reached up and rubbed Ramsey's shoulder, silently thanking him for his magical healing. His suit was actually repairing itself. Bit by bit, I watched as all the leather slowly covered his shoulder. It looked brand new.

"So what's the plan?" I asked.

Bray cleared her voice. I could tell she was feeling nervous. Her spirits were still guarding the corridors behind and in front of us. "We keep moving, eliminating anyone we come across until we reach their command center. Then, we can destroy the ships."

"Why can't you just use your pets and shred them right now?" Wayne asked.

"Because we need to make sure none of them will come back," Willie said bluntly. "They have suits too, and can survive in space. Once we return to our universe, we can see how things are going." He touched his pdPhone. "James, do you still copy?"

"Gotcha, big bear," James replied. "There's a lot of red dots above and below you."

"I still think we should split up and go at them in groups," Wayne suggested.

Everyone literally shook their heads and Wayne got the hint. We followed Willie down the corridor to another staircase, which we used to ascend through the ship.

"James, do you have a location for the bridge?" Willie asked.

"It's about ten floors above you," James answered over the phone.

"Is that an elevator?" I pointed at a wide double-sided door. It looked like one. A control panel was attached to the right side of it.

Willie nodded while heading over to the panel. He pushed a button which opened the door and showed a huge elevator. "Let's use it," he said. "It'll be quicker."

Wayne and I glanced at each other with shrugs and a few nods. We both agreed with Willie. After our furry bear walked inside, we all followed him with plenty of room to spare after the door closed. I assumed the controls were similar to other systems Willie had used. He tapped two holographic buttons that floated in midair over a panel, and the elevator started to rise through the ship. But, who or what would we encounter once the doors opened?

Willie cocked his rifle with his oversized hand. Wayne held his handgun and I did too. Both of us were more than ready to fire a shot. Bray lifted her hands. She was ready to summon spirits, and Woofa got prepared to cast his magic. Duluth and Ramsey stood behind us all. However, when the elevator stopped and the doors opened, we only encountered another white and lengthy corridor.

Willie stepped out first. He looked both ways and listened for any rustling agents who might be headed down the hallway, but nothing came. Maybe they were waiting to ambush us.

"How far is the bridge?" I quietly asked.

Willie shook his head. "I'm not sure. I do recognize the layout of this particular design. It's very familiar. I've been on rogue ships before when they were part of the MST."

Bray summoned her two serpent spirits, which stayed close to us in order to block any gunfire which we soon encountered.

Several agents had raced around the corner of a connecting hallway, and started firing at us with their guns and rifles. Bray's spirits deflected every shot and then quickly raced ahead to slaughter the rogue troops. Her pets knocked them all down and then chewed at their faces and chests, ripping them apart and spilling blood all over the floor as they screamed in agony.

I was shocked to see Willie laughing, but then I wasn't familiar with all he had witnessed over the years. I had no way of knowing all the headaches and trouble these agents, and the MST had caused his people, or any unsuspecting worlds they felt like conquering. I could tell his actions were justified, although Wayne and I weren't laughing. However, my handsome man was smiling as he watched, obviously content with seeing these troops slaughtered.

Wayne faced me. He stared in my eyes. "I know this is out of your league. But, they deserve it. You know they do."

I nodded a few times, but started to feel sick to my stomach. I could smell their insides and all the blood. It was gross. I cringed. Wayne rubbed my shoulder in a comforting manner then shot me a smile. I saw the love in his eyes for me, and I knew he would never leave me or let anyone harm me.

Willie continued forward with the rest of us carefully following him. Bray and Woofa didn't mind if they walked through the blood, but I wasn't about to. Severed fingers and hands lay around us. Two of the agents had their arms torn off, along with their legs below their knees. I focused on Wayne's attractive butt while stepping over the mess, so I could move forward. His shapely ass looked fantastic in the tight-fitting brown leather. Watching him pacified me and calmed my nerves.

"It looks like there are only a few red dots on the bridge," James said over Willie's phone's intercom. "Looks like it shouldn't be a problem to take out that horned dude, if he's there."

Willie chuckled while carefully aiming his rifle ahead. "Oh, we're going to take them all out. Trust me, little captain." It warmed my heart to see how Willie and James loved each other so much, and how they could exchange funny remarks.

We continued down the corridor for about two hundred feet before we reached another elevator near a staircase. It was oddly quiet. No agents were coming for us, even though they obviously knew we were aboard their ship.

Bray's spirits had stayed behind us, and Duluth and Ramsey seemed somewhat reluctant to continue ahead. "Something doesn't feel right," Ramsey said, as he and his boyfriend came to a sudden stop.

I assumed along with their magical abilities they might be able to sense bad situations. Ramsey projected a minor force field ahead of us, while Bray commanded her two spirits to come closer and protect our rear.

I felt unnerved. Wayne and I stood closer to the staircase, but before I could even take hold of his hand, a huge explosion rocked the ground around us. It ripped apart the floor beneath our friends, and completely demolished the stairs. The two of us, along with Duluth, fell down with the rubble as he produced a semi-transparent force field that surrounded each of our bodies to protect us from all the sharp metal.

Smoke filled the shaft, and the sound was so loud I couldn't hear myself shouting to Wayne as we fell several floors down, before landing on a heap of jagged metal surrounded by small fires.

"What the fuck are they trying to do?" Wayne sounded incredibly pissed.

"Kill us, I imagine," Duluth said, in an aggravated voice. He tried to stand and make his way over the debris and tiny fires to get out of the staircase area.

After the force fields dispersed, Wayne helped me get up. He held my hand and made sure I didn't fall over the pile of steel and injure myself. He was just as cautious with his steps, pressing his boots against the biggest pieces of metal, so he didn't topple over the twisted beams.

As soon as we stood outside in the corridor, we looked back at the destroyed staircase. It was a heaping pile of crumbled steel and paneling.

"So, now we're separated from everyone else," Wayne pointed

out. He sounded frustrated as he pulled his handgun from its holster, holding it ready to fire. He nodded at mine, suggesting I do the same, which I did.

"Maybe we should find another elevator and take it back up to join them." Duluth sounded hopeful. He looked it, too. "Or, I can open a portal to our friends."

"Let's find an elevator," Wayne said. "Then we can go to the bridge."

We walked together down the corridor, guns in hand and Duluth kept his hands ready to cast magic if we ran across any agents. A glowing blue light hovered around his fingers.

The hallway was white and pristine, like the other levels of the ship, although some smoke lingered in the air. I could still smell the fires after we had moved down the hallway. We turned a corner and found another elevator.

Wayne had a skill for observation, and he recalled the buttons Willie had tapped. The elevator door opened, and it was as large as the other one we had been in. Wayne stepped inside first, and I followed with Duluth right behind me, after he checked the hallway for any activity.

There was none, so Wayne pushed some green holographic buttons, the doors closed, and we started moving up through the ship. A few times the elevator stopped suddenly, moved to the side for a few seconds, and then continued ascending. I wasn't sure if Wayne was that skilled in directing our ride or not.

"You think we're going right back to everyone?" I asked.

Wayne shrugged. "I hope so, sweetie. I just pushed the same buttons Willie did."

The elevator stopped and after the doors opened. We all gasped after realizing where we arrived to. We stared at the bridge of the rogue vessel, with three agents accompanying Korath, the smartass and burly horned guy we had met back in the woods.

It was a wide area with a huge movie-theater-size viewscreen located along the wall to our left. Several workstations sat around its perimeter.

Korath turned around to face us. "Welcome to my ship. You and your friends have been stirring up a lot of trouble for us." He sounded smug and sarcastic with a look to match. He even stroked his horn on the right side of his head.

Korath wore a brown vest which he had left opened, giving us a view of his hairy, muscular chest and dark gray skin. He completed his look with blue jeans and brown leather boots that had thick soles and rounded toes. The other three agents were aliens; two males and one female. They were all clad in armored suits similar to ours. One of the males was a demon with red skin and small black horns. The other two must have come from a race comparable to Dean's. They both were covered in dark blue skin and similar facial features to his.

Korath gestured for us to enter, which we did slowly and cautiously. We had no way of knowing how arrogant or accepting of us he would be. I assumed because of the attack from Bray's sprits, he was going to be an asshole. Guess we'd find out.

He stepped down from his upper section of the bridge. It was surrounded with workstations and floating holographic displays. There were only three steps. His area was the highest part of the bridge. An oversized command chair sat upon its center.

The others watched us with scrutinizing looks while Korath rubbed his gray hands together while standing near a console. "I feel you three have been turned against us without knowing all the facts," Korath said. He looked at each of us in the eyes.

"You attacked and tried to destroy the elshons world," Wayne hatefully blurted out. "I think we know all the facts about your intentions."

Korath shook his head while locking his hands around his thick waist. "You have *no* idea what suffering and chaos our organization has gone through. The universe we come from is under new leadership, and they want nothing more than to see us dead. We've been their protectors and overseers for millions of years. We're only fighting for our right to exist. Is that so bad?"

"There's nothing wrong with wanting to live," Duluth said, "But, trying to conquer a peoples' planet that is already established is unbelievably horrible. You have no right to do that. Find somewhere else to go."

I had never heard Duluth sound so adamant with his opinion. I liked hearing it.

Korath shook his horned head again while walking back and forth in front of his raised platform. He looked disgusted and annoyed with us. "Then I guess there's no more to discuss," Korath said. He then gestured to one of his troops who quickly pulled out a handgun and fired directly at Wayne.

Duluth must have anticipated an attack. He instantly projected a force field which completely blocked the deadly blast of energy. He then shoved his hands through the air which dispersed the field and knocked all four agents down on their butts. They scrambled back up on their knees and then stood. Each one aimed their gun and fired, but Duluth protected us with his magic.

Wayne fired his gun and hit the blue male directly in the chest. The blast from his weapon was bright and bold. His powerful shot completely blew open the front of the agents leather suit, spraying lots of blood through the air. He fell on his back where he lay lifeless.

The other rogues fired their weapons, but it was pointless. Nothing could penetrate Duluth's protective barrier.

Korath rushed forward, running toward us, but Duluth jutted out his arms and knocked him back on his ass with a magical blast of energy. The female agent tried to do the same, but I was quick to respond with my handgun. I fired at her and hit her in the shoulder which knocked her down to her knees. Wayne then finished her off with a shot to her chest.

The other male agent squatted behind a workstation and kept firing his gun at us as he held it over the top of his desk. Every shot was off and they randomly hit the walls, ceiling, and a few hit the steel floor. He must have been terrified of us after seeing his associates killed. I wasn't sure what damage level Wayne had his gun set to, but it was firing off some deadly shots.

Korath held his hands up in a pleading gesture. "Stop!" he demanded. "We don't deserve to be disrespected like this."

"The hell you don't!" Wayne shot at him and hit him in the knee.

Blood sprayed over the floor as he fell on his butt and wrapped his hand around the wound.

The other agent stood up and held a rifle in his arms. He aimed it directly at us then fired, but the shot was deflected by Duluth's barrier.

Wayne fired off a shot that hit the agent directly in his demon face. It blew off a large piece of his head and he collapsed on the ground, soaking in a growing pool of dark red blood. One of his black horns had tumbled across the floor after he fell.

Duluth gave Wayne a pat on his shoulder. "Nice aim."

I glanced in the eyes of my handsome man and he seemed to be searching for my approval after what he had done. I smiled and conveyed my acceptance of his shot.

Korath tried to push himself back across the floor as we walked closer toward him, but being in a lot of pain he didn't get very far.

He spit at us from his gray lips, but it didn't get very far. He must have gotten weak. "You and your friends are going to suffer after fleets of rogue ships invade your universe." He sounded out of breath.

"Too bad you won't live to see that." Wayne raised his gun and fired off a shot directly at Korath's horned head. It blew off half of his face, plus one of his large horns. He fell on his back with copious amounts of blood pouring out from the gapping hole.

Duluth dismissed his magical shields, and we stood silent for a long moment as we gazed at the bodies and around the room. It was oddly quiet. I wondered how Willie and the others were doing.

Wayne reached over and held my hand. I looked in his eyes. Hopefully, he didn't think I would judge him or condone his actions. Honestly, I didn't think Wayne had the strength to kill people. He enjoyed his violent and bloody movies back at home, so maybe watching those over the years had prepared him to dish out some justice.

"It had to be done," I told my tough man.

He nodded and smiled, then stared directly in my eyes. "I will do whatever it takes to keep you safe, Adam. Believe me, I will."

A heartfelt tear ran down my cheek and Wayne raised his hand to wipe it away from my face. He was so loveable to me. The best memories of being with him filled my head, and a few more tears trickled down from my eyes.

He stepped closer after holstering his gun and then gave me a warm hug for a long moment. He added a few kisses on my cheeks and lips.

"I love you with all my heart, Adam," he whispered beside my ear. "And, someday, I hope you will do me the honor of being your husband."

I leaned back then stared straight in his beautiful eyes. "The honor will be mine, Wayne." I passionately kissed him and he slipped his tongue in my mouth showing me considerable amounts of love.

From the corner of my eye, I saw Duluth glancing at us while we kissed and I hoped Ramsey was safe and well. I could tell Duluth wanted to get back to his husband.

The elevator doors opened and we all spun around to face them. Wayne and I pulled out our guns while Duluth produced his force fields in front of us. I assumed more rogue troops were going to step out, but instead it was our friends. Willie led the way with Ramsey, Bray, and Woofa right behind him. They all stared at us cautiously, and then noticed the dead bodies lying on the ground.

"We're fine," I blurted out. "And, look what Wayne did." I pointed at Korath's body and then gave Wayne a mild tap across his back, congratulating him for such perfect aim.

Bray and Woofa came close to us while staring at the bodies. They seemed surprised but delighted knowing he was dead. Duluth quickly walked over to Ramsey and gave him a hug and plenty of kisses. I was relieved to see they had all survived, and that our magical friends could be together again.

"How did you guys get to the bridge?" Bray asked.

"Just by luck," Wayne told her. "We found an elevator and I pushed the same buttons Willie had in the other one. Once the doors opened, we dealt with these assholes." My sexy man sounded much more confident and proud of himself, but not in an arrogant sort of way. He was merely satisfied with our outcome.

"I'm glad you guys took out these bastards," Willie said. He had a crooked and delighted grin plastered across his face as he walked around the bridge, looking down at the blood and bodies. I'm sure if anyone enjoyed seeing rogue agents dead, it was him.

"So how many rogues are still on the ship," Wayne asked. "And, are their other ships still nearby?"

"Yes," Woofa answered. "But, we're going to need to step up our game if we mean to defeat them all."

Willie stopped and faced Woofa. "What do you have in mind?"

"I think I know," Bray answered. She mildly laughed. "I'll have to use spirits to destroy their ships. That's the only way to take them all out at once. Their reactors will explode and take out everyone."

"I can keep a portal opened where you can command them to your will," Duluth said. "We can control the gateways so no one will be able to pass through them. No fires or explosions will come through either."

"We can fire from the ship, too," Willie added. "I'm sure James will enjoy doing that."

"Then let's get out of here and finish this fight." Wayne sounded content with our decision.

Ramsey swirled his arms through the air and opened a portal back to the bridge of James's ship. Wayne held my hand as walked through, and Duluth and Ramsey did the same. Bray and Woofa followed with Willie bringing up the rear.

"Welcome back," James said in a happy voice. He rushed over to give Willie a hug. Our captain's arms couldn't reach halfway around Willie's stomach. He was incredibly thick and built like a brick shithouse.

I watched as the portal's outer ring changed colors. Originally it was blue and white, but now it changed to a swirl of reds.

"This will make sure nothing can come through," Ramsey explained. "Only magic can be used on the other side." He turned and looked at Bray. It was time for her to summon her pets.

On the main display, Dean pulled up a detailed holographic view of the rogue vessels, along with dozens of red dots sprinkled within each ship. Every ship was outlined in orange and green colors.

Woofa nudged Bray's arm, and she leaned down a bit to give him a kiss since he was shorter than her. "Show us what you can do, babe," Woofa said to her. They shared one more kiss. Her long auburn hair dangled over his shoulders.

Bray walked over to the portal and stood in front of it. Duluth and Ramsey stood on opposite sides of their magical gate. Slowly, Bray moved her arms, twisting and turning them fluidly, bending her hands and fingers, standing straight or hunched over until several gigantic serpent spirits appeared on the other side, directly on the bridge of the rogue vessel we had come from.

Each of her pets was identical to the others, but much larger. They had fangs that were longer than my legs with whipping lengthy bodies. I watched the main display and saw her spirits ripping apart the rogue vessel. They were moving in and out, altering the density of their bodies, tearing through the metal hull like it was tissue paper.

Explosions came forth in a variety of magnitudes. Steel shards and huge pieces of metal flew off in all directions. Many red dots were hurled out into space, but soon after they disappeared from the display. I assumed that meant they were no longer alive. Bray's spirits swam through their masses and were likely chewing them apart. Even with their protective helmets each suit could generate, they would be no match for those fangs.

"Your spirits really know how to rip apart a ship," Wayne said. He had a delighted smile on his face while watching the holographic show.

"They're directed by my guidance," Bray explained. She had never stopped moving her arms and hands in graceful motions.

Her spirits attacked the other ships, and did the exact same thing to all of them, shredding each one piece by piece until all that remained was a field of debris. Bray lowered her hands and dismissed her ghostly serpents, and then stood up as we all gazed through the portal watching chunks of the rogue ships drift by.

"So that's it. We've won?" Wayne raised his hands in the air in a questioning gesture.

Willie and James both chuckled while shaking their head. "Knowing the MST and these rogue bastards," James said, "I doubt this will be the last time we'll encounter them. They'll never stop, which means we're going to have a lot more of them to deal with over time."

Woofa stood beside Bray. He gave his tall girlfriend a loveable hug and kiss on her cheek for doing such a great job. They both smiled while making eye contact. It delighted me to see them so happy together.

"Should we check on our gopher friends," I asked. "They did mention some kind of celebration that was coming up."

Everyone headed back to their workstations. Duluth and Ramsey stood beside me and Wayne. They held hands.

"Dean, how long would it take you to scan for more rogue signatures?" James sounded confident yet cautious.

Dean shrugged. "Maybe thirty minutes, give or take a few." He started pushing various buttons on his console.

"So what do we do for thirty minutes?" Wayne asked.

Duluth instantly opened a wide glowing portal and I recognized the landscape. It was the woods surrounding their cabin back on their home world. "Let's take some time out for a few snacks," he said to me and Wayne.

I wasn't about to refuse. Willie and James gave both of us approving nods.

"Be back soon," James told us happily.

"Promise," I answered.

The four us stepped through the portal and appeared right outside of their cabin near the front porch. It was warm with the sun shining brightly. Duluth dismissed his magical gateway while Wayne adjusted his harness suit. I could tell he was feeling overheated. I was too. He lowered his head and spoke near his chest area where the control device was located. The entire top of his suit disappeared and showcased his super hairy chest and back. Seeing him half-naked pleased me immensely.

Wayne nudged my arm and aimed a wink my way. "You can take your top off too, Adam. Show us your wonderful tattoos."

He made me laugh. I deactivated the top of my suit and Wayne rubbed his had over my hairy chest while moving his eyes over every inch of me.

"Come on you two," Ramsey said with a chuckle. "Let's go inside and grab some food."

We followed them up the few stairs and then inside their home. I would love to have a place like this someday with Wayne. I could only imagine how much fun it would be.

The four of us went in the kitchen. Wayne and I sat down on the stools around the center island, right next to each other. Everything was exactly as I remembered; the wooden cabinets and stove, all the landscape images hanging on the walls.

They both kept stepping around each other while taking food and drinks from the refrigerator and cabinets. They laid out some wonderful smelling bread and then heated up some sautéed chicken breasts with a few sides of vegetables. They were such great cooks.

They sat a large pitcher on the table and filled four glasses with a cherry scented juice. I took a drink and was surprised at how great it tasted.

"This is fantastic," I said.

Wayne nodded with raised brows after he took a drink too. Cherry was a favorite flavor of his.

Duluth turned on a small radio which began playing some music, which sounded a lot like a video game soundtrack. He then sat down beside Ramsey and they shared a quick kiss before taking a bit of their food. I could see the love they shared in both of their eyes. I reached over and massaged Wayne's thigh. He gave me an appreciative smile and wink as he rubbed the back of my hand.

We each pieced together a sandwich using the chicken breasts. Our hosts provided a thick cheese to layer over the meat along with some tomatoes and lettuce.

I took a bite and my mouth watered. "Oh, this is really delicious."

"Thank you," Ramsey said. He leaned to the side and gave his hubby a mild nudge along his arm. "My sexy man is an incredible cook."

"You got that right!" Wayne kept devouring his sandwich and shoving forkfuls of veggies in his mouth. He tended to eat much faster than I did.

"So how do you feel after killing Korath?" Duluth asked Wayne. He showed a concerned yet pleasant look on his face. "I hope what you did isn't tearing you up inside. That horned jerk deserved what he got, and you know our gopher friends would enjoy a future without worry."

Wayne sighed as I kept tenderly massaging his thigh. He glanced at me with a blank stare and I sweetly smiled at my handsome man, conveying how much I loved him.

"It hasn't fucked me up too much," Wayne told Duluth. "I've spent a lifetime of watching horror movies and imagining myself in terrible situations." He faced me and placed his hand on my shoulder where he massaged me with a tender smile. "I'll get through it."

My eyes began to fill with happy tears, but I held them back for a later more personal time. It warmed my heart knowing I was Wayne's foundation of strength when he needed support.

They both smiled while taking some bites of food. "Don't ever let anyone try to control you," Ramsey said. He gazed right in our both of our eyes. "Feel free to agree with other's opinions, but don't give in to someone who enjoys dominating others. That's no way to live."

Despite the fact that Wayne was chewing a big piece of chicken breast, he leaned over and gave me a kiss on my cheek. "Love you so much, Adam," he whispered beside my ear.

I moved my hand further up his thigh so I could squeeze his armored crotch a few times. I felt his manhood growing firm even beneath all the padded leather. My adoration put a wide smile on Wayne's face.

"So, are you two going to come to the gopher festival on their planet?" I wasn't sure if they had plans or not.

They both nodded happily. "We'd love to attend," Ramsey said. "I'm sure they're going to celebrate a lot more considering the rogue threat is gone."

Wayne cleared his throat loudly while holding his fist over his mouth. "James told us that more rogue ships might come across from their galaxy. I don't think we should dismiss that possibility."

Duluth raised his glass in a toast to Wayne. "And, now that we've opened portals to the gophers home world, we'll have no problem checking in on them whenever we have time."

The sudden thought of no longer being a part of all this hit me hard. I wished Wayne and I could stay and join James's crew, but we had our lives back on Earth. What would our families think if we both just disappeared? Our house wasn't even paid for yet, not to mention our car payments, and credit card bills.

All three of them must have noticed my depressed look. They were all staring at me with concerned looks on their faces.

"What's wrong, sweetie?" Wayne returned the favor by rubbing my thigh beneath the tabletop.

I glanced at them all and then confessed my concerns. "I'm going to miss this place," I told them both. "I'm going to miss James's ship, the gophers' world, these incredible harness suits, and all the friends we've made. It's going to be depressing."

Wayne slid over and pulled me closer so he could give me a caring hug. He kissed the side of my neck. "We get to keep the harness suits, silly."

Duluth giggled. "You know me and Ramsey could always come to your home. We could open a gateway whenever you two were feeling bored or have nothing to do."

"That's right," Ramsey added. "We'd be happy to hang out with you both. Think of all the fun we could have in the hot tub or out in the woods, or we could go back to the restaurant we all visited."

I wept with Wayne's face so close to mine. His adorableness always melted my heart. He leaned back, shot me a smile, and then wiped away my tears of joy using the edge of his thumb.

"You guys are the best," I told them, before I gave Wayne a passionate kiss on his lips. "But you're the greatest of all," I whispered to him.

Wayne slipped his arms around my body and gave me a passionate hug, while Ramsey reached across the table to pat my arm.

I leaned back and imagined my face was soaked with tears as I gazed in Wayne's beautiful eyes. I couldn't have better friends or a more outstanding boyfriend to share my life with.

"Don't worry about anything, Adam," Wayne told me. "I'm going to make sure you have everything you want in life. I promise."

I placed the side of my face against his the slipped my arms around him while we both sat on our stools. He had such a special way of touching my heart and soul. Joyful tears ran down my cheeks as he held me close.

I never wanted moments like this to end.

12

The four of us sat at the table and enjoyed our great meal for about an hour before James contacted us. Our captain's voice came through our suits. The headsets automatically appeared around both mine and Wayne's ears so we could talk back to James. They were small and fit perfectly in our ears.

"The gopher people contacted us and said the celebration has already started," James told us. "I'm having Dean shift our ship over to their planet, so I figured you four could open a portal and come join us."

"Sure, we're looking forward to going to their party," I told him. "We'll be there in a few minutes."

"Perfect," James said. "We'll see you soon."

Duluth and Ramsey started to clear the table and put the leftovers away. They piled the dishes in the sink.

"We'll wash them later." Ramsey batted his hand through the air. Neither of them looked concerned about cleaning the plates or the silverware.

I stood up, and so did Wayne. We both lowered our heads and spoke near the invisible control device attached to the chest area of our suits. Immediately, our tops and arms reappeared, covering us with its padded leather and extra armor over our shoulders, biceps, and forearms.

"Looks like you guys are ready for the party," Ramsey pointed out.

"You're coming too, right," I asked. I assumed they both were joining us.

"For a little bit," Duluth informed us. "We have a local town meeting tonight, but we'll join you guys again after its over. It shouldn't take more than an hour or so."

Wayne moved behind me, wrapped his arms around my stomach, and then kissed my neck a few times while holding me close against him.

"Well, somebody is excited to get going," I said, with a minor laugh. I enjoyed his affection so much.

Duluth and Ramsey smiled at us before they exchanged a lengthy kiss.

"We can wait a few minutes before opening a portal," Duluth told us. They kept kissing each other. "I don't think there's a huge rush to get there."

That made sense, since I wasn't sure how soon James's ship would appear. Hopefully, it would be soon. I doubted Dean would waste much travel time. He seemed like the kind of guy who liked to get things done as fast and accurately as possible.

I heard a beeping noise coming over my earpieces, and then an automated announcement played, letting me know the ship had shifted to the gophers' planet.

"That was fast." I spun around and gazed at Wayne. He obviously had heard the same thing through his headset.

"We're ready," Wayne told them. "Where are you guys going to open the portal at?"

"Probably near the docking port where we were earlier," Ramsey answered. "That'll be the easiest spot, and I'm sure there'll be a ton of our gopher friends there."

I let out a minor laugh while picturing the scene. Ramsey would likely be right. I'm sure there would be a huge gathering of them for the celebration.

Duluth raised his tree-bark-looking arm and used his magic to open a small view of the docking port.

"Wow," Wayne said with gusto. "That place is packed!"

It was early in the evening on the gophers' planet, and if I had to guess, I'd say there were probably a thousand of them gathered around, many with drinks in hand and dressed in various colored pants or shorts, T-shirts, and shoes or boots.

Ramsey worked his magic. He opened a portal in a section that wasn't occupied by our small furry friends. As soon as it appeared, Wayne and I stepped through and stood beside each other on the dock. Our magical friends followed us. Several gophers came rushing over to me and Wayne who we had met before. They seemed excited and happy to see us.

Duluth outstretched his hands and projected his tiny glowing orbs onto all of them, so we could easily communicate with each other.

"It's good to see you again," a small gopher said. He brushed his hand down the length of my thigh. He was dressed in beige pants with an opened dark green vest, and he wore stylish, shiny brown boots.

"Nice to see you too," I told him.

He smiled and nodded happily. He was covered with light gray fur and the top of his head barely came up to my waist. He was actually tall in comparison to most of them.

A gopher band was performing some loud dance music and everyone was having a great time. The streets were crowded with their people and everyone was lively and having fun.

"Let's go mingle," Wayne said with a smile. He held my hand and led me through the waist-high crowd, with Duluth and Ramsey right behind us.

We walked down the flight of steps to the cobblestone street and then proceeded through the numerous gopher people. All of them were giddy and laughing. It made me happy to see them all so satisfied and entertained.

The avenues had been cleaned and many of the store fronts had already been repaired entirely from the earlier chaos. Lots of vendors stood beneath covered booths with tons of stuff for sale. Much of it looked like antiques, or items you'd find in a thrift store. There were ceramics, clothing, hats, vases, kitchen wares, garden stuff, a variety of knives, and many personal grooming items. All of it looked good. None of it appeared cheap or trashy.

We walked about halfway down the avenue before we saw Willie and James. They were with the entire bridge crew and the maintenance team members. Willie stood so high that many of the gophers were no taller than his knees.

I waved my hand high in the air and they saw us. Slowly, we made our way over to our friends. I could only think what the gopher people were thinking about the Devil Bunnies, with their dark curved horns and purple-colored skin. They were definitely unique.

Willie gave each of us a hug and James dished out some handshakes.

"Did you guys have a nice meal?" Bray asked. She was dressed in her usual red attire of tight-fitting pants with tall boots, and a jacket with a tank top beneath it.

Wayne patted his stomach. "We did, but I could definitely eat some more."

Mortenna, one of the Devil Bunnies, pointed at a nearby restaurant and bar. "We could go there and grab some food and drinks. Maybe have some fun." She sounded excited.

James and Willie showed delighted smiles, along with Bray and Woofa. Kurt from the maintenance team also looked thrilled. Amp and Reese did too. I'm sure the mentioning of drinks is what made them happy. They wore biker-style clothing; black leather jackets, steel toed boots, and worn jeans. I was sure they would enjoy mingling with the Devil Bunnies. They all kept gazing at those ladies shapely bodies.

Our group started to walk over to the restaurant, but Duluth stopped me by placing his hand on my shoulder. "We're going to head over to our meeting now," he told me. "We'll be back soon."

"Okay," I said with a smile. "I'm sure we'll all still be in the bar having a good time."

They both gave me and Wayne hugs, and then Ramsey opened a portal back to their cabin in the woods. They stepped through to the other side before it disappeared.

"Let's go party!" Willie said in a loud voice. He draped his huge furry arm across James's shoulders and walked beside his boyfriend up the three steps to the front doors of the restaurant.

Willie had to duck in order to step through the doors, though once inside we had plenty of room to stand. The chairs turned out to be a little small, but they were comfortable and we all managed to sit around a long rectangular table, except for the maintenance team and the Devil Bunnies. They headed over to the bar and sat on stools near the counter, laughing and flirting with each other. I expected as much.

Luckily, the menus had pictures of meals and drinks, so when the waitress came over we simply pointed at several items and she understood. James offered to pay for everything. His pdPhone was able to transfer funds to the restaurant.

"Duluth and Ramsey seem like really nice guys," Willie pointed out. Occasionally he had to shift himself while sitting on the small chair.

"They are very nice," I said. "They're cabin is terrific, too." I turned and looked at Wayne right in his eyes. "I think we need a cabin like theirs."

My handsome man nodded happily as the waitress brought over some drinks and placed them around the table. We ordered more than usual since the glasses weren't that large. Willie alone would probably be able to drink several really fast.

I slipped my hand under the table so I could massage Wayne's thigh. He smiled and gave me a wink as he rubbed his hand over my back.

"So how soon do you both have to be back?" James sounded concerned, yet relaxed as he took some sips from his beer.

"Well, our vacation is over on Monday, so I think we have a few days left to enjoy all of your company," I told them.

"It's really going to suck having to go back to our ordinary jobs," Wayne added. "It would be so much better to just stay on the ship with you guys."

Everyone chuckled at his remark. "Well, we don't want to put any pressure on you," James said, "But you're both welcome to stay on the ship and travel with us. Of course, that's if you want to. I know you have family and friends back on Earth."

"We'd love to," I said, "But maybe you guys could come back once a month or something and visit us. Would that be okay?"

Willie nodded happily then raised his small glass of beer to both me and Wayne. "I'll leave my pdPhone with you so we can communicate. Its battery is unlimited. It never dies."

"That sounds perfect," Wayne said. He and I, along with the rest of our friends, then all raised our glasses in a salute to each other before taking a drink.

"Cheers," I said.

Our friendly waitress came over with some food, along with two other servers and they placed all of it right in front of us.

I leaned over and took a whiff of my food. "This smells amazing."

Wayne had already shoved a huge forkful in his mouth. "Wow," he mumbled while chewing his food. "This is the best steak and potatoes I've ever had."

I ordered a breaded fish and baked chicken meal, with a pasta salad on the side. It was delicious. I mimicked Wayne and kept shoving loads of it in my mouth. In fact, everyone was gobbling up their food. Our gopher friends were excellent cooks. Everyone decided to get some desert, too. We ordered several cheesecakes, which were sweet and tasty. Willie ate two by himself.

We sat for about an hour around the table, chatting and drinking until James decided it was time to go. Kurt and his maintenance team were still at the bar beside the Devil Bunnies. They were all standing and laughing together, until a few gophers raced in through the front doors with terrified looks on their faces. They were out of breath, panting while hunched over as they stood near the entrance.

James and Willie both jumped out of their seats, and stood up as they stared at these gophers. They both had terrified looks on their faces, and after dealing with the rogue agents, I was certain their startled response was justified.

The three gophers spoke in their language, shouting out loud, and then dozens of patrons freaked out and panicked. Some of them hurried toward the front doors and left the restaurant, while others headed toward the back of the building.

The rest of us stood up and stared at each other. "What the hell is going on?" Wayne asked James and Willie.

"If I had to guess," Dean said, "I'd bet more rogue trash has shown up."

"Are you kidding me?" I wasn't expecting to hear that, but then again we weren't entirely sure about the situation either.

James and Willie headed over to the double doors at the entrance. They stopped dead in their tracks after a huge explosion sounded in the distance from outside. It shook the floor beneath our feet for a few seconds, freaking out everyone in the room.

"What the fuck was that?" Willie shouted out loud. He bolted over to the doors and pushed them both open so we could see outside.

The rest of us hurried over to stand beside our tall furry friend, and although it was getting dark outside, I saw in the distance several small fires and billowing clouds of black smoke rising up from a street not far from our location.

All the music had stopped playing, and the vendors were scurrying to package up their products as fast as they could. The distinct sound of intermittent gunfire could be heard about a block away.

Many gophers raced around us and fled down the three steps to the street, where they ran away from the destruction. All of them seemed terrified and were crying and shouting out.

"Fucking rogue assholes," Willie said. And, to confirm his belief, we saw an agent out in the street holding a long rifle in his arms. He was shooting at our gopher friends, killing as many of them as he could.

Before I could even say anything, Bray summoned a menacing serpent spirit with thick arms, claws, and huge jagged teeth. Her pet appeared right beside the agent. It opened its wide and gapping mouth and then twisted its glowing body. It chomped down on him, sinking its long sharp teeth through his thighs, stomach, and chest, which sprayed a lot of bodily fluids into the air.

Her spirit killed the agent instantly, and he dropped his rifle on the street which was now covered in several pools of his blood.

Willie and James pulled their handguns from their holsters strapped around their thighs. Wayne and I did the same. Dean was without a weapon, but Bray told him to stay close to her. "I'll protect you," she said.

The Devil Bunnies along with Kurt, Reese, and Amp all came over and walked down to the street with the rest of us. All of them had guns in their hands.

"What do we do?" I asked.

"We fight," Wayne said bluntly. He rubbed his hand over my back in a comforting gesture.

Several more agents appeared down the street, and Woofa instantly summoned a huge glowing ring high above them that dropped several gigantic frozen chunks of ice down on them. Each was easily the size of a car, and they crushed the agents, flatting their bodies completely.

Bray summoned more serpents, and each spirit raced out over the street, flying directly toward the remaining agents, where they savagely tore them to pieces as they tried their best to shoot at Bray's pets, but had no effect.

Dozens of gopher people lay dead or injured throughout the streets. Some were crying out for help as they bled and tried their best to get away from the anarchy. Others pulled them to safety, but there were too many to rescue all at once.

"Kurt," James ordered, "you, Reese, and Amp go with the Devil Bunnies and see if you can't help them clear the street. Me and Willie will head over to the other block and see what the hell is going on."

"What about us?" Wayne asked.

"You two stay here with me and Woofa," Bray said.

Dean kept close beside Bray. He looked absolutely frightened. I don't think he was much of a fighter. But, then again, I wasn't either. That was Wayne's department.

The maintenance team and the Devil Bunnies headed out in the street and started helping the wounded victims, but they kept watching just in case they were ambushed by any agents.

Willie and James ran over to the side of a building along another street. They glanced around the corner, and then proceeded down the avenue with guns in hand until we lost sight of them.

I saw so many injured gophers lying out in the street. They were crawling on their hands, crying out, trying to flee from this nightmare as they slowly made their way toward the fronts of stores.

"We need to help them," Wayne told me.

I nodded, completely agreeing with him.

We hurried out in the street and started helping the injured victims, just like Kurt and the others were doing. Bray and Woofa kept working their magic as more rogue agents came down the road from both directions. Her spirits attacked them, biting right through their bodies or ripping off their legs or arms. Woofa cast his destructive magic spells, dropping tons of vehicle-size, icy chunks down on them which completely destroyed the cobblestone streets.

The agents kept firing their rifles or handguns at Bray's glowing spirits. A couple of shots raced by me and Wayne, barely missing us as we crouched down and helped some gophers to sit up against the front of stores. Many of the doors were locked, so all we could do was make sure they were okay before moving on to the next ones while dodging bolts of energy.

Wayne and I stuck close to the sidewalk and the storefronts while helping the victims.

"We're getting kind of far away, aren't we?" I was worried the further we moved from Bray and Woofa that we might get ourselves in trouble.

However, our magical friends were holding off the agents really well. Every spirit was immune to weapons, no matter how powerful the blasts. And, a few serpents gathered around Bray and Woofa to protect them from random shots.

Two agents came rushing toward us, and for some strange reason they weren't firing their weapons. But, Wayne pulled out his handgun and shot at them several times, hitting them in the legs and chests, which soon knocked them both out cold. They collapsed on the sidewalk, lying unconscious.

There were more gophers further down the street, and I rushed off to help them while Wayne kept close behind me.

"Sweetie, we really should get back to Bray and Woofa," he said. "You were right. We can't risk being this far away from our friends."

"We will. Let's just help these gophers over to the sidewalk and then we can head back."

I felt Wayne tap my shoulder and then he pointed at several agents who were walking toward us. We both stood up and stared in shock at who we saw. Leading their pack was a female version of the horned guy that Wayne had killed. She looked similar to Korath, with large dark horns and the same colored skin. She had big breasts and a hateful scowl plastered on her face. Both of her eyes were fixed directly on me and Wayne.

I pulled my handgun from its holster and started firing at them. Wayne did the same but we didn't hit a single person. They ducked or jumped to the side, avoiding every continuous blast we fired.

Wayne and I crouched down along a stairway leading up to the front of a store, but it proved to be no good as far as protecting either of us. A yellow blast of energy hit Wayne directly in his chest and it knocked him on his back. I stared in horror, gazing at the energy as it swirled over his body from head to toe before he lay still and quiet.

I dropped my gun and knelt beside him on my knees, crying my eyes out. I rested my hand on his chest and felt he was still breathing. It must have been some kind of stun effect. Behind me, I saw the horned female rushing toward us with her entourage of troops behind her.

She stopped directly in front of me and stared down at me with a detestable look. "You and your friend are going to suffer immensely for what you did to my brother!"

Before I could even ask or say anything, one of the agents behind her fired off a shot which hit me directly in the chest and knocked me out completely.

13

When I woke up, I was in chains and my entire harness suit had been removed, which left me naked. I was standing, but my back was flat against a concrete wall. The chains were thick and rusty around my ankles and wrists. It looked like I was in a prison. The large room was dimly lit from a few overhead lights, and there was an odd smell lingering in the air, something comparable to vomit or intestines. The ceilings looked dilapidated and old, with lots of holes in the roof.

About twenty feet from me I saw Wayne chained to a flat wooden tabletop that looked like it could tilt back and forth. He was also completely naked.

"Wayne," I called out as quietly as I could. "Are you awake? Can you hear me?"

He raised his head up as much as he could to look at me. They had put a chain around his neck.

"Sweetie, I'm so sorry," he said in a tearful voice. "We should have never left Bray and Woofa."

"It's okay," I said softly, attempting to calm his nerves. "I'm sure James and his crew knows what happened, and they'll be here to rescue us before we realize it."

I felt terrible for him. I had no idea where we were or what was about to happen to either of us. My eyes filled with tears as I watched him trying to move, but the chains around his ankles and wrists were pulled tight and attached to large steel hoops mounted along the floor. His legs were spread far apart, and his arms were too. I could see his armpits.

I noticed three prison cells lining the room on opposite sides, and as I looked around I saw a few dead bodies lying on the floors that seemed to have been there for a month or more. That was probably where the foul stench in the air was coming from.

My heart started to beat rapidly. I felt sick to my stomach. I didn't want Wayne to suffer or die at the hands of these freaks. I felt responsible for getting us into this situation. Why didn't I just stay with Bray and Woofa? I shouldn't have bothered to go further down the street. That was stupid on my part. I felt terrible for what I did.

A tall and wide metal pocket door opened across the room, and the horned female with two male demon agents came inside with her. She was tall and broad, muscular and thick, much like Korath, and she looked capable of beating the shit out of anyone who would piss her off.

Her subordinates were gray skinned with short black horns growing above their temples. They were dressed in harness suits, but she wore a sleeveless black shirt, jeans, and tall brown knee-high leather boots.

The two minions stopped beside another table and loudly dropped several items down on its wooden top. I saw thick pins, long steel needles, a variety of knives, and two objects that resembled battery powered drills. I about vomited after imagining what they were going to do to my sweet man.

The horned female stopped right beside the table Wayne was lying on. She pushed a few levers and the table moved upright with Wayne still plastered to its wooden surface. She gave him a hateful look, and then raised her whopping big fist and struck him right across his face. I saw blood spray out from his jaw and Wayne seemed somewhat dazed after her strike. But, he never cried out, and soon he spit at her which landed on her shirt.

"What the fuck do you want with us?" I bluntly asked. "We were only trying to defend the elshons home world. *You* are the ones who invaded their planet and tried to kill them."

"You murdered my brother!" she screamed out loud. "And, for that, you must both pay the ultimate price. We had surveillance cameras onboard his ship, and I saw what you did to him. I, however, am going to make both of you suffer much more."

She glared at me then raised her fist and slammed it down hard against Wayne's stomach. I watched in horror as he loudly gasped and struggled to breathe, groaning in pain as he tried his best to squirm and move about the surface of the table. I even saw a bit of vomit spew out of his mouth from all the food we had eaten.

I never stopped crying. My face had become soaked with tears. "Please don't hurt him," I begged. My throat began to feel course and dry.

She wickedly laughed and gave me a squinted devilish gaze, which conveyed she wasn't going to listen to anything I said. She walked over to the table where those weapons sat and picked up a long silver knife, much like a hunting blade, about seven inches long. She then walked over to the table Wayne was against and then lowered it back to a flat position. She stood right beside him.

The look in his eyes was of sheer terror. I imagined his heart was racing with fear.

"Don't do this, please," I pleaded to her.

Wayne said nothing. He only projected a hateful look toward this horned bitch.

She held the blade over his chest and then slowly sliced him across both of his pecs. Blood poured out from his hairy chest as he tried to resist crying out, but the sounds soon came. Wayne cringed in agony. He spat at her too.

"Fuck you!" Wayne said. "You can rot in hell, slut!" His eyes were covered with painful tears.

She laughed at him after pulling the knife away. "Maybe you need something more than mere cuts." She glanced over at her minions, then nodded her head toward the bottom of the table.

One of the demon males picked up the drill and stepped over to Wayne. The closer I gazed, it actually resembled a nail gun, and soon the demon raised it, put it against the center of Wayne's right foot and then pulled the trigger.

My handsome man cried out in excruciating pain after the huge nail went halfway through his foot just below his toes. They were thick and long steel rods with sharp pointed tips. I felt dizzy and sicker than I had been. I felt vomit building up in my throat. I couldn't imagine how much pain Wayne was in.

The demon holding the gun laughed, and then shot two more nails through Wayne's other foot. Blood covered the wooden table as it ran down his feet.

"Stop!" I cried out. "Please stop!"

All three of them ignored me and kept focusing on Wayne. The other demon picked up two of the long steel spikes and handed them to the horned female. They were each about twelve inches long, and she leaned over the table and placed one of the spikes near Wayne's inner thigh. Slowly and maliciously, she shoved it in deep, penetrating him probably down to the bone.

He screamed in unbelievable pain, as he jerked and tried to thrash as much as he could while being chained down so tightly.

The horned female then shoved the second spike deep into Wayne's other thigh. The pain must have been overwhelming, because it wasn't long before he passed out. There was so much blood covering his chest and his feet. His legs jerked back and forth.

I gasped in shock as the horned female then picked the knife back up and slowly jabbed it deep inside Wayne's abdomen. After it was inside him, she started to pull it to the side, slicing him open.

But, as I wept heartbreaking tears while watching the love of my life getting butchered before my eyes, a small magical image appeared across the room which caught my attention. It was one of Duluth's and Ramsey's viewing ports they would use to communicate with others.

The horned female kept slowly slicing through Wayne's stomach. She had opened him from one side to the other and my voice was shot. I couldn't beg or plead anymore. But, before I gave up on all hope, a portal opened in the middle of this room and an enormous spirit came charging out from it. It resembled a glowing bear, and it quickly took out the two male demons, slashing at them with its huge paws and savage claws, spraying their blood through the air. It took hold of them with its mouth, biting their shoulders, and violently tossing them across the room where they both hit a brick wall and lay dead.

Our magical friends stepped through the portal followed closely by Willie and James. Our captain and his boyfriend held a rifle in each of their arms. Ramsey projected a magical barrier just in case the horned bitch decided to attack them.

James and Willie stared at Wayne on the table with horrified faces. Blood poured out of him and pooled around his body on the tabletop. I wasn't sure how he could have survived this torture.

Willie snarled and aimed his rifle at the horned female. He fired off several shots, purposely missing her each time so she would step back and cower across the room away from Wayne.

Duluth and Ramsey quickly moved over to Wayne and started projecting their magical healing effects on him, covering him in a radiant blue and white light. Ramsey used some shots of magic which hit every nail and dispersed them to ashes. Blood poured out of every hole along his feet. It made me so sick to watch, but I couldn't take my eyes away from him. I loved him in so many ways, even memories of all the flowers he would bring me on Sundays raced through my mind.

"We killed your agents," James told her in a bitter tone, "And now we're going to take care of you too. All of you rogue assholes are too much of a threat to leave behind. I swear I'm going to hunt all of you down until no one is left breathing."

She laughed. "You are fools if you think eliminating me is going to change anything. There are thousands of us, and we know exactly how to get into this universe." She shook her head and smiled. "You will never stoop us. We will come back to the elshons world and destroy them all."

"Not today you won't," James said. He aimed his rifle and fired off a powerful blast that hit the horned woman directly in the chest. It blew a hole directly through her and she blindly stared ahead before collapsing back on the ground.

Duluth projected some magic toward me which made all the chains dissolve away from around my ankles and wrists. Willie rushed in and caught me before I hit the ground. He lifted me up, holding me like a child in his arms.

I could barely speak. All I kept thinking about was Wayne and if he would be okay. My heart was devastated. He didn't deserve to suffer. I swore to myself from this day on, if he made it through this, I would focus on making his life much happier than it already was.

Ramsey used the same type of magic to release Wayne from his chains. Every piece of metal turned to dust and fell from around his ankles and writs.

Willie held me near the table and I was able to watch as their bright healing cloud of energy repaired Wayne. Slowly it took away his wounds. The slashes from the knife disappeared and the holes they put through his feet did, too. The gashes over his stomach were no more, but my caring and sweet man still laid there unconscious, probably from the blood loss.

I cried while resting the side of my head against Willie's furry arm. My face was soaked in tears.

"He'll be okay," Willie whispered to me. He tenderly massaged my back in an attempt to comfort me as best as he could. He turned us toward James. "Are there any more agents here we need to take care of?"

"I sent a message to Dean to move the ship to this planet and scan for more of them." James sounded sad and withdrawn. I noticed his eyes were shiny with the beginning of tears that never fell. He was probably thinking about how he would react if something like this had happened to Willie.

"Well, if there are more of them, I'm going to blow each of their heads off," Willie said.

The blood covering Wayne's feet, chest, thighs, and abdomen had disappeared and his flesh had been fully restored to its perfect condition. I watched his chest rise and fall, proof that he was breathing.

Ramsey walked over to me and Willie where he cradled my face in his tree-textured hands. His eyes started to glow with hews of green and yellow. "I'm going to gaze inside your mind for a few seconds," he told me. "I want to open a portal back to your room on James's ship."

I nodded and barely mumbled, "Thank you."

He smiled appreciatively and then worked his magic. As he probed my mind, I seemed to have entered a dreamlike state. From my perspective, I seemed to float through James's ship, drifting down the corridors, hovering inside the elevator and much more until I reached the door to our quarters. It opened, and I floated inside our room until I stopped beside our big bed.

Ramsey lowered his hands from my face and then smiled. "I've got it. I can take you both back to your room to recover."

Before I thanked him, he opened a portal beside the table with glowing white edges. I could see our bed and the table beside it. Willie wasted no time. He stepped through it with me in his arms and he gently placed me on top of my bed.

"Thank you," I told him.

"You're welcome," he answered. "I'll grab Wayne and lay him beside you."

I watched Willie step back through the portal and I could see James talking on his pdPhone as he stepped around the room. It was likely Dean about other rogue agents in the area.

Willie carried Wayne through the gateway and my handsome man was still passed out. He gently laid him down in our bed, and then helped me pull back the sheets so we could turn Wayne on his right side. There was no trace of blood on him, but I caught a faint whiff of odor from the room on his skin. It didn't bother me. The fact that he was alive and near me was the greatest gift ever.

Willie headed back to the prison room and the portal shrank before it slowly closed, leaving the room dimly lit from the planet's light that shined through the bedroom windows. I assumed Dean had moved the ship to our coordinates, positioning it near some unknown planet.

Beneath the covers I slipped my arms around Wayne, pulled him close, and then rested the side of my face against his chest. I cried while lying here. I felt thankful for the help from my friends. I imagined being back at our home in Spanish Lake, in our bed together, comfortable and warm. I could feel Wayne breathing and more tears streamed down my face as I whimpered. I raised my head and gave him a kiss then mashed our beards together, which I loved doing with him. It felt incredible, and my heart slowed while holding him in my arms. I scooted up in the bed so I could rest the side of his face against my chest. I gave him some kisses on his bald head.

"I love you," I whispered. "And I'm so glad you're with me. I promise, I'll make your life the greatest it has ever been when we get back home."

I rubbed my left hand over his back and shoulders while brushing my right over his chest. I couldn't even begin to say how good it felt to be touching and holding him like this. I was in heaven and I never stopped weeping. I couldn't imagine my life without Wayne beside me. He is my source of strength and the only man who I've loved so deeply.

I held him closer against my body and felt incredibly relaxed. All bad thoughts had left my mind. Only love filled my heart.

I gave him one more kiss on his head before closing my eyes. My soul was content and at peace. I would sleep here beside him, holding him all night long, the love of my life, the best man ever.

I could hear Wayne snoring when I woke up. The sound pleased me more than anything. I wasn't sure how many hours had passed, but none of the bridge crew had disturbed us while we slept.

My tough guy was turned on his side with his back facing me. I leaned over and gave him a kiss on his shoulder. He stirred a bit, waking up some. He reached behind himself and took hold of my hand so he could pull my arm around him, where he placed my palm against his chest. I cupped the left side of his muscular pec then gently massaged it.

I rested the side of my face against his back.

"Good morning," Wayne whispered.

"Good morning," I said. "Are you feeling better?"

"I had the strangest dream. I dreamt I was being tortured and cut with knives, and my feet were burning like really bad."

I kissed his shoulder. "That wasn't a dream, Wayne. Don't you remember the horned female who was torturing you, and those two demons that drove nails through your feet?"

He immediately slid his right foot out from under the blankets and held it up, where he looked it over thoroughly, turning it from side to side. He flexed his cute toes. "Was that real?" He then flipped over to face me and bounced in the bed a bit.

I put my hand against his handsome face. "It was real. Remember, we were helping those injured gopher people on the streets and then those rogue agents stunned both of us? We woke up in some kind of prison cell. You were lying on the table. We were both naked and then she started torturing you with that knife and those pins."

His face went blank and his eyes veered to the side. I could tell the memories were starting to come back to him. A single tear ran down his face and it touched me deeply. I raised my hand and wiped it away from his cheek.

"Duluth and Ramsey opened a portal to us. Remember? Then Willie and James killed her." I leaned close and gave him a kiss on the side of his face. "They healed you using magic."

He gazed directly in my eyes and then whimpered. "I'm so sorry, Adam." He kissed me and then nuzzled the side of his face against mine.

I smiled. "There's nothing to be sorry about. You know how those assholes operate. If they can't control people then they'll make them suffer."

Wayne scooted closer until our chests pressed together. He fell back against his pillow and wrapped his arms around me where he held me close against his body. He gave me a kiss on my head. "I'm sorry you had to witness that."

I smiled and kissed the thick patch of hair on the center of his chest. "I'm just glad they rescued us and that you made it back in one piece." I slowly slid my hand down his enticing stomach then moved lower where I fondled his manhood, stroking him and brushing my fingers through his hairy bush.

Wayne comfortably sighed before giving me another kiss on my head. "You mean the world to me, Adam. You truly do." He brushed his bearded chin along my forehead. "Nothing would make me happier than making love to you right now."

I moved my face all through his hairy chest, savoring the feel of every thick and long strand against my lips, nose, and cheeks. He was getting a massive erection. "That sounds perfect. But, let's grab a shower first."

He rubbed his hands over my back with another kiss on my head. "Maybe we both should jump in the shower."

I kissed and sucked on his hard nipple a few times. "Maybe I'll give you a special treat in there, handsome."

He squeezed his strong arms around me, delighted from my suggestion.

I slid my legs out from under the covers and then jumped out of bed. Wayne did the same and then followed me to the bathroom while he playfully tapped my butt several times. We peed together, flushed the toilet, and then turned the water on in the shower to let it get to the right temperature.

"You first," he said happily.

I stepped in the shower and there was plenty of space for both of us. One end had a shelf with small hooks below it where two loofahs hung and there were three bottles of body wash above them.

Wayne's chest was soaked with warm water and he looked so much hairier. He hugged me and kissed me, then slipped his hands lower where he massaged my ass. The water from the showerhead kept spraying in my face and it made me laugh. Wayne didn't seem to care. The only thought in his mind was filling me full of his warm love. Both of us were hard and we kept rubbing against each other.

We soaped and then scrubbed each other, then slowly rinsed off. But, before we turned off the water, I got down on my knees and gave my handsome man a special treat. I swallowed all of him and it felt heavenly to feel his enormous dick down my throat. I moved my hands over his hairy thighs and made sure I kept a tight seal around his manhood while sucking it. That was the best way to pleasure a man, in my opinion.

He rested his hands on top of my head. "Damn, Adam, that feels incredible. You are so good at doing that."

I used my right hand to fondle his boys while I kept sucking on him. A few times, he held my head tight and force-fed me his erection, slamming it in, and then slowly working it down my throat over and over again.

"Oh, baby," he uttered, "We need to get back to the bed so I can make love to you nice and hard."

I stood up and rubbed my hands along his sides and arms. He kept kissing me and our dicks slid along each other several times. "Okay, let's get out of here."

Wayne opened the shower door while I turned off the water. He had already dried himself off and was lying out in the bed before I even stepped out of the shower.

I laughed. "You're done that fast!"

"Come on in here, baby!" he said. "I'm ready to make you groan and moan."

He made me laugh while I dried myself off. I turned off the bathroom lights and then stood in the doorway where I stared at him on the bed. He was on his back slowly stroking his erection. It looked super hard and he wiggled it back and forth with his hand, enticing me to come over and sit on it. He was holding a bottle of lube in his other hand.

I walked over to the bed. "Where'd you get the lube from?"

"I found it in the bathroom cabinet," he said. "You look so fucking sexy, Adam. Your tattoos really turn me on. It's not going to take me long to get off."

"Me, neither," I told him. "You look hot laying here and playing with your dick."

Wayne enjoyed it when I sat on top and rode him. So I climbed on the bed, spread my legs over his thighs, sat down on my knees, and then worked my ass down on his beefy and thick cock. He had already greased it up, and he helped me spread my cheeks. I slowly reached behind myself so I could guide it inside me, moving down until all ten inches were inside me.

I leaned down so I could kiss my handsome man.

"You are so nice and tight," Wayne whispered. "You feel so good, Adam."

While I was hunched over, he was able to pound my ass several times nice and hard, forcing himself in and out of me until I felt his hot load fill me. He had braced his feet against the mattress and squirmed several times as he got off. It felt so good it gave me shivers. I kissed him passionately, shoving my tongue deep inside his mouth and he did the same to me.

I sat up and rubbed my hands over his hairy chest. It felt incredible to feel his muscles and fur. "My turn," I told him.

He nodded happily and ran his tongue over his lips. "I want to taste you, sweetie."

I chuckled. "It's probably going to be a heavy load."

Wayne smiled. "I'll take every drop, babe."

He pulled out of me so I could scoot up closer and sit in front of his face. He took all of me in his mouth, swallowing every inch over and over again. I wasn't as well endowed as he was, but it still felt amazing. Wayne could give head just as good as I could.

"Oh, that feels wonderful." I moved my fingers down the side of his cheek and then rubbed them along his beard. "You do that very well."

Having his mouth full, he tapped my butt cheeks, signaling how much he was enjoying himself. He then placed both of his hands against my stomach and pushed me back a few inches.

"You taste so good, Adam." He raised his head and buried his face in my bush, sniffing and working his lips through every hair.

I started stroking myself and he looked eager to swallow my load. It didn't take long for me to get off. I moved forward and aimed right for his mouth. He stuck out his tongue and it wasn't long before I filled his entire mouth with a warm and tasteful treat.

As promised, he swallowed every drop.

"Wow," I said. "That was amazing. You treat me so well, handsome."

He nodded a few times with his eyes wide open. He looked so happy.

I lifted my leg over his, and then dropped down beside him where I cuddled next to his muscular body. He slid his arm around me and I lightly moved my hand over his chest and stomach. He always enjoyed my soft touch, and I enjoyed putting a smile on his face.

"What do you think we should do now that they've taken care of the rogue agents?" I asked him.

Wayne sighed. He sounded uncertain or indifferent. "I guess we should probably head back home, if that's alright with you."

I kissed his nipple. "I'd be happy to go back home with you. Think how many phone calls we've probably missed from family and friends."

We laughed while thinking about that.

He held me close. "I think I've seen enough of the ship and different worlds. Don't get me wrong, it would be awesome to come back some day and hang out with everyone again. But, I just feel like I want to go back home and be with you." He kissed my head. "I love you, Adam. You're the best thing in my world, and I want to spend some time with you having sex, watching movies while drinking wine, or hanging out in the backyard gazing at the stars. I want *you* to be happy, nothing more."

I wiped away a tear from my eye. Wayne could be such a sweet and caring man. He always touched my heart with his words and actions.

"Then let's see if James can take us home," I said. "They shouldn't be too sad about us leaving. I mean, they can come back to us anytime they want to. Plus, they said we could have a pdPhone so we could call them whenever we wanted to."

Wayne rubbed his hand over my back. "You feel so good, sweetie. I don't want to take anymore risks that might get one of us killed. I don't want you to go through anything like that ever again, or me. It's not fair to either of us."

I scooted further up along the bed so I could face Wayne and gaze into his beautiful dark eyes. "I completely agree with you," I told him. "Let's make happy times for both of us."

We shared some kisses and slipped our tongues in each other's mouths a few times.

"So, I'll break the news to James and his crew," Wayne told me in a soft tone. "They shouldn't be too surprised, don't you think."

I raised my hand so I could feel Wayne's beard. I never got tired of running my fingers through its fullness. I nodded. "They'll understand."

He gave me a few more kisses before I scooted down a few inches so I could rest the side of my face against his strong body. "You feel so good, sweetie," he said. "I always love holding you in my arms."

"You're the greatest man ever," I told him, after I kissed his hairy chest.

We cuddled in bed for about twenty minutes before deciding it was time to get up, get dressed, and then head up to the bridge. Since we lost our harness suits we put on our shorts and T-shirts, socks and sneakers again. I don't think we had worn them since they'd been washed. It was getting difficult to remember one day from the next, at least for me.

"Are you ready, sexy man?" I asked.

Wayne smiled before approaching me with a kiss. "Lead the way."

As soon as our bedroom door opened, Wayne rushed toward me and playfully tapped his hand across my behind. His affections made me smile. After the doors closed, we held hands and proceeded down the hallway to the elevator. Once inside, Wayne tapped the necessary buttons and we started to rise through the ship with a couple of turns.

"I'm going to miss a lot of this ship and the friends we've made," Wayne confessed. But he sounded happy.

"Me too." I raised his hand then kissed the back of it. He had such strong and manly hands. I loved them.

Once the bridge doors opened and we stepped inside, everyone happily gazed at us. In fact, Willie came over and gave both of us a warm hug. "Glad to see you two are back with us. We missed you."

"Yes, we did," Bray said. She had come over and gave us hugs, too. She stood as tall as me and Wayne.

Woofa and Dean both looked pleased to see us, and so did the Devil Bunnies.

"Welcome back," Mortenna said. "Those rogue agents had no idea what they were getting in to when they messed with you guys."

Dean nodded, agreeing with her. "That's for sure."

James stood by the main holographic display with his arms crossed over his chest. "So, are you two ready to leave yet? We'd love for you to stay, but I can understand if you both want to leave after everything that's happened."

Wayne shrugged and took a moment to answer our captain. "Well, Adam and I talked about it and we both think we'd like to go back home to Earth."

Everyone seemed suddenly shocked and surprised. I heard a few sighs, too.

"Now we're not saying we don't like being on board your ship," Wayne added. He held his hands up to convey that we did enjoy being here. "We've had a really great time and we love seeing all of you. We just feel a bit weighed down by all the situations and stuff. It's a lot different than watching a movie, that's for sure."

Willie gave Wayne a few gentle taps across his back before heading over to stand beside James at the center of the bridge.

"We completely understand," James said. He sounded as though he understood our predicament.

"Well, we're going to miss you both," Bray told us. Her eyes were glossy with the building of a few sad tears.

"Definitely give them a pdPhone so we can keep in contact with each other," Dean said. "We've got several spares over here in a drawer."

"That would be perfect," Wayne said.

"So, are we going to have a fancy party before you two leave?" Neese and her fellow bunnies were all standing together with their heads tilted and a single brow raised waiting for our response.

"Hell yeah we can have a party," Willie said out loud with gusto. "We can cook some food and have it down in the dining area."

Everyone liked his idea. They all seemed intrigued.

"Are the rogue agents all gone from the area?" Wayne asked.

James sighed, and so did Willie. "We've detected a few small ships shifting throughout this galaxy," James told us. "But, overall, I think any major threats from them are not going to happen for quite a while."

"With so many of their agents getting killed, I doubt they'll stir up any more problems," Dean added. He kept pushing buttons and analyzing his readouts. He then pulled up a view of our galaxy on the main holographic display.

Willie pointed at three minor dots. "See them," he asked. "They're far off from any habitable worlds. Dean will keep monitoring them for any malicious activity."

"So far," Dean said, "They're merely drifting through space."

"Good," Woofa said bluntly. "Hopefully those dumbasses will stay away and stop stirring up so much trouble."

"So, when are we having this party?" Bray clasped her hands together in an excited way. The wide smile on her face was priceless.

Willie stood with his huge hands locked around his waist. "We can start as soon as I cook some food for us to eat!" He wore blue jeans and a brown leather vest he had left opened. The difference between his human side and his growda ha'tar side was clearly visible.

"We can help," Mortenna said. Her and the other Devil Bunnies walked over to Willie and stopped right beside him. They each showed him some appreciation by gliding their hands down his large furry arms. He towered over them all.

"Thanks, ladies," Willie told them. He sounded delighted from their attention. The four of them headed out through the main doors, then turned down the hallway.

Bray gave each of us a pat on our shoulders before moving over to Woofa at a workstation. As soon as she stood next to him, she lifted two harnesses up and showed them to me and Wayne. "You guys can have these since you're other ones got stolen," Bray said.

We both smiled. "Thank you," I said. "We really enjoy wearing them."

She nodded happily. Woofa gave both of us a wink.

James came over to stand beside us as we gazed at the holographic image of our galaxy. "I've got a surprise for you two when we get back to your planet," James told us.

"What kind of surprise?" I asked.

"You'll see when we get there," James said. "I think both of you will really enjoy it."

"Thanks for coming to our rescue." Wayne sounded humble. "I don't remember much of what happened, but Adam told me you took out the horned female." He reached over and patted James's back a couple of times. "You and Willie are an awesome couple."

James smiled. "He's my big loveable bear, that's for sure. I can't imagine not having him around. I enjoy every furry inch of him."

"I feel the same way." Wayne slipped his arm around my waist and pulled me close against his body. He kissed my cheek and my heart melted beside my beautiful man.

I lifted my arm then patted his tummy.

James walked away. He headed back over to his captain's workstation where he pushed a few buttons and flipped some switches.

"Looks like the rogue agents are taking things carefully," Dean informed us. "They don't seem to be stirring up any trouble at all."

"Good," James said. "Hopefully, they've learned their lesson."

Bray and Woofa both shook their heads. In the back of my mind, I assumed there would be more problems in the future. Hopefully, they would call us.

Wayne pointed at Dean. "You said something about extra pdPhones?"

"Oh, yeah, I forgot about that." Dean walked over to a different workstation, pulled open a drawer, and then took out a phone. He brought it over to us and handed it to Wayne. "Here you go."

"Thanks." Wayne looked it over. "I guess it works just like any other cell phone."

Dean nodded. "Just push the button and you can start talking. I've put all of our numbers in it so you can contact any of us. Speak someone's name and it'll connect you to their phone. It's super easy."

Wayne looked excited. He slipped our new phone inside the pocket of his athletic shorts then gave me a kiss. "Now we can relax on our couch back home and talk to them whenever we want," he whispered.

I smiled while giving him a wink. I reached around with my left arm and squeezed his behind a couple of times. "You're a wonderful man."

"So are you, sweetie." He leaned in and gave me a much longer kiss.

"So I guess we need to wait for the party to start," Wayne said. He had a huge grin on his face, obviously excited.

Bray, Dean, and James all nodded. They were all eager for some fun time too.

14

We stayed on the bridge for about an hour. Bray and Woofa showed both of us how to use the workstations, and then Dean taught us how to pull up details on the main holographic display, which included rogue signatures. Wayne got excited as he pushed all kinds of buttons and flipped switches. I could tell he felt in charge for a few minutes. It made me smile seeing him having fun.

Willie's voice came over the intercom. "We're all ready down here. You guys can come and join us."

James was the first to walk over to the bridge doors. They opened and he stepped out in the hallway. He patted his stomach a few times. "Come on, everybody. I'm hungry."

The five of us followed him to the elevator. After its door closed, James pushed some buttons which started us moving down through the ship.

"Is your dining area big and spacious," Wayne asked.

"Oh, it's roomy, for sure," Woofa said. "If we were in the Expanse we could open the bay doors and get a nice view of stars, nebulas, or a planet."

"That would be nice." I know I sounded intrigued. Too bad space in our galaxy was lethal and not breathable like theirs was.

As soon as the elevator stopped, we hopped out in the long white hallway then proceeded to the dining area. I was anxious to be in the area. I could tell Wayne was, too. He kept touching me along my arm or playing with my hand. His level of joy and satisfaction was at an all-time high. I was pleased to see him like this, especially after what those agents had put him through.

We stopped in front of a large pocket door and I faintly heard music playing from inside the room. James reached over and pushed a button on the control panel and the doors opened, disappearing within the walls.

The six of us stepped forward and gawked at all the work Willie and the Devil Bunnies had done.

"This looks incredible!" Wayne said. He and I gazed around the mess hall, admiring all the decorations while taking whiffs of all the food they had laid out. It smelled wonderful.

The Devil Bunnies were finishing up some decorations. They had tied red, blue, and orange streamers along the high ceiling, and all were twisted so they looked more exciting. They had blown up balloons, some of which hung from strings, while others lay on the ground for us to mildly kick around.

There were six tables, three on each side, and a restaurant-style bar along the left side of the room. I could see the bay doors Woofa had mentioned. They were large and wide. I'm sure we would have gotten a great view of their universe. I noticed several speakers positioned around the room in the corners. Dance music played with a hip-shaking beat.

We had brought along our harnesses suits too, and laid them down on a table.

Willie approached James, leaned over, and then gave his captain a warm and caring hug. "How's it look?"

James surprised us all. He actually stepped to the side and tapped Willie's behind a few times. "Looks great, big bear. You, Mortenna, Skiss, and Neese did a lot of work in a small amount of time."

"Well, we wanted to show Wayne and Adam how much we care," Neese said happily, as she stroked one of her horns above her temple. She and her two companions had pulled down the zippers of their uniforms, exposing more of their cleavage.

One of the tables looked like a buffet. It had large trays sat out with several types of pasta dishes. There were vegetables, a mix of rice, cookies and cake, steaks and potatoes, all beside plenty of bottles of booze and other non-alcoholic beverages.

"Dig in!" Willie raised his furry black arm and invited us to start eating.

James gave him another playful tap across his rear and then kindly allowed me and Wayne to go first.

"Thank you," I told James. I brushed my hand down Willie's arm as I passed by them.

"You first, sweetie." Wayne paused after picking up a china plate so I could go first.

I playfully tickled my fingers over his stomach and then dished out a huge spoonful of pasta on my plate. It had pieces of meat mixed throughout it with red sauce and veggies. I picked up a piece of steak and filled the rest of my plate with some delicious smelling potatoes. I could tell Wayne was eyeballing the steak. He loved a good piece of meat, and not just mine.

After Wayne filled his plate, we both poured ourselves some drinks (something that looked like red Kool-Aid), and then we sat down at one of the tables. Wayne smiled and pulled my chair out for me, and then sat next to me. There was plenty of space for everyone else to join us at the table. They were long and had eight chairs on both sides.

I turned around when I heard the door open up. Kurt, Reese, and Amp entered the dining room.

"We figured it was time to chow down!" Kurt said in his scruffy voice.

All three of them got in line and filled their plates. There was plenty of food for seconds and thirds, so all of us would be stuffed by the time we were done.

The maintenance team joined us at our table and we all scooted closer together so we could talk without shouting. Willie raised his pdPhone and adjusted the volume of the music, so it wouldn't be too much of a distraction.

"How did you make all this food so fast?" I asked. It was delicious. My mouth kept watering as I shoved forkfuls in it.

"We have a stocked kitchen behind the counter," Willie said. "We usually have meals ready so any of us can just heat something up and then chow down on it."

Wayne raised his glass and then glanced at everyone sitting around the table. "Well, I would like to thank everyone here for welcoming us aboard and for this great meal. All of you are amazing people, and I appreciate everything you've done for me and Adam, especially saving my ass from those rogue jerks."

"It's been a pleasure having you two around," James said, with a smile.

Everyone raised their glass then courteously toasted me and Wayne. I could see a great amount of love and appreciation coming from their faces. It pleased me immensely. I reached under the table and massaged Wayne's thigh. I couldn't get enough of his muscular legs. It put a smile on his face and then he wiggled his fingers over the back of my hand in a tender show of affection.

"So, what do you all plan on doing after me and Adam go back home?" Wayne shoved a large piece of steak in his mouth. "You guys going to hunt down more rogue agents?"

"Most likely," Willie answered. He was consumed with the steak and potatoes too. "We can't let them flood your universe with their bullshit. Who knows what crazy shit they would do to your world, or any others?"

James lifted his hand and rubbed it down Willie's arm. "We'll continue to block them and eliminate them if need be. Dean is an expert at tracking their signatures."

Dean laughed a bit. "It comes from your awesome ship, James. You've got a ton of advanced equipment and scanners. It's really impressive."

"Well, you can thank my arms merchants for constantly upgrading my stuff," James said. "They live in the Expanse and they love coming aboard whenever they've got new programs or components to try and sell to me."

"What are their names?" I really didn't need to know, but I was curious.

"The short demon is called Finger Pop and his tall android companion is called Shake," Willie explained.

I raised my glass in a celebratory gesture. "Here's to Shake and Finger Pop! I hope they have a load of upgrades for you when you get back home." Everyone happily took a drink from their glass.

We sat for a long time and listened to stories about the Expanse and all the wonders it had to offer. Kurt dropped some maintenance tales once in a while, and Willie talked about his furry bear people while all of us kept going back to the buffet to fill our plates.

"It would nice to see the Expanse someday," Wayne said. He sounded somewhat saddened from all the amazing details everyone kept talking about.

"You can always contact us," Dean reminded me and Wayne. "We can shift to your planet pretty fast. It won't take long for us to flood your home with a party."

"And, we'd be more than happy to show you both some breathtaking sites from our universe," Bray added. She smiled at both of us.

Woofa reached over and raised Bray's hand where he gently kissed the back of it. Her face lit up with warm and tender feelings.

Willie ate a bunch of food and so did the maintenance team. Amp, the reptilian, focused on different pieces of meat. He enjoyed every slice he tossed in his long, scale-covered mouth.

"So, is there anything you two would like to see before we take you home?" Willie asked.

I shook my head. So did Wayne. "We have to be back at work on Monday," I told them. "I hope you all don't mind us leaving so soon."

"Not at all," Bray said. "You're welcome to come back anytime. Like Dean said, give us a call and we'll come and pick you both up."

"Of course if we're in the Expanse, you'll have to leave a voicemail message," Dean told us. "Our pdPhones can't communicate between universes."

"Oh, we'll definitely call you guys," Wayne said with excitement. "It'd be nice to travel to some popular stars I like to gaze at during the night."

"We can take you wherever you'd like to go." Willie held up his furry hand and gave Wayne a thumbs-up. "There's just one important question that still needs to be answered."

"What's that?" James asked.

Mortenna jumped in with a silly remark. "How much sex Wayne and Adam are going to have once they get back home?" She had a wicked grin on her face.

We all laughed at her comment.

"Or how much they're going to miss us," Bray happily added.

"No, no, no," Willie said. He flapped his hand through the air and dismissed everyone's jokes. "The important question is *who* is going to do all of these dishes?"

Everyone sat quietly for a moment and then exploded with laughter.

"Let's *all* help clean the table then wash the plates and pans," Bray suggested.

"Sounds good," James said.

Each of us got up and helped clear the table as well as the buffet table. The kitchen was roomy and it had a deep, double-sided sink. The tall water faucet was removable from its handle, so you could spray soap off a lot of dishes while they sat in the sink. There were also two gigantic refrigerators sitting next to each other with silver doors, and plenty of cabinets were hung around the kitchen to shove the plates and pans back in.

The maintenance team kept dawdling and acting anxious. Clearly, they had some jobs to do, so they each gave me and Wayne handshakes.

"It was nice meeting you guys," I told them.

"Likewise," Kurt said.

"Good luck and we hope to see you both again sometime soon," Amp said. His reptilian hand felt rough and textured. He stood about a foot and a half taller than me or Wayne, probably a bit over seven feet tall.

"Hope you both have a goodtime back at home," Reese told us. He was shorter and tended to be quiet, though he always had a smile on his face. A cheerful guy, for sure.

They left the kitchen along with the Devil Bunnies who simply waved their goodbyes to us. Call me crazy, but I think something was going on between them and the maintenance team. I wasn't sure if they were having sex or just hanging out with each other, but Kurt patted Mortenna's back a few times when they left the kitchen. Reese kept close to Skiss, and Amp seemed attracted to Neese. Friends or lovers, it was hard to say. I just wished good times for them all.

James stopped beside us after most of the dishes were washed. "So are you two ready for my surprise?"

I noticed smiles suddenly appearing around the room. I could tell everyone knew what our captain was talking about.

"Yeah," Wayne replied. "We're ready for some fun."

Bray and Woofa both chuckled. "You're going to enjoy it so much," she said. "It's incredible."

She sparked my curiosity. I couldn't imagine what James was going to show us.

"Dean, will you move the ship to the coordinates I gave you earlier," James asked.

Dean nodded while smiling. "Sure, I'll head up to the bridge and take us there." He left the room with a delighted look on his blue face.

Bray came over and gave both of us a warm hug. She even gave us each a quick kiss on our cheeks. I could see the beginnings of tears in her eyes. As soon as I noticed hers mine started too. "Be safe, in all ways," she told us.

"You too," Wayne said.

Woofa came over and gave us hugs. "Call us anytime. We can pick you up and take you on a tour around your universe."

Wayne smiled and nodded his head several times. "You can count on it. A trip would be awesome."

Bray and Woofa held hands while they exited the kitchen and made their way back up to the bridge.

Willie came over, leaned down, and then gave us hugs. I purposely brushed my hand down the length of his furry arm. Every hair felt like silk. His bear limbs were incredibly smooth. "I'll wait for you guys down in the cargo bay." He winked at us. "We can use the bikes to take you back home, once we get there."

James gave his boyfriend a scrutinizing stare. Perhaps, Willie had said too much? I wasn't sure, but they both smiled at each other as Willie left the room.

"Follow me," James said.

We picked up our harnesses and then followed James out of the kitchen and dining area, until we walked down the hallway to the elevator where we all three stepped inside. James pushed a few buttons and we started moving.

"So what are you going to show us?" I was curious. I knew Wayne was too.

James let out a mild laugh. "I don't want to spoil it for you guys. Trust me. You both are going to enjoy it immensely."

The elevator came to a stop, but when the doors opened, we weren't presented with a hallway. A round and wide room with a domed top appeared before us with a flat, dark floor, and the only thing present was a waist-high, vertical black pole at the center of the room. It had a few glowing buttons across its top. The walls were an odd color of metal. They looked like they were covered in thick brown gravy and it was slowly moving, like after you cook it too long on the stove and then tilt the pan back and forth.

We followed James out to the center of this room and we stood around the upright pole.

"I'm going to leave you both alone so you can enjoy your time together," he told us. He pointed at the control buttons. "When the green one starts flashing, push it. You'll see what I'm talking about after that. Take as long as you want. There's no rush. Willie and I will be down in the cargo bay making out while we're waiting for you. Have you both noticed how frisky he's been lately?"

Wayne and I both cheerfully nodded with raised brows, confirming James's observation.

"So are you taking us home after whatever this is we're going to experience?" I asked.

"Yes," James said. "I don't want you two to be late for work Monday morning." We both laughed at his comment.

Wayne moved in and surprised our captain with a friendly hug. He held James for a long moment. "Thanks for saving me," Wayne said.

"My pleasure," James replied. He patted Wayne's back a few times. James stood about five or six inches shorter than us. He briefly rested the side of his face against Wayne's chest. "Me and Willie will always be there for you both. I promise. In fact, I consider you guy's part of my crew." He leaned back and looked directly in Wayne's eyes. "You're just on an away mission for right now, but you'll be back soon."

They parted and then James gave me a nice, tight hug. He then walked over to the elevator, stepped inside, and then waved at us before the door closed.

Wayne stepped over to the control buttons and raised his hand over them.

"He said wait for it to start flashing," I said.

"I'll wait." He lowered his hand and scrutinized all the buttons on the pole. "I'm just curious about what's going to happen."

I shook my head. "I guess we'll find out shortly."

Wayne smiled and then moved closer to me so he could kiss me. His lips felt wonderful against mine. I rubbed my hand over his chest and stomach. His defined muscles calmed my heart and mind. Touching him always proved to be incredible.

From the corner of my eye, I noticed the green button began to flash.

"It's time," I told Wayne.

He turned his head and looked down at its glowing, bright green light. "Can I push it?"

I shrugged and gave him a goofy grin. "Sure you can. Let's see what happens."

Wayne reached over and slowly pushed the green button. Instantly all the walls and floor vanished, leaving only the pole at the center of the room. Outer space surrounded us with a high-orbit view of Earth directly in front of us. The sun sat further away to the side, and the moon lay in the distance.

"Holy shit," I blurted out while gazing around. "I didn't expect this to happen!"

Wayne grabbed hold of my hand to calm me down, and I could hear a joyful sadness in his voice. "It's amazing, isn't it?"

He walked ahead a few steps, dragging me along until he stopped and we stood before our home.

The view of Earth was breathtaking. We were above it, but it was close. Stars shimmered in the background and there were even a couple of constellations I recognized. The sun was bright but not annoying in any way. Through a variety of different clouds, I could see the eastern edge of the United States. It looked like evening was approaching where we lived. The Midwest was slowly getting covered by darkness as we watched our planet slowly turn and drift through space.

Wayne stood behind me. He wrapped his arms around my body with his chin resting over my shoulder, so we could both watch together.

"Do you hear that?" I asked.

Wayne took a moment to listen, and then he nodded. "It's soothing."

Music had started to play. The volume was low, but we heard a drawn out tone with subtle piano keys softly covering its baseline. It matched perfectly to the view of Earth and sounded like the music Wayne would play while he sat out in the backyard gazing up at the night sky.

Wayne kissed my cheek. "We're home, Adam. Our journeys over."

From the sound of his voice I could tell he was weeping. He sniffled a few times. My stargazer clearly felt touched by this profound moment of standing before Earth.

"It's beautiful." I lowered my head and kissed his hairy forearm since he had it across my chest but close to my chin.

Earth appeared large before us. Every detail showed wonderfully as it slowly turned. Wayne pointed at where Missouri was located. "That's where we live." He kissed my cheek again. "This view is incredible. I never thought I'd be here above our planet, gazing down on it with such calm music playing in the background."

"Can you imagine if our race stopped all the petty bickering and focused on global issues and space travel," I mentioned. "Think how wonderful life would be, and how our species would advance overall."

Wayne rested the side of his face against mine while holding me close against him. I could hear him breathing, and I got a bit misty-eyed knowing we were going home together and that soon I would be cuddling beside him in bed.

"That would be an incredible way to live our lives," Wayne whispered beside my ear. "Maybe we should ask James to fly his ship over the White House so everybody gets a nice view and knows that aliens really exist."

I chuckled at his comment. "Somehow, I think that would only freak people out even more than they already are."

"You're probably right, Adam." He kissed my cheek again.

"Do you think the ship is in orbit right now?" I asked.

Wayne nodded. "It probably is, and I'm sure James has some way of disguising it from any observers down on the planet."

I rubbed my hands along his forearms then sighed happily. Wayne felt good and I could have stood here forever with him holding me in his arms. My heart was thankful that he survived and my life would continue with the best man ever for a long, long time.

"Think we should make our way down to the cargo bay?" I wasn't trying to rush us or anything like that.

"Well, maybe we should give James and Willie a few more minutes so they can finish making out with each other." Wayne laughed a bit before nibbling on the edge of my ear. He swirled his tongue along its edge, showing me an abundant amount of love.

We stood together and admired Earth for maybe thirty minutes. The entire Midwest area had turned dark while we watched, and I assumed they would shift the ship back to Spanish Lake and take us home on their flying motorcycles.

"I'm guessing this will end exactly like it started," I said.

Wayne kissed my cheek. "Oh, I don't see an end to this. We'll come back someday, and think how excited everyone will be to see us again. I'm sure they couldn't get enough of your shapely butt."

He thrust his hips twice against my behind and it made me laugh. "You're so sweet and silly."

"It's all for you," he whispered beside my ear. "I'm never letting you go, Adam. You make me happy in so many ways. When I'm with you my soul feels complete and my heart is content."

I turned around so I could give him a kiss while inside this room, while we stood among the stars with Earth just a few dozen feet from us. What better place to enjoy a passionate moment with my loveable stargazer.

Wayne slipped his hand down my stomach and tenderly massaged my crotch. I'm sure he could feel my hardness, so I reciprocated and his had grown hard, too.

He giggled. "You'd better stop before I start leaking and get you all wet." Wayne tended to precum a lot.

I gave him a smile then cradled his face with my hands. "I love you so much, Wayne. You're such a great man, and I'm so thankful for having you in my life."

He leaned closer to give me a kiss. "I love you too. My life would be so dull without you in it, Adam."

We hugged each other for a few minutes, savoring the feel of our hands over our backs while gazing at Earth from the corner of our eyes. Without warning, Wayne pushed the green button on the vertical pole and the room changed back to its original appearance.

"Let's go home, sweetie," he said.

15

Wayne pushed the appropriate buttons after we stepped in the elevator, and it took us to the hallway that led to the cargo bay. We checked and made sure we had both of our harnesses and all of our phones as we walked along, including the pdPhone Dean gave us. We held hands while walking down the corridor.

"So did you have a good time?" Wayne asked me.

I raised his hand and planted a kiss along the back of it. "I had a fantastic time, especially with Duluth and Ramsey. We really need to go back to their world and take a dip in their hot tub again."

"You know we could get one of our own," Wayne suggested.

I squeezed his hand. "Then we could have our own fun in the water."

"My thoughts exactly." He laughed then raised *my* hand so he could give me a kiss along its back.

We reached the cargo bay and the wide doors slid open, revealing Willie and James who were standing near a row of motorcycles. They both looked at us with happy faces.

"You guys ready?" Willie asked.

We both nodded, but I could tell Wayne was feeling a bit saddened by our departure. His face showed clear signs of his emotional state as he glanced around the room. I imagined he was trying to record this moment in his mind for later times.

James used his pdPhone to adjust the lighting. He dimmed the overhead lamps considerably and then opened the main bay door. "We're right above the lake where we met you guys at."

I glanced out the opened door and saw trees in the distance as well as lights coming from people's homes. It was late at night and the park was closed. The only people that might have seen us would be anyone that lived along the edge of the park, if they decided to take a midnight stroll through the woods.

I could smell the scent of trees and the lake from below us. A mild breeze blew through the bay and saturated the air with several pleasing and familiar aromas.

Willie walked over to the largest bike. He sat down on it and then signaled with his furry hand for Wayne to come over and take a seat behind him. James did the same, and I followed so I could sit behind our captain. They both started their bikes, revving them a bit before they both flipped a switch which made the engines run quiet.

"Here we go," James said.

I slipped my arms partially around his waist then watched as Wayne held on to Willie's wide hips as best as he could. We both had slipped our harnesses over our shoulders, but we didn't lock the center piece to the straps.

Both bikes slowly rose into the air and they maneuvered them over to the door, until we moved out in the night sky. It was clear with plenty of stars shining above us. It felt strange to be home while flying over the still waters of Spanish Lake, considering everything Wayne and I had experienced and seen. Would life still be the same for us? Would our everyday jobs become boring, knowing we could have stayed on a spaceship and explored the vastness of space? I guess we'd find out soon enough.

But, the one thing that stood out the most came from within me. No matter how dull or mundane our lives might turn out to be, I would always be thankful for having Wayne beside me. No man has been more caring to me than he has. He soothes me with his touch, and warms my heart with every kiss.

I smiled while glancing over at him behind Willie. He was having some minor issues while trying to hold on, but he managed to do so without falling off. He even giggled a few times. I could hear him.

They moved us closer to the surface of the lake and we ended up probably six feet from the water, slowly gliding over it, engines quiet and still, until we slowed before reaching the shoreline right where we were originally picked up.

James and Willie expertly moved both bikes around trees and over dense gatherings of bushes and shrubs, until they landed in a small clearing right beside a path I recognized and had walked along many times before.

After the motorcycles landed, Wayne and I hoped off. James and Willie used their boots to push large kickstands against the ground, and then they both lifted their legs over the seats and stood beside us.

We stood and stared at each other for a brief moment.

"Looks like a nice evening," Willie said. He smiled at us. James stood beside him and Willie rested his gigantic hand on James's shoulder. "How far do you live from here?"

"Just down a few trails," I answered. "Our house is right near the edge of the woods."

"Sounds like a nice and quiet area," James said.

"It's a great place," Wayne told them. "Maybe the next time you see Duluth and Ramsey they can open a portal and you guys can all come over for some drinks and food."

They both nodded with abundant smiles. "That would be nice," James said. "And, we can bring everyone, including the Devil Bunnies and the maintenance team."

I started to cry a bit while thinking about all of our experiences and new friends. Wayne wrapped his arms around me, comforting me the way he always did. He cradled my head, holding my face against his chest.

"Don't be sad, sweetie," Wayne whispered. "You guys will come back, right?"

Willie came over and patted my back. "We'll definitely come to visit you two. You guys are great and fun, plus, I could use some drinks and food. So could James."

James laughed. "Like Dean said, call us and we can come over anytime. It's not a problem. I'm sure we're going to be in your galaxy for a long time chasing down those assholes."

I stood up and wiped away my tears. "You guys promise you'll come back." I know I sounded all emotional and sad.

Willie grabbed hold of me and gave me a hug. "We will. Push all the bad thoughts out of your mind, Adam. Enjoy your life and keep in mind that you guys will have to come aboard our ship again. We'd love to have you both back, and think of all the new and exciting places we can show you."

"Maybe you guys could take us across to the Expanse sometime," Wayne said.

They both nodded happily, and James spoke. "We'd be happy to take you guys to our universe. There's a lot of amazing things to see. You guys will be blown away. And, outer space isn't lethal like it is here. It's no different than a cool, autumn evening."

I walked over and gave James a warm hug. I held him close, appreciating all they had done for us and then Wayne did the same.

"This isn't goodbye," Willie said.

"I know, I know," I said. "I'm just going to miss you all so much."

Wayne slipped his arm around me and added a kiss on the side of my head. "We should let them get back up to their ship before someone sees it."

I waved to my friends as they hopped back on their motorcycles. Willie blew us both a kiss and James gave us a farewell salute before they started to rise through the trees and ascend into the night sky. Wayne and I watched them move through the sky until they slowed down and moved back inside the ship. The cargo bay door closed. After a few seconds, a flash of bright light appeared with a mild sound of thunder as their ship shifted away.

"You okay?" Wayne rubbed his hand over my back several times.

I nodded with a couple of sniffles. "Yeah, I'm fine. Let's go home."

We held hands while taking our time to walk along familiar paths that were bordered by dense patches of bushes, trees, and the occasional clearing where we could see the lake in the distance.

Wayne squeezed my hand several times showing his compassion in regard to the end of our journey. He sometimes nudged the side of my arm in an attempt to make me laugh. I wasn't feeling terrible or withdrawn, only a bit sad. But, in my heart, I knew Wayne would be able to cheer me up. He tended to be very strong as opposed to myself. I tended to let emotions overwhelm me at times.

We finally reached the end of the trail, and I could see our house beyond several tall trees. Seeing our home made me smile and I lifted Wayne's hand and kissed the back of it. The back porch light was still on, but I knew no one had entered our house. Our cars sat out front, so I'm sure the sight of them would have deterred any strangers while we were away.

Wayne stopped while still holding my hand. He pulled me close then leaned down to give me a kiss. "How many times have we done this beneath the night sky?" he asked.

I smiled at him while gazing directly in his eyes. "It does feel good to be back."

We continued on, and after opening the fence gate to the backyard, we both laughed after noticing his telescope was still standing there. I forgot we left it outside. He picked it up while I stepped up to the back door and slid it open to let him in. He sat the telescope near the kitchen island, and then stood straight up where he pulled off his harness and then his shirt. He tossed both on the countertop.

We usually didn't have many lights on, so he went around and lit some candles that sat in round glass jars. Watching him pleased me more than anything, especially his hairy shoulders and back. I loved kissing them when I snuggled with him.

I took off my harness and then walked over to him, so I could lightly brush my hand over his shoulders while he lit one more candle. He turned around and allowed me to admire his chest. I moved my hands though his dense sea of hair and then cupped his pecs. His nipples were hard and he smiled at me.

"Nothing looks better than your eyes in the candlelight," he said to me.

"And, nothing feels better than being with you," I told him. I kept moving my hands over his chest and then asked, "So, what would you like to do now that we're home?"

He laughed, and then slipped his arms around me to hold me close against his body. "I want to be with you in every way possible, sweetie. In fact, I think we should cuddle on the couch and watch some television. Would you like that?"

I nodded happily, then reached down and pulled my cell phone out of my pocket so I could plug it in. Wayne did the same. He sat Dean's pdPhone down beside ours.

My loveable man reached down and grabbed hold of my shirt so he could pull it off. He tossed mine right on top of his, and then leaned down to kiss my left nipple. He took hold of my hand and walked us over to the couch. He grabbed the remote control, turned on the TV, and then laid down across the sofa. He gestured for me to join him, so I stretched out in front of him where he put his arms around me. He kissed my shoulders, the side of my neck, and the back of my head, all while rubbing his hands over my chest and stomach.

"You feel so good, Adam." He softly brushed his beard over my neck with several more kisses.

"Being with you is so comforting, Wayne." I wiggled back against his body, and he locked his hands around my stomach.

"We can watch whatever you want to." He kissed the side of my neck.

"I think laying here with you will be the best part of my evening." I reached over and rubbed my hand along his thigh, squeezing it and savoring the feel of every hair after I pulled his shorts up and exposed his manly leg.

I could feel him getting hard through his athletic shorts. His erection poked my lower back. It felt amazing and I was sure his arousal would lead to more intimacy later this evening, which I would gladly take. His thick and meaty manhood felt so good.

Before I knew, it Wayne started to lightly snore and I turned my head to the side to see that his was laid back against the couch. I guess he was content and glad to be home. I wished only the best for him, for the both of us.

I flipped through some television channels, and finally found a horror movie. I turned down the volume so it wouldn't bother my sweet man. I relaxed my body against his. He still had his arms around me, though they weren't as tight as they had been since he was sleeping.

I felt comfortable, relaxed and at peace. It was nice to be home while watching the candle lights flicker off of the ceiling. I didn't realize how much I had missed our house and sitting together on the couch. I was in heaven, and someday soon, I imagined James and Willie would contact us for another adventure.

I smiled and leaned my head back against Wayne's chest before closing my eyes. Who knows what tomorrow would bring. We still had one day left before we returned to our jobs, but for right now, I would enjoy my time here on the couch, snuggling with the love of my life.

Printed in the United States
By Bookmasters